MY ONE REGRET

CLAUDIA BURGOA

My One Regret

Michelle:
Thank you for all your
love, support and patience.
Love you so so mucele!
Te Quiero amiga
Claudia

DEDICATED TO:

Nirza, your departure came like a swift wind. You'll be missed.

EPIGRAPH

"It is impossible to live without failing at something, unless you live so cautiously that you might as well not have lived at all — in which case, you fail by default."

— J.K. Rowling

Chapter One

SADIE

I don't think I'll ever understand why she tried to take her own life. And I worry about what's going to happen to her. She needs help but who'll be around to give it to her?

Sadly, I'm not part of her life. Not anymore.

I twist my engagement ring as I wait for Kade to arrive.

We need to talk, said his text.

I hold my breath, hugging my stomach. This can't be happening. Just this morning, we talked about looking for a bigger home. We booked the honeymoon. Two months visiting the most beautiful gardens in the world with the man of my dreams.

The sound of the apartment door closing makes my heart beat faster. He's here. I take my ring off. A one-carat solitaire diamond he gave me almost a year ago. I set it on top of the nightstand and look around our room. His apartment, not mine. Everything belongs to him; I only brought a few things when he asked me to move in.

"Sade?" His voice is loud, his tone neutral.

"In the room," I croak. "How is she?"

I look up, as he enters. My eyes study him from top to bottom. It's been a hard day. I'm not expecting his charming grin or his seductive smirk. But I can't stand that his mouth remains in an uncharacteristically grim line.

Now that the end is coming, I feel numb. My heart beats, but my chest is hollow.

"Hey," he mumbles.

He runs a hand through his dark, longish hair. It's messy, covering half of his rugged face. His jaw is overshadowed by two days' worth of stubble is set into a scowl. Those silver eyes search around the area avoiding mine. I hate his rigid posture. My hands itch to reach out and comfort him. He's going through hell. This is as bad as what happened to his sister...or worse.

He's blaming himself. Does he blame me too?

My heart hurts for him and his daughter. Nothing I can say or do will make it better.

"Recovering." His husky melodic voice is calm yet distant.

His eyes find mine. The storm inside them makes them look dark, yet they are still so clear. Everything in his expression screams rejection.

It's over.

I lower my gaze, staring at my freshly painted toenails. Just earlier I was getting a mani-pedi with his daughters, Hanna and Tess. For the first time, I believed that things were going to settle with them. They had finally accepted me.

"Is there anything I can do?" I stupidly offer, knowing that they don't want me around, nor do they want my help.

The air thickens, almost choking me as I wait for him to end this. My eyes still see, but the walls are closing in, and everything is getting dark. *Breathe, breathe. You need to be strong.*

I try hard, but my mind is shutting down. Maybe it's just the shock of today's events. From the best news in the world to ... everything shifts, crumbles. I'm not sure what to expect next. The only thing I know is that I kept pouring out love, hoping that one day it would be enough.

But it's over.

My heart knows it; we're done. The journey ends here before it even began. I watch his boots move away from me and then back again. He does it several times until they stop right in front of me. My eyes travel over his long legs, all the way up until they meet his face.

"Thank you for leaving before things got out of control," he states.

Out of control is an understatement. Alicia, his ex-wife, lost her shit and was blaming me for something I didn't do. *I didn't kill Tess. Your daughter isn't dead.* Tess hates the idea of me so much that she ... my lungs collapse, and I hold my tears back. It hurts that we almost lost her. But I don't have the right to cry, because she's not mine.

Three years of loving her, caring for her as if she were my own doesn't count. I'm still nobody. This entire situation wrecked my heart with endless emotions: sadness, pain, guilt, rage. I drop my head because the guilt weighs more than anything else.

Kade almost lost his daughter the same way he lost his sister.

My heart hurts for him, for Tess, and a little for Alicia. A parent should never have to face this kind of pain. I lift my hand to take his, but he takes a couple of steps backward. My lungs deflate when I see the void in his eyes.

No, please don't do it. We're a family. We should talk this through, fix it. Don't leave us.

"I care about you," he begins. It's such a cliché.

No, I want you to say, you love me.

Last night he said it before I fell asleep tucked between his arms.

You woke me up with the same words, insisting that you couldn't wait for the day you could call me your wife. Mrs. Hades. You can't just toss away a three-year relationship.

I can't lose my best friend, my lover, my soulmate. I feel as if my heart is being ripped away from my chest.

"My children are my life. My reason to exist. Their wellbeing matters more to me than anything in the world."

More than me, I finish what he can't say.

I want to scream at him. Yell until I turn purple, until he understands that I matter too. That I'm worthy of his love, that we can work this out as a family. But can we really? There's no use in fighting it. His children will never accept me. His ex will always poison them against me.

"The last thing I want is to hurt you or leave you. But I don't see any other solution. I have to protect them, even from you."

Does Alicia know how much he sacrifices for their two children? Do they?

Not many fathers put their children first. Mine isn't like him. I recall the multiple times I had to endure my father's wife, or my mother's boy toy. My parents always put them before me. This moment, what he's doing—choosing his daughters over me—makes me fall in love with him all over again. My heart bleeds for our love, but is happy knowing his daughters have a fantastic father who loves them more than anything.

"I love them."

"And I appreciate that you were nice to them, but this can't continue. Hope you understand," Kade says.

Since I met him, he's never talked to me like this. As if I were a total stranger invading his space. Overnight, I've become no one to Kaden Hades. My heart explodes inside my chest, the pieces becoming dust, disappearing as the wind blows through the room. I count my breaths, reminding myself that I'm a strong woman.

From the beginning, I was aware that this was just a fantasy. A love like the one I shared with him can only last for so long before it changes. Growing up, I learned that nothing is permanent. Why did I believe that this time it'd be different?

Composing myself, I smile at him. "It'll take me a couple of days to pack my things." I breathe a few times, finding some strength left inside me before my legs and my body give up. "Tonight, I'll take the essentials, let me know when the best time is for me to come by and pack the rest. Plus, I have to find a new place."

"Fuck," he exhales, his broad shoulders slump. Kaden's breaking apart. If only he'd let me be there for him, but he doesn't want me here.

"Sadie..." his voice trails away.

My body jolts when I hear a smashing sound. His fist connecting with the wall.

"I'm hurting you, after I swore I'd never do it..." He runs a hand through his dark hair, taking several breaths. "I'm sorry for breaking my promise."

"Don't be." I brush him away heading to the closet while searching for my luggage. "This is one of the reasons why I love you, Kade. You hang the moon and the stars for them."

I bite back the rest of my thought. Words that might convince him that this could work, that we could try to defy the odds. But maybe I'd just be postponing the end for a few more days or weeks. Alicia was right.

He has a family, you're just an intruder passing through.

She won, not that anyone won after what just happened. Everyone lost a piece of themselves, and it'll take time for us to recover. Focusing on the task of packing, I try to remain quiet. But suddenly, I feel sick to my stomach and run to the bathroom.

"Oh my God, are you alright?"

"Fine." I heave, holding my stomach while he rubs circles on my back with his big hand.

"Did you go to the doctor?"

"It's nothing, you don't have to worry about me anymore." I brush my teeth and my face before heading to the closet.

Packing and holding in the tears is like juggling with fire balls. Something is going to fail, and I'll catch on fire. *Remain calm, wait until you get to the car.*

"Tess wants to recover here, instead of going to Alicia's," he says after I close my second bag. "Would you mind if I have someone pack for you?"

"Tell you what," I offer walking to the bathroom to collect my toiletries. "I'll pack and bring my things to the flower shop. That way, I'll be out of your hair before tomorrow morning. In the meantime, why don't you go back to the hospital?"

Leave me while I bleed and plan my next step.

Tell him.

You said you'd talk to him.

No, there's no point. Think about Tess.

"Not sure if it'll help, but I know a few counselors," I channel a neutral voice.

The self-preservation mode I adopted when I was a little girl is fully activated. He won't know how much this is affecting me; that I'm dying on the inside. For once, I let myself believe I could be part of a family, in a happy place.

"Sade," he calls my name. His voice is deep with longing.

I turn toward the door and spot him leaning against the frame, his face etched with excruciating pain. It hurts me seeing him agonizing, torn between his daughters and me. He deserves to be loved, to be taken care of. He's such a troubled soul, but the best man I've ever met.

"Kade," I mumble his name, slumping my shoulders and getting back to the task at hand.

Nothing we say will fix what's happened to Tess, what's happening to us.

We're over.

"Ask me to be selfish, to say fuck it all," he begs.

"As much as it breaks my heart, I refuse to cause any harm to your girls." I shake my head, taking my jewelry box. "I didn't do anything, but you're right, this is for the best."

"Babe, I don't want to lose you." His voice breaks.

I set my bag on the floor, and cover my eyes with the heels of my palms. I take a few deep breaths, soothing myself.

Hold the tears, Sadie. Be strong.

His sandalwood and tobacco scent hits me before he embraces me, trapping me into those strong arms while he fights his own decision. Leaning my head on his chest, I listen to his heartbeat, letting it calm me for the last time.

"I never wanted to hurt her," I cry, unable to hold the pain. "Or for her to hurt herself because of me. I love her."

"You've been good to them."

"I love them as if they were my own."

"You're the love of my life," he murmurs close to my ear. "My perfect half. But I can't put my children in danger."

I look up, finding his handsome face so close to mine that I can feel his breath caressing my face. Lifting my hand, I caress his jaw. We're both the product of broken homes and irresponsible adults.

That's not the future that either one of us would like to give to our own little ones—or the children he already has. Our minds understand each other, just like our hearts and souls. I recognize his internal fight, and I respect it.

Kade just wants to be the best father he can be to his daughters who already have to deal with a horrible mother.

"They'll be fine, because they have you. I'll leave, because I love you," I whisper entwining my hands behind his neck and kissing him long and deep one last time.

This is where the story ends. For the last time, I share the energy of my soul with him. Tonight, I open myself to him. I feel alive. I'm strong enough to take a chance to love him one last time—to dream of what will now never happen.

Chapter Two

KADEN

Six Months Later

The music thumps so hard through the speakers, my bones vibrate. Sad and angry rifts play through my guitar, accompanied by lyrics filled with pain and regret. Desperation. *Guilt*. I blame her for not holding on to me, for letting me be the most stupid man in the world.

I lost her, and I'm dead inside.

"You denied me your body," I sing, closing my eyes. My angel. My magical fairy. The woman who stole my heart from the first moment I saw her. These days that's the only way I can feel her; when I'm on stage singing—just for her.

The progression of the melody doesn't stop. The drums are pounding on a wicked sequence of beats, hammering against my chest. Once the tempo builds, I open my eyes, run to the left of the stage, and continue bleeding lyrics.

"You deprived me of all the things that feed my soul." My voice trembles reliving the last moments with her.

You deprived me of your love.
I begged you to stop me, not to let me destroy us.
How do I live without you?
Without your scent,

your magic,
Don't let me go,
Hold on to the memories
Hold on to my love
One day I'll find you
Here or in another world
One day I'll find you
And when I do, I won't let you go.

My guitar weeps along with my heart at her absence. The images of our last night play in my mind. Her long, chestnut with purple and pink locks tangled between my hands. My lips pressed against her sun-kissed skin. My cock thrusting inside her while I poured out my love to her and branded myself in her soul.

"Marry me, Hades!" Someone from the audience screams, another one professes her love for me.

The applauses and shrieks from the crowd last long enough for the sweat to clear along with the tears.

Fucking tears.

Who the fuck cries while working?

But tonight of all nights, I feel like my heart's been ripped from my chest—for a second time. That I'm losing her, this time forever.

Despite my body shakes and dripping sweat, I gather all my strength and smile at my public. The world doesn't have to know that I'm broken, and that the music I play is my life support.

"We love you, LA," I say, playing the last riff of my latest song. The one I composed for her the day I pushed her away from me. "You were wonderful tonight."

I nod at Jax who takes over, performing his last drum solo as I walk toward the backstage. Thank-fuck this tour is over. Visiting thirty-three cities. Playing thirty-four concerts in less than sixty days was my salvation to avoid what would've been my honeymoon. But I'm physically and mentally exhausted.

How am I going to survive when I get home?

From the moment I met Sadie, she made me feel like I couldn't live without her. Everything about her was addicting. A unique drug made just for me. The elixir that saved my soul.

It's hard to hold myself together without her. There's a strong need to be by her side. It increases with every second that passes. I carry a craving I can't satiate, and I know not even the strongest kind would erase it.

Fuck, I've been broken, but I've stayed sober. Though, I'll admit that since we broke up, I've been tempted more than a few times. What if I drank my weight in alcohol or snorted enough cocaine to forget my own name?

But my heart knows she's the only thing that can soothe my soul.

I can't have her. I shove my hand into the pocket of my pants, touching the ring she left behind after we broke up.

I never follow the rules. Not when I met Sadie or after. I should break the one she imposed when we ended our relationship and call her. Her voice would control the demons, her light would brighten the darkness at least for a few seconds.

I miss the way I felt when she was with me.

Sadie Bell made me believe that everyone deserves to be loved. That life could be different for me. My past didn't define me. She loved me with it and because of it.

I miss her.

All of her.

Those soulful dark brown eyes, her long hair. The melodic, sweet voice that called to me like a siren in the middle of the ocean, completed me and gave me hope.

With her, Kaden Hades was a regular man whose sins didn't matter. She didn't judge me for my past. Never claimed me for my fame or wanted more than my heart.

"Kade," Duncan, my manager marches toward me.

"Duncan," I greet him, grabbing the towel he hands me.

"Encore!"

"Encore!"

The auditorium shakes as the audience claps, stomps their feet and continues demanding one last song. Their energy is incredible, but I just can't give them more. I'm empty. Though, I hate to leave them hanging. Their support is what keeps Killing Hades in the number one spot.

"Are we going out again, man?" Jax pats my back, tossing his drum-sticks toward the ratty, old couch.

I let out a long breath. As I'm about to turn around back to the stage, Duncan snaps his fingers.

"Kaden, I'm talking to you," he repeats, exhaling harshly.

Finally, paying attention to my manager, I noticed his pale face and haunted eyes.

"What's going on?"

"We received a call," he says, his gaze studying the area, he pauses, "Kevin, from home."

Kevin's a friend of mine. I met him years ago when Killing Hades opened for his former band, *Without A Compass*. We all became friends, and sometimes still meet at the studio to play around and make music.

But why would Kevin call? And what's up with Duncan's attitude. His worried tone and long pauses don't sit well in my stomach. He usually talks non-stop, and I can barely keep up with him.

"Is everyone okay?" My pulse begins to beat fast because fuck, something must have happened back at home.

"What's going on with Kevin?"

"It's not about him, but you." He licks his lips. "I'm not sure if it matters or not, because you never talk about her. But he wanted you to know."

My gut clenches. "*Her*?" I arch an eyebrow.

"Are you talking about Tess?" I hold my breath waiting for his response.

Just six months ago, my oldest daughter tried to commit suicide.

What is it this time? I check my watch, trying to remember the time difference between LA and ... where is she today? I can't remember exactly in what city they landed, but I know she's safe. She's in Europe with her mother.

He shrugs one arm. "Well, I wouldn't know, but this isn't about her. It's about..."

He clears his throat. "Sadie."

"Sadie?" I repeat, holding my breath. "What happened to her?"

"Kevin said that you should head to Seattle ASAP."

The air around me disappears.

"Is she alright?" I demand because my gut tells me that he's hiding something from me.

But I don't wait for him to respond. I rush through the backstage toward the dressing room that was assigned to the band. Once I'm there, I search for my phone. The screen has a few missing calls from Kevin, and several Seattle numbers I don't know register on my phone.

I dial Sadie's number. Her voicemail picks up right away.

"Hummingbird, it's me, Kade. Can you please call me? I just need to know that you're okay," I beg her frantically. "Tonight, I've been more miserable than ever. There's this fucking pain inside me that's growing at a scary pace. Help me numb it and make everything better. Forgive me, please. We can work this out."

I close my eyes, and breathe harshly before calling the flower shop, but it's closed.

"What else do you know, Duncan?" I look up at the ceiling waiting for an answer, or for Sadie to call me telling me that she's okay.

"Just go back to Seattle."

"You're hiding something," I growl, grabbing his tie and pulling him closer to me. "You either fucking tell me what you know, or I can't be responsible for my actions."

"There's been an accident," Duncan says, flattening his suit once I release him. "She's in surgery, they don't know if she's going to make it."

My head pounds. Every cell in my body screams for oxygen—and for Sadie. I feel like my head's about to explode. I need to take a breath. But I can't. I begin to fall into the nothing. I fall further and further into the darkness, until it threatens to swallow me whole.

"Hades." Duncan shakes me.

"No, fuck, no." I gasp for some air and hold my head with both hands as my entire world begins to spin out of control.

My phone rings. I answer it automatically. "Hades."

"Hey, it's Kevin."

"Where is Sadie?"

"At Seattle Medical," he confirms my suspicions. "She's in surgery. Brynn was attending in the ER when she arrived. She called me before going into surgery. You need to come like right now. They need you."

"I'm on my way," I say, looking around for my manager. "If you can, tell Sadie not to leave me."

"Duncan," I call my manager who's on the phone. "Get me a plane. I have to fly to Seattle, now."

"Got it." He gives me the thumbs up, walking away.

It takes me only a couple of minutes to shower. I needed to wash away the sweat and the tension.

"What's going on?" Jax enters the room changed and carrying his stuff.

"Sade's in the hospital," I inform him, pushing away the fear and anguish that's ripping my insides.

"Everything is set, Hades," Duncan says, entering the room. "The car is outside waiting for you. I'll make sure to send your things to your house."

"Ship this too, man," Jax throws his duffle bag toward Duncan and follows me.

I look around, remembering the last time Sadie and I were in this stadium. I wish I could turn back time.

Chapter Three

KADEN

Two Years Ago

I loved my life: jumping from one city to another, one country to the next, playing every night at a different venue nonstop. At least I did, until Sadie. Tonight, I wanted to exchange the sold-out concert for an evening at home with my girlfriend.

"Man, you're sulking again," Jax mentioned as he enters the dressing room. "Like your woman would say, you've been grumpy all day."

"Don't mock Sadie," I warned him.

"I take that you haven't heard from her yet?"

Still no word from her, I repeat in my head for the millionth time today.

Sadie's been out of reach all day. I tried calling her several times, but she never answered my calls or texts. All fucking day long, I wondered if I did something to piss her off. But she wasn't like that. When I upset her, she called me on it right away.

"Awe, he misses his little flower girl."

Fuck, I hated when he called her that. Instead of acknowledging him, I grabbed my phone and fired up a text.

Kade: Hey Snuffle Bunny, I missed you all day. If I upset you,

let me know what I did so I can fix it. If not, let me know you're okay because I'm worried sick. I just want to hear your voice and tell you that I love you.

"Ah, so that's why you've been calling me all day?"

My pulse quickened, and my head snapped at the sound of her silky voice.

"You're here," I lifted my gaze and found her.

Just like the first time I saw her, as soon as our eyes locked, everyone around disappeared. It's just us. Her dark eyes twinkled as I marched to meet her. She wore a pair of jeans and a t-shirt of Killing Hades. The newest one with the hummingbird logo of our latest tour. My good luck charm was here.

"You think I'd miss your birthday, Booboo Bear?" She raised her hand that held a cupcake and with the other, she lighted up the candle.

"Happy Birthday to you..." Sadie, my bandmates, and the crew sang.

I couldn't believe it. She's here with me. The one person in the world I wanted to be with is right in front of me. And if it was possible, I love her even more.

"Make a wish," she whispered, biting her lip.

Fuck I wanted to be the one nibbling on it, tasting her. This was the best fucking birthday ever. She was my best present. I only wished to be with her forever. After I blew out the candle, she pulled it out of the frosting. Then the Little Minx smeared some of it around my mouth and nose.

"You're going to pay for that," I joked, grabbing her by the waist and pulling her to me.

"Happy Birthday, Nightingale," she mumbled close to my mouth, licking some of the frosting before capturing my bottom lip between her teeth and tugged it.

Before she teased me, I took a hungry kiss from her lips. If I had time, I'd take her somewhere private and bury myself inside her. It's been so long; nearly three weeks since the last time I saw her.

"Get a room!" Someone yelled.

"If we could," Sadie laughed with that deep throaty laugh that hit me right in the groin.

"You fuckers are just jealous!" I groaned.

"Are we grumpy, Mr. Hades?" She caressed my jaw with her lips.

"Don't tease me, Little Minx," I begged her. I fucking wanted more. "How long are you staying, beautiful?"

"I'm going to be with you for the last leg of the tour. Tonight, Portland, Vancouver and then we go home."

"Will you be okay on the bus?"

She smirked, shaking her head. I thought so, and I had no idea how to fix it tonight. Sadie loved my crew, and they did her. However, she could only take so much noise, and the bus was anything but quiet.

"Not to be a prude but your bandmates are too much to handle for that long, Kade. But, I have it all under control. Duncan and Jax helped me book planes, hotels, and even a fancy restaurant to take you for dinner." She tossed her head back as she laughed at me.

"You're pulling my leg about the fancy restaurant, aren't you?"

"Of course," she patted my chest.

"That'd be torture for you. I have other plans. Like whipped cream ..." She licked her lips, trailing and bit her lip.

My semi-hard cock twitched. I was going to have blue balls during the set.

"Hades, it's almost time. The Roadrunners are done, they are switching the stage."

"It's okay," Sadie cupped my chin. "We have all night and plenty of frosting."

"But I need you now," I whispered in her ear. "Your sweet little pussy milking my cock. I'm so fucking ready, it wouldn't take long."

"Sorry, Mr. Hades. After the last time we got caught by Jax, I refuse to have sex backstage. Lock or no lock."

"You're a cruel woman, Sadie Bell."

"Yet, you love me."

I pressed my lips against hers, kissing her slowly. It's almost a chaste kiss.

"Where are you going to be while I play?" I nibbled her neck, my hands roaming around her body.

"On the sidelines, listening to you." She pushed my hands. "Stop it. I swear it'll be worth the wait once we're out of here."

"That's it, we're canceling the gig," I joked, but everyone glared at me.

"Let's go, fucker," Jax yanked me away from Sadie.

"Thank you, Jax," Sadie waved at him and blew me a kiss. "Sing your heart out, Hades."

We walked toward the stage, I grabbed my guitar from Esteban, one of the roadies, and waited for the crew to finish switching the Roadrunners' equipment out with ours.

"You knew she was coming and didn't tell me, asshole," I feign anger, but squeezed his shoulder. "Thank you, man. I owe you."

"Sadie makes our leader happy, the least I should do is help her to keep you in line." He laughs. "So, are we following the same lineup or are you adding your usual acoustic 'I'm going to get fucked after the concert' crap for her?"

I grinned at him and pushed him toward the stage and started playing our first song.

Chapter Four

KADEN

Present

After an almost four fucking hour flight, I'm in a helicopter on my way to Seattle Memorial.

Sadie's going to be fine, I mumble, resting my arms on my thighs. *She's the strongest person I've ever met.*

I close my eyes and concentrate on her melted chocolate eyes. Her smile. That dimple that appears on the left side of her mouth when she's laughing. But the need to numb my pain grows bigger and bigger.

Be strong.

She's all that matters, not the fucking craving, the thirst for whiskey that squeezes my throat as the minutes pass.

It's been a long time since the need has won, but there's always the risk of losing my sobriety. The first time I tasted the alcohol my mother hid under her bed, I was ten. It burnt my tongue, but my body felt unlike anything I'd felt before. Like my mind occupied a different space than my body. I felt superior, unstoppable. It gave me the courage to get through the beatings that my mother's boyfriend gave us. It got me through the winter nights, and bitter cold when she forgot to pay the electric bill. The loss of my sister was easier to bear when I couldn't remember my name. It helped me through those days when we barely had food on the table. It helped me forget what I was missing, and it brought me closer to my guitar.

Alcohol became my poison, my weapon, and my way out of life.

Booze was my closest companion until my ex-wife used it against me to take my daughters away. That sobered me up for a while. Sadie though, she is the one who replaced the craving for being numb with the pleasure of living. I lived to make her happy, to enjoy her.

The pleasure of being buried deep inside her, high on her scent and her taste, intoxicated me. She's my addiction. The only drug I need to survive this life.

Duncan's words, 'they don't know if she's going to make it,' only increase the need for a bottle of bourbon. I need a liquid flame burning down my throat, setting my insides on fire while I forget my fucking life. At least for the next few hours. But I can't. Not when Sadie might need me.

Fuck, I rub my face and grab my phone one more time. Ella doesn't answer the phone.

Hades: Have you learned anything new?

Dunk: No, she's still in surgery.

I called the hospital and pretended to be her husband, and they said that they won't know anything new until she's out of surgery.

"We can't release any information over the phone," the lady repeated as I begged her to tell me how she was doing.

In no time, the helicopter lands on the helipad at Seattle Memorial. I rush toward the door, taking the stairs two at a time. I open the metal door, walking toward the elevator. The stench of chemicals burns my nose. The smell of sickness and death mixed with antiseptic and the vivid fluorescent lights make my stomach churn.

I hate hospitals.

"They said third floor," Jax follows behind me. "Kevin is waiting for us."

"We'll take the elevator." I walk toward the metal doors, pressing the button.

"She's going to be fine," he reassures me for what feels like the fucking millionth time.

I enter the elevator and lean against the cold steel wall. I close my eyes, regretting the last five months without her, wishing I had chosen her. Would she be okay if I hadn't left her? I open my eyes and look at my left hand, reading my knuckles.

S-A-D-I-E.

One word, five letters. Her name tattooed on my hand. Her soul branded to mine. Her heart fused with mine.

When I arrive at the waiting room, I spot Kevin.

"How is she?" I ask.

"Still in surgery." He gives me a hug, patting my back. "Everything is going to be fine, man."

"Do you know what happened?"

"A car accident," he explains. "She was doing the last delivery of the day."

"That's all you know?" He shrugs. "Have you seen her?"

"No, but follow me." He tilts his head and begins to walk toward the elevator. "There's someone you have to meet."

"No, I have to stay here," I halt, calling after him.

"Go, man, I'll stay here," Jax pats my back. "If there's any change I'll get you right away."

"Who am I meeting?"

"You'll see." He stops right in front of the NICU unit and rings the doorbell.

A nurse waves at us as the door unlocks automatically. We enter the first set of doors and are stopped by a second set of glass doors.

"Put on a gown and a mask," Kevin orders, pointing at the pile of scrubs. "I'll be in the waiting room with Jax if you need me."

As I do what he says, I look through the glass spotting five incubators. Only three of them occupied with tiny babies that have tubes in their little noses and their bodies. I wash my hands, drying them well and step into the dim room.

My pulse speeds as I get closer to the babies. I walk faster and stare at the tag on the side of the crib. *Baby Bell.*

"A baby," I mumble unable to tear my eyes from the little thing lying in front of me.

I stare at him for several beats. Unlike my daughters, this little boy is so tiny. His arms are smaller than my thumb. His eyes are covered with a tiny black mask. He looks like a doll with needles in his fragile arms, tubes attached to his nose. I have a little baby boy. I read the tag one more time. Baby Bell, four pounds, nineteen inches. No, he should be baby Hades-Bell. Just Baby Hades, because Sadie hates hyphenated last names.

"Is he going to be okay?" I ask, wanting to hold him and protect him.

"This little guy only needs to stay in the incubator for a few days or weeks before he can go home."

But how could he when he's alone, surrounded by machines and people who barely know him. This little guy should be with his mom.

"Mama is going to be fine," I whisper reaching for his hand.

"Of course, she'll be fine," the nurse who is checking his vitals tells me. "Dr. Ward is attending the operation. She's one of the best doctors in Seattle."

I pay closer attention to the nurse and realize she's my kids' pediatrician. "Sorry, Dr. Hawkins. I didn't recognize you."

"Hey, you're fine. This is a lot to process." She adjusts the tubes close to the baby's nose. "But I ask you to trust us. They are both in good hands. This little angel is going to be fine. He came out nine weeks earlier than expected, but he's strong. He's able to control his body temperature. That's a big step."

I touch the crib, yearning to hold him. My baby boy.

"Your hands are washed. You can touch him, but be careful. His skin is still sensitive."

"Hi," I mumble feeling his wrinkly skin. The warmth of his body soothes my soul and strengthens my heart.

Turning my attention to Dr. Hawkins, I dare to ask, "Couldn't you let him stay inside his mom for a few more weeks?"

"Believe me, we considered every option."

"What do you know about the accident?"

"The other car t-boned hers. It pinned the van against the light pole. They had to cut her out of the car. There's internal bleeding, broken ribs ... the placenta separated from the uterus. With her injuries ..." she sighs. "To simplify, both baby and Mom had a better chance of survival if we delivered him early."

"How is she doing now?" I ask in hopes that she has more information.

"Still in the OR. So far, there's no news, which is good news. As I mentioned, Dr. Ward's one of the best surgeons in the country. She'll take good care of her. Until surgery is over, we won't find out more. In fact, we might not know much for a couple of days."

"So we wait?"

"While we care for them." She sets the pen and chart down and touches my baby one last time. She looks at me. "He's perfect, just too small, but he'll catch up soon. I'm going home."

"He needs you," I say, my heart beating fast. "You can't leave him."

"We have a team of nurses watching him twenty-four hours a day," Dr. Hawkins explains. "I'll be back here early in the morning."

"Thank you, doc." I nod and turn my attention back to my little boy.

"You're going to be fine, and Mom will be too. We'll be okay," I assure him.

God, I know we don't have a relationship. But please, please, *don't take her away from me. This little guy needs Sadie. We both do.*

Chapter Five

KADEN

I stare at the round wall clock for the millionth time—scrutinizing the big hand which seems to linger an extra minute with every passing second. I take my gaze off the clock. The wait is killing me. I've never been a patient man. But from an early age, I learned to suck it up and wait for the storm to end, pushing myself out of the debris. The only positive news I've gotten so far is that my baby will be okay. Aspen, his pediatrician, assured me that even though he was born nine weeks premature, he's healthy.

The little one will stay in the NICU for a few days or weeks. It all depends on his growth.

My primary concern is Sadie. The woman who let me go without a fight. I understand she was thinking about Tess's mental health. She always put the girls first, as if they were her own. Would anything have changed if she had told me about the baby?

I can't believe, Jax and I are the only ones here. Kevin left a couple of hours ago but promised to return once Sadie was out of surgery. Where are her parents and her friends? Should I call someone?

I blow some air through my mouth, closing my eyes and picturing my woman.

Sadie's bright smile. That's all that matters right now, Sade.

I pull out my phone to text Duncan.

Kade: Were you able to get that done?

Duncan: We're still working with the hospital to get a location where Sadie and the baby can be close together.

Kade: Good, make sure they have the best care.

I lean against the wall, waiting for someone to come out with an update. As I stare at the blank white wall in front of me, avoiding the clock, the tension and anxiety continue building up, squeezing my chest. I stare blankly; my mind full of emptiness and panic.

What if she doesn't make it?

Then there's our baby. He's not ready to deal with life in this world. He's underdeveloped and what if his mama... I massage my sternum, soothing the ache. Don't think about it, she'll be fine.

I wipe my sweaty hands on my pants, pushing the negative thoughts from my mind away. If not, the panic is going to eat me alive. I begin my breathing exercises to help me relax. Just as I regain a steady heartbeat, I hear the familiar continual tap of a heel against the floor, and my pulse rate shoots up once again.

Moving my gaze forward, I spot a woman wearing blue scrubs, her light blue eyes peering at me.

"Kade," she sighs, tapping her clipboard simultaneously.

The doctor removes her blue surgical cap, releasing her dark braid. I recognize her when she removes the mask covering most of her face. Brynn Ward. She's the head of surgery at Seattle Memorial.

"Brynn?" I step forward, staring at her. "How's Sadie?"

"Stable," she breathes the word.

She shakes her head. "She's in critical condition, but stable." Her shoulders hunch. "We stopped the internal bleeding. We extracted her spleen. She has three broken ribs, a broken arm, and a punctured lung. On top of that, she hit her head against the window. She has a cerebral edema."

I frown, but as I'm about to ask questions, she continues, "It's swelling on the brain. She's in an induced coma that prevents further brain damage from occurring while the swelling goes down."

My mouth dries as I listen to Brynn. Swallowing hard, I ask, "Is she going to be okay?"

"As I said—"

"Be honest with me. Don't give me the bullshit runaround. I have to know if she's going to recover."

"I don't know." She breathes deeply, looking at the floor.

"She's my friend. I want her to heal and be able to hold her baby." Her breath hitches. "But as her doctor, I know that it's a waiting game."

"Waiting game?"

"We've done everything we can to save her. But I can't tell you if there will be permanent damage to the brain until we try to wake her up."

"Brain damage, that's a broad term isn't it?"

"It is, the spectrum is wide. Brain injuries are tricky." Brynn presses her lips together, looking at the floor for a second and then back at me. "There's also a possibility she might not wake up..."

I drum my fingers on top of my heart as I try to breathe in and out while I repeat her last words inside my head. The last words that left her lips are like daggers puncturing my heart. I can't comprehend them, but they keep bouncing in my head, replaying like a broken record.

She might never wake up.

There's a pain in my chest, so strong I don't know if I'll be able to survive it.

"But you have to have faith," Brynn continues, wiping the corner of her eye. Her free hand reaches my arm. She squeezes it reassuringly. "We'll wait and see how her body reacts. And in the meantime, we pray for a miracle."

My mind begs me to numb it. My heart bleeds. There's a vast difference between not being beside me, and not existing in the world.

After several seconds, I find my voice. "How long are you keeping Sadie in a coma?"

"At least a week," she states. "It all depends on the severity of the swelling, and how she responds. She's strong and young. We'll do our best to help her heal."

"When can I see her?"

"They're setting up a room in the left wing for her and the baby."

Brynn looks around. "For all intents and purposes, you two are together," she whispers. "She'll be close to the baby. Once he's better, we can move him with her."

"Thank you, Brynn," I mumble, tossing my head back and closing my eyes.

"She's going to be fine," Jax says as he pats my back.

☆ ☆ ☆ ☆

The hospital room is as devoid of beauty as I am of hope. Its walls are white. There are no decorations. The place has an undertone of bleach, and the floor is purely grey. There're no windows. By the door are dispensers for scrubs, rubber gloves, hand sanitizer, and soap.

My heart stops at the sight of the woman in the bed. There's a stand of intravenous drips, cables, and tubes hooked to her arms and face. She looks nothing like my Sade. Her petite body lies in bed, lifeless.

Black obscures the edges of my vision, and the only thing I can hear is my heartbeat. My breath comes in ragged, shallow gasps. Seconds pass as I stare at Sadie. Her eyes are closed. The left side of her face is swollen. There're monitors on both sides of the bed. An IV on the right connected to her wrist. Her left arm is wrapped with plaster and elevated.

The pain of looking at her burns like a fire.

"Baby," I whisper, walking toward the bed.

I lean forward, caressing her delicate, bruised face. Kissing her cheek lightly, I try to find her signature jasmine, gardenia, and peach scent. A signature fragrance that her grandma gifted her when she turned eighteen, and she still gets it from a signature scent studio. It's weak, but the aroma diminishes the ache in my chest, numbing it slightly.

Reaching for her right hand, I intertwine our fingers. Her pulse is slow, her breathing faint, but I feel closer to her than I've felt in a long time.

"I missed you," I murmur, kissing her hand. "I missed you so fucking much it was getting hard to breathe. And seeing you here..."

I close my eyes. My tears roll down my cheeks. I was torn inside; I wished I were dreaming. But all I hear is the faint sound of her voice. Not knowing if I would never see her again, I just keep feeling this terrible pain inside my chest. It's too intense. I have a hole in my heart.

"We have a son. Our little boy is beautiful." I brush the strands of hair away from her face. "You have to wake up and meet him. He's so tiny. Your room is close to the NICU. Once he's out of the ventilator we might be able to move him over here."

I clear the tears running down my cheeks.

"Kade," Brynn calls to me from the door. "They're setting up the room next door for you."

"I don't need a room."

She shakes her head and smiles. "You have to rest for at least a few hours. The staff will be available around the clock to take care of Sadie and the baby's needs. Kevin is bringing you some clothes. He wants to know if you need anything else."

"My guitar, tell him to bring my guitar."

As I look at the bracelet they gave me to identify me as the father of my little boy, I think about all the videos I have of Sadie. He should listen to her voice.

"My laptop and the box with SD cards that are next to it...and the camera too. It's in my closet on top of the shelf."

"We'll get some clothes for the baby too," Brynn states as she walks toward the door. "He can only wear booties and hats for now, but we'll have everything for him."

"Thank you for looking after them."

"Hey, I'm here to help as much as I can. They'll be fine. There's a nurses' station next door. They'll be monitoring both 24/7. Studies have shown that talking to people in a coma helps them wake up sooner. Once the little man is ready, you can hold him—skin to skin contact helps them a lot during this time."

Chapter Six

KADE

"Hey, little man, you need a name," I say, while I put a pair of blue booties on his tiny feet.

Careful not to hurt him, I change his hat for a knitted one that Brynn brought for him.

"Did Mama have a name for you?" I hold onto his hand for several seconds, staring at this little miracle.

Our miracle.

He's fragile, tiny, and yet, he feels like a gift. The best gift that Sadie could've given me. If only she could see him.

"Do you want to hear how I met your Mom?" I pull a chair closer to the crib and take his hand one more time. "We might have to do some censoring because things heated up after I wore her down."

My lips finally smile, as I remember the day we met.

☆ ☆ ☆ ☆

Three Years Ago

"We're back to playing in coffee houses," Jax complained. "You wouldn't think that we just arrived from a sold-out concert at the

Staples Center in Los Angeles or that our latest single has been on the top chart for ten weeks in a row."

"It's only a couple of nights, and for a good cause. Don't be such a snob." I leaned my guitar case against the wall. "Think of this as your good deed of the decade."

It took us a long time to be where we are. Killing Hades started as a garage band when we were sixteen. Once we moved to Seattle, we worked twice as hard and played wherever we could. Like this café, or the bar that's a couple of blocks away from here. Many business owners gave us a chance to play during weekends to get some exposure. For that, I'll always be grateful.

Logan, the owner of the café, was a friend of ours. Afraid that his sales might drop due to a Starbucks opening a couple of blocks away, he thought including acoustic concerts on the weekends would help sales.

"Whew!" Jax stared at the door. "I wouldn't say no to those hotties. The blonde seems like an easy one."

My eyes diverted toward his line of sight. Two beautiful women stepped inside the café. The blonde shook her long mane while taking off her raincoat, unlike the second one who just took off her beanie hat and shoved it inside the pouch of her hoodie. Then, when she took off her sweatshirt, her blouse lifted enough to show some of her sun-kissed skin.

"I'll definitely take blondie," Jax called out as if choosing a player for his softball team. "Or both if they're willing."

"The brunette one is out of your league," I said, concentrating on the cables. Our roadies were on vacation, but we didn't need help setting up a couple of microphones and the speaker.

Logan had designated the far-left corner of the café for the band. He assumed that the patrons would stay around their seats, maybe sit on the floor if he ran out of space.

Right at seven, we were ready to play. The place was full, a few people stood at the back and others around the bar. We played our old songs first, and then Jax began to take requests. Two hours of playing and chatting with the audience flew by in what felt like only a few minutes. It's not often we got to be in a small space and jam as if we were with friends at a party.

Or serenading a beautiful woman who'd held my attention ever since I set eyes on her. She knew the words to every song. While I sang, it was like it was just the two of us feeling the music and keeping the tempo. I itched to touch her beautiful face. I was dying to learn her name, listen to her voice.

As I ended the last song, the spell broke. The patrons began clapping, standing and asking for autographs and selfies. I tried to keep an eye on her, hoping she wouldn't leave before I talked to her, but after an hour I lost track of everyone around me. I tried my best to chat with the fans, and my face was surely stamped all over Instagram and Snapchat.

But my mood changed when from the corner of my eye I spotted *her* walking with an easy saunter toward me. The woman who had brightened the entire place when she'd arrived. She smiled with ease. Everyone around her felt compelled to greet her and smile back.

She was a beauty. And her luscious curves woke up my sleepy body. Her long legs were wrapped in a pair of leggings and knee-high boots.

I didn't want to be obvious, but I observed her as her hips swayed. Her steps were assertive, and her pouty lips drew a beautiful smile. It wasn't flirty, just determined. She was a woman on a mission.

Did she feel the connection?

Fuck I hoped so, but I wasn't sure how to feel about her coming to me. With her, I wanted everything to be different. After fourteen years in the business, I was used to groupies throwing themselves at me and offering sexual favors. Not that I had taken them up on the offers. What had happened with my ex-wife made me cautious.

My ex had been a hardcore groupie, and I was too young and only cared about getting pussy. The joke was on me when I learned that I'd knocked her up. After things ended with Alicia, I'd fuck around, but I was always cautious.

But this woman seemed different from all the ones I'd crossed paths with. Something about those bright, whiskey color eyes of hers told me that I was in for a treat.

"Hi," she greeted me using a silky voice that sounded like a siren call.

"Hey." I threw a smirk and continued packing.

She didn't have a phone for a selfie or a pen for an autograph. Maybe she wanted the same as me, one night of sex. I bet she felt the connection too. And for her, I'd break some of my rules and take her home. My daughters were with their mom for the weekend. We had more than forty-eight hours to satisfy the sudden craving I had for her.

I waited for her to throw some line. But after several seconds of silence, I was the one asking the question, "Need a selfie, an autograph?"

"A date," she requested, pressing her lips together. "Well not anything serious, more like a rebound."

"Rebound sex?" My brain froze at her request, my attention shifted toward the owner of that sweet, melodic voice whose request was making my cock twitch. "A deal that includes sex?"

"A rebound date. Not sex," she clarified, enunciating each word. "I'm sure that a man like you has already booked an entire weekend with some model and are planning on having hot sex. Though, a weekend of sin might help exorcise the ex-"

"A weekend to exorcise someone?" I chuckled.

My eyes roamed over her gorgeous body, stopping as I found her beautiful eyes challenging me.

"One weekend full with sex to make you forget," I licked my lips checking her out one more time.

She was one of those women who was so beautiful she didn't need any makeup. Her wavy chestnut colored hair had a few strands of honey, burgundy, and purple highlights. She looked young, yet mature. And I wanted her so bad. My dick hardened as I imagined how it would be to touch her soft skin. To be inside of her, pounding her against the wall while sucking her tits.

I examined her delicate features. The button nose, the luscious lips, and those crinkling, dark brown eyes that smiled at me. If I had her for one night, I'd make those eyes burn with lust and turn them into liquid chocolate. She'd be trembling and screaming my name, again and again.

"Sweetheart, I'd only need one time to make you forget any man who's ever touched you before me."

She released a full-blown laugh, touching her chest lightly and shaking her head. The sound was magical, soothing. Like a melody made just for me. At that moment, her laugh became my tune. The rhythm I wanted to live by.

"Oh my, you think so highly of yourself," she said once she sobered up, but the smile remained on that beautiful mouth that I wanted to devour. "But I'm not asking for myself."

She turned slightly toward her table and pointed at Blondie. "Ella, my friend, is the one who needs a good rebound guy from the asshole she dated."

"What makes you think I'd agree?" I narrowed my gaze.

"We aren't assuming." She looked at her friend, whose forehead was pressed on the table with her arms covering her head. "But it never hurts to ask. I mean, how amazing would it be to say that Kaden Hades exorcised the lowlife out of her system."

I rubbed my chin, pretending to think about the proposal. "What's in it for me?"

"A date with a hot, sexy woman. She's tall, slender, busty, and beautiful." She wiggled her eyebrows. "If you play your cards right, something more could happen."

"How about you?" I grabbed her hand and kissed it, my lips stayed pressed against her hand as I enjoyed the heat created by our touch. "Any kind of satanic ritual you'd like me to perform on you?"

She touched her chest lightly and shook her head. "No, I'm good." Leaning forward, she whispered. "My dating policy excludes players."

"Only players?"

"Well, and slimy assholes." She studied me with those perfect eyes. "But I don't want to *assume*."

"Glad you're withholding judgment. In the name of full disclosure, I'll confess that I am a recovered asshole. But I was never slimy."

"Noted," she scribbled something in the air. "Anything else we should add to your file?"

I chuckled and pulled out my phone. "Why don't you give me your number? We can discuss your plan this upcoming Thursday, over dinner."

"Thursday?" She frowned. "Dinner. This is a simple yes or no."

"There's more at stake than you think." I checked my watch. "If I had time, I would do it now, but I have to leave. What's your number?"

She chewed her lip as her eyes focused on me. The woman was trying to guess my intentions, but I have a great poker face.

She couldn't see the heat burning inside me—for her. A spark ignited a fire that created an urge to kiss her.

Make her mine.

"Five-seven-zero-three-two-one-one." She recited it. I put it in my phone and dialed right away.

I wanted her to have my number, to know that I was calling her. Because I wouldn't wait until Thursday to hear her voice again—or to see her.

Her eyes grew wide as I put the phone close to my ear.

"Gino's pizza, what would you like to order?"

I stared at her, shaking my head. "Is pepperoni fine with you?"

She opened her mouth, closed it and shook her head. "What?"

"Well, I'm guessing you want to have dinner now seeing as you gave me the number of a pizza place."

She pressed her lips together, but her body shook as she tried to swallow the laughter.

"Hello," the man on the other line said.

"Yes, give me a second. We're trying to decide if we're going for your meat lovers or vegetarian." I went on, serving her with my best grin. "They're waiting for you."

"This is so embarrassing," she moaned, and that throaty noise hit me right in the groin. "I don't usually do this, but Ella has a big crush, and she just broke up with a dirt worm scumbag."

"A fucker?"

"Yeah, that."

"Well, think about Ella. You and I can discuss her situation over pizza."

The beautiful woman shook her head and rolled her eyes. "Forget that I asked."

She turned around, but I stepped forward and reached for her elbow.

"Wait," I begged her. I wasn't ready to let her go. There was a need inside me urging me to stop her. "What's your name?"

I swallowed hard as the warmth of her skin sent an electrical current through my fingers, shocking my entire body. My heart beat so hard in my chest, that it threatened to break loose. I fought the need to pull her to me and kiss her senseless.

"Her name is Ella," she mumbled. "She called first dibs on you when we were fifteen. You're on her list of guys she'd do if she ever met them. And she's my best friend."

I lifted my hand, running my thumb over her jaw and then her beautiful lips. "But I want to get to know *you*," I whispered, leaning closer to her, pressing my lips so close to her ear that I could smell the sweet floral scent of hers. "What's your name?"

"Sadie," she mumbled with a throaty voice. She stared at me with heavy eyelids.

"Sadie," I repeated, tasting the word for the first time and hoping to repeat it over and over. "Give me your number. I want to have dinner with you. Give me one date."

Those words didn't make sense. I'd never been on a date. Ever. Not even with my ex-wife.

Sadie rose on her tip-toes. She kissed my jaw. "Sorry, I don't date."

I closed my eyes and groaned as the most beautiful woman in the world walked away from me.

Thinking fast, I pulled out a paper from my backpack. After doodling a few lyrics, I wrote my number. Walking toward her table, I handed it to her. "As lovely as it'd be to perform the ritual, I couldn't. Not when my only goal is to see you again."

I gave her a chaste kiss on the forehead and left.

Chapter Seven

SADIE

The atmosphere in the café thickened. Sparks flew around us as Kaden Hades' scruffy stubble rubbed against my cheek and he gave me a lingering kiss.

Everything inside me ignited when he kissed my hand. My skin tingled. It felt hot and tight.

"Call me," he appealed one last time using a low, rough voice that melted every cell in my body.

And walked away leaving only the scent of tobacco, coffee, and sandalwood behind and my heart flipping around in my ribcage.

"I told you he wouldn't be rebound guy," Ella sang the words in an *I told you so,* tone.

She snatched the note that Kaden Hades left for me. "But still. He's mine—forever. You promised."

I was fifteen and stupid when we split the members of Killing Hades. She got Kaden and Jax, while I got the ugly keyboard player who left the band years ago. That's the story of my life. Ella always chose the best ones, and I kept whatever she didn't want. Like Justin Timberlake, Luke Perry, Mark-Paul Gosselaar, and James Van Der Beek. Van Der Beek didn't bother me, I preferred Joshua Jackson anyway. After all, Pacey was the one who got the girl on *Dawson's Creek.*

"He's just another unreachable celebrity," I reminded her. "But you can always dream."

We could dream.

I had something Ella didn't. A kiss. Hot, sinful, sexy Kaden Hades kissed me. He touched me. I ran my fingers over my elbow. My skin shivered as I remembered the electricity that ran through my entire body when his callused fingers touched me.

"Oh, my fucking God, I'm in love," Ella screamed from the top of her lungs, hugging the note.

"Read this, Sadie. You have to read it." She handed me the paper.

A brief kiss
A searing touch
It's only one moment
But your scent is engraved in my mind
In my heart and soul
Give me more than just one moment
I need
A thousand more kisses
And a million moments with you
K
Sade, here's my number (206) xxx-xxxx. Call me.

"Hate to say this, but you have to call him," she insisted.

Call him? I read the poem several times, then I examined the paper. It was clearly ripped from a notebook and had a few musical notes and scribbles that I couldn't understand. The words that he wrote were bold, artistic. Almost perfect. So much so that I was sure they meant nothing to him.

He was a musician who composed for many other artists. He could create a song as fast as I could fix a flower arrangement. The words were beautiful but hollow. They came from a man who knew how to seduce women and men of all ages with lyrics and melodies.

"He's a player," I concluded and folded the paper.

"Your loss." She snatched it away from me.

"Well, you should try not dating anyone right now."

"That's where you're wrong. After you fall off the horse, you have to get back on," she told me with conviction. "The only thing I need is a few drinks, a hot man, and my life will be back to normal."

Her attitude didn't sit well in my stomach. There was a hint of jealousy lingering around me. What if she called him? She wouldn't, would she? I had to trust her. Ella was my oldest friend, my *person*. The one who would go to the ends of the Earth for me. Nothing had ever come between us. After my parents' divorce, I crashed at Ella's house during holidays, weekends, and summers.

It bothered me that I couldn't grant her big wish—a weekend with Kaden Hades. I wished he had let me give him the sob story about her latest breakup. Then again, her breakups were always messy.

"Should we come again tomorrow night?" Ella pushed my mug closer to where I stood.

"I don't go out on Saturdays," I reminded her as I finished my chai tea latte. Do you want to crash at my place?"

"Nope, as much as I adore spending time with you. Your home is boring. I need wine to lose myself for the next couple of days. You don't have any alcohol at home. And you'll be up at the crack of dawn."

I pressed my lips together and nodded, biting my tongue because Ella's condescending tone reminded me of my mother.

Sadly, this grown-up version of Ella struck a chord. One of the most painful of my life. My mother's attitude. She was right. It'd be best that we didn't spend the night together. Since I was nine, I'd taken care of my mother every single time a man hurt her. First, it was my father, then her line up of deadbeat boyfriends. I knew the pattern—and hated it.

Ella was in a state of emotional pain. Anything I said would be dismissed. Joe, her ex, was a lot like my father. A narcissistic, cheating bastard. I loved my Dad, but I didn't like him. He was a terrible human being.

My mother didn't accept who he was and how much he hurt her. She chose to numb her pain with alcohol, sleeping pills, and painkillers. None of those remedies made her feel better about herself. After Dad divorced her, she had a revolving door of boyfriends and husbands. Sadly, she also frequented rehab centers every year.

It wasn't the first time I'd dealt with women like Ella and Mom. Up until a year ago, I'd worked as a social worker in Child Protective Services. I dealt with many women who neglected their children due to their love of narcotics and alcohol.

I tried to help as many women as I could, but not all of them stayed clean or kept their children. They craved love, but they had no idea how to love themselves, let alone others.

While being a social worker, I focused more on the children. Innocent kids who lived in toxic environments where addiction reigned. My main focus was finding them a foster home, making sure they were safe. Part of my job was to talk to the parents. Mostly the mothers who had lost themselves and their lives. I didn't judge the women. All of them had been there for one reason or another. They deserved my understanding and support. But I hurt when they gave up on themselves.

My heart sank as I studied Ella. Her make-up was perfect, her smile fake. Nothing fulfilled her. She craved love, but she couldn't deal with relationships. Ella didn't know how to share. As the years passed, I worried more and more about her.

I'd hate to see Ella behaving the same way for the next thirty years.

"If you need me, you know where to find me," I said.

"You're judging."

"No." I fixed my beanie hat. "Just worried about you. You had a hard time getting over your last boyfriend, Raphael. You used a lot of pot and vodka to get you through. Now it's Joe."

"Well, I worry about you too." She patted her purse. "One of the hottest men alive gave you his number, and you rejected him. Any woman would come in her panties after reading that poem. But you don't, because you won't let yourself *live*. There's nothing wrong with drinking, partying, and fucking."

"You're right. There's nothing wrong with either one—in moderation." I exhaled, massaging my temples.

I loved Ella, but sometimes getting through to her was more laborious than taming a lion.

"I don't have alcohol at home because my mother—who is an alcoholic and a drug addict—visits me unannounced. But I enjoy a cocktail or two when I go out. I drink wine with my dinner when it's possible.

For me, there's no point in hooking up just because it feels right. I did it during college and a few years after that."

"Did you?" She tilted her head; her condescending tone made my blood boil. "Because I recall you pining for Alex like a sick puppy. Remember him?"

Alex, I mumbled his name for the first time in years.

My college boyfriend. Well, we didn't have a label. I chewed my lip as I recalled what I thought was the affair of the century. A romance that would last for years. My rose-colored glasses didn't allow me to see him for who he was. An immature, good looking college guy who slept around campus.

I tried so hard to be the one who would change him.

"Babe, you can't dictate my life. Love is free," he'd say each time I confronted him.

My world collapsed each time I found out about his new flavor of the month. But I always forgave him because if I was patient, I'd fix him. After a couple of years, I broke up with him, but that didn't stop me from dating guys just like him.

"I remember Alex and every other guy I went out with after him. Which is exactly why I don't date scumbags," I gave her a sharp nod. "Unfortunately, I mix sex with feelings."

"You're not your mother," she said, snapping her fingers. "Wake up! Live! Stop being afraid that you'll end up like her. I won't stop being me just because you think I'm wrong. One day, I'll find the right guy."

I bit my tongue. Because she might have been putting herself out there, but every time she ended a relationship it took her months and several bottles of vodka to repair her heart. Our discussion was heading toward a fight. Any other time I wouldn't mind, but she needed me to be around.

"I think it's best if I leave, we're not getting anywhere." I bent down and gave her a hug. "Take care of yourself, El."

"That's right. Run from the truth."

Was there any truth in her words? No. She was hurting so badly that she was trying to take me down with her. I adored Ella. But when she burned, she tried to set everyone around her on fire, so they'd share her hell. This time, it wouldn't be me.

"You're wrong. I just choose not to date the wrong guy." I clenched my fists.

Somedays, I hated her. If anyone knew how to get under my skin, it would be Ella DeVonaire.

"Nobody likes to be alone. But I won't hook up with a well-known playboy just to forget that I don't have anyone." I tapped my foot while pointing a shaky finger toward the door. "He's not going to soothe the need. I want a soulmate."

"Ugh, that soulmate shit again."

"What can I say? I believe that souls come in pairs," I explained. "I'd give anything to find mine."

Fall for a guy who'll treat my heart with gloves and my body with rough love. Someone who won't slash my insides when they walk away.

I stroked my neck, calming my voice. "Because they won't walk away."

I waved my hand toward the door. "I'm too old to be kissing toads, knowing they'll never become princes."

"Your loss." She fished Kaden's note out of her purse and kissed it.

"Give me that," I ordered her. "It's mine."

She opened it, scanned it and handed it to me. "Sometimes you're so fucking boring."

"Call me when you're in a better place." I said, leaving the café.

Chapter Eight

KADE

"What are we waiting for?" Jax lit up his cigarette and handed me back my zippo. "It's cold, wet, and late."

"She has to come out." I clamped the cigarette between my teeth, taking a drag of it and filling my lungs with smoke.

Smoking was bad, but I chose the vice over all other addictions. It helped me calm my nerves before a concert, when I was stressed—or just waiting.

"Who's coming out?"

"Never mind, you can leave," I suggested not wanting to give him an explanation. We drove in separate cars, and he lived in Renton, about thirty minutes west of the city. "It won't be long, and I'm going home afterward."

The café was about to close in less than twenty minutes. She had to come out soon.

"Hmm," He took a drag of his cigarette, let the smoke out in a sequence of circles and gazed at me. "The pretty brunette?"

"Can you blame me?"

"No, but you go more for the blonde type. Easy, fast, and goodbye."

"There's something about Sadie."

"She has a name," he laughed. "She's way out of your league. If I were you, I wouldn't waste my time with her."

"I have to try."

"She got to you, didn't she? I never thought I'd see the day that you'd chase someone."

I shrugged, unable to respond to his comment. There's something about Sadie that pulled me to her. I wanted to taste her, to find out what it was about her that I wanted so badly. No one had ever gotten under my skin—and it only took her a few beats.

"Good luck, Hades." He extinguished his half-smoked cigarette before tossing it away in the trash can.

Ten minutes after Jax left, she came out of the café. Turning to her left, she walked at a fast pace.

"Stop following me. It's creepy," she stopped at the red light, waiting for the green to continue walking.

"It's after midnight."

I hated that she wasn't taking a cab or walking with someone else. Downtown Seattle wasn't a safe place after midnight. Following her wasn't just about finding out more about her, but also making sure she arrived home safely.

"Interesting. Eleven thirty is after midnight?" she sassed me.

"It's not safe for you to walk by yourself."

"Seems like I'm not alone." She continued walking fast, not stopping for anything.

Once we arrived at a tall steel building, she halted looking for something inside her purse. Once she opened the main door, she turned toward me and smiled. "Thank you for the company. Next time you might want to try walking beside me."

"Try not to walk by yourself so late at night."

"Good night, Mr. Hades."

She entered the building without letting me say more. I typed her address into my phone and walked back to my truck. Tomorrow I'd call Kevin. He was one of my best buddies and had his own band. The guy knew people who could help me track her information. I had the nagging feeling that she wouldn't call me.

But I was wrong. Two hours later a text arrived.

Thank you for your number. Why don't you come to see me? We have all night.

The address she sent was different from the one I'd written down, but still in the area.

It surprised me she would text at almost at three in the morning. She didn't seem like the booty call kind of woman. However, I didn't really know her, and after the blue balls she gave me, I threw caution to the wind.

"Oh goody, you're here." It was Sadie's blonde friend who greeted me upon opening the door.

"You're drunk," I declared, my nostrils flared as I took deep breaths.

I'd given Sadie my number, not her friend. Why did she give it to her? The lyrics I wrote were dedicated to her. It was something I was working on in my head but wouldn't finish until I know more about her. Until we kissed.

"Tipsy," she hiccupped, taking off her shirt. "Where do you want me, playboy?"

"This isn't happening." I exhaled, turning around ready to walk away.

Though, I halted as I heard the retching noise followed by a *thunk*. Ella was on her knees, holding her stomach and puking her brains out. I'd been there many times, and I didn't have the heart to leave her alone.

"Let's get you to the bathroom."

"Yes, baby, take me in the bathroom, against the wall. We can do it in the shower."

Chapter Nine

KADE

Karma's a bitch. It never forgot, and always served me what I deserved.

Jax dealt with my addiction for a long time. He'd stay with me all night when I was on a binge. He called me an asshole many times. Bailed me out of jail, and other shitty situations I got myself into, without ever complaining.

After spending the night with Ella, I understood part of what he'd dealt with while my brain was drowning in alcohol. However, I never tried to have sex with him. Ella was relentless. She rubbed her naked body against me a couple of times.

She wasn't my temptation though. It was the amount of liquor she had around her house. Heat flushed through my body all night as I fought the need to grab one of the bottles of vodka she had on the counter and drink it all. I felt weak, my body ached, and I struggled to maintain my sobriety. Between the anger and the amount of alcohol that she owned, I was about to relapse. I focused on my daughters instead.

That morning, Ella flirted some more, but at least she wasn't naked trying to fuck me. To finish my babysitting duty, I took her to have a hearty, greasy breakfast since her refrigerator was empty. It wasn't an act of charity, but a way to get closer to Sadie. It had been a big mistake. I couldn't stand the woman. She was demanding, irritating, and entitled.

"Next time we go out, I expect you'll be taking me to a much better restaurant."

My mouth opened as wide as my eyes. She was fucking unreal. A piece of work that I dealt with because I'd trusted Sadie with my number.

"There's not going to be a next time. I stayed with you last night because you were too drunk to be alone."

She clamped her lips and watched me for several beats.

"Well, then I have to ask, are you gay?" she finally asked as she drank her Bloody Mary.

"What the fuck?" I spit my coffee, laughing at her. The waitress appeared right away and helped me clean up the mess.

"You need help. What you did last night was dangerous."

"Oh, for fuck's sake, you sound just like Sadie."

At the mention of her name, I stiffened. Last night happened because Sadie handed my number to her friend. If she didn't want anything to do with me, she should've just tossed it away.

"Why did your friend give you my number?"

I drummed my fingers against the table waiting for her response. The fact that I had to deal with Ella angered me. But I wasn't upset at the brown-eyed girl. She hypnotized me. In fact, as I waited for her answer. My fingers played the melody Sadie's voice inspired when she first spoke to me.

"Because I wanted it." She shrugged one shoulder, fidgeting with the napkin.

"Somehow, I don't believe you."

I used my index finger to lift her chin and look into her eyes. "Sadie didn't give it to you." I guessed.

Her green eyes avoided me. Ella reminded of my thirteen-year-old daughter, Tess. The times when she tried to blame her little sister, Hannah, and I caught her. Defiant, yet remorseful. The distinct pout of a spoiled child who believed that everyone should be serving them. They thought that nothing nor no one could ever punish them.

"Why do you have my number?"

"I memorized it. Saved it on my phone after she left the coffee shop."

"This is enough to pay for breakfast." I rose from my seat and threw down a fifty-dollar bill. "Tell Sadie that number is no longer in service. I'll reach out to her."

"She will never let you fuck her," she yelled. The entire restaurant went silent. All eyes were on me.

I pivoted around and gave her a sharp nod. "Good, because that's not what I want from her. *I want more.*"

The last words came out of nowhere. More wasn't part of my life or my vocabulary. The only time I'd dared to have it, I lived in a little hell called my ex-wife's world. But something inside my heart told me that Sadie wasn't Alicia. And for the first time in years, I dared to believe there was something beyond a night of fucking, rubbing skin against skin, and nameless women.

"You think she's innocent, don't you? Well, she's not."

"What is it?" I dared her to respond. "Is she a harlot or a saint?"

"She doesn't fuck trash like you," she concluded.

I didn't pay attention to her hurtful words. She wasn't the first woman who'd insulted me for pissing her off. While walking out of the restaurant, I texted Duncan.

Hades: I need a new number.

Duncan: How many times have I told you to keep your phone locked?

Hades: Just get me a phone.

Duncan: I'll bring it to your house in a couple of hours.

Hades: Good, I'm turning this one off.

Ella gave me the impression of a trouble maker. If I ever wanted to have a shot with Sadie, I had to move quickly. One phone call and her friend, the bitch, could ruin everything.

"Were you here all night?" a voice asked as I turned from Pine Street onto 9th Avenue.

I looked up and found Sadie. My heart beat faster, and my legs froze at the sight of her. She was more attractive than I remembered. She glowed, and her eyes twinkled. The softness of her expression showed her inner beauty, and maybe that was why she was the most gorgeous woman I'd ever met.

Sadie barely wore makeup. Her face glowed. It could be her natural, flawless, bronze skin. Her brown eyes like the color of mahogany wood were framed by long, curly eyelashes that looked like majestic butterflies when she blinked her eyes. She radiated confidence and tenderness. A rare combination.

"No, but I've been in the area since three AM. Where are you going this early in the morning?"

She sighed, checking her phone. "Work, but I have to make a pit stop since I got a nine-one-one text from Eleanor."

"Eleanor?"

"Ella," she sighed. "I'm sure she fucked some parasite who trashed her place or stole something. And I have to pause my life and go to her rescue." She rolled her eyes. "Because she doesn't care that I have to work."

"Work on Saturday?"

"Yes, I work six days a week. Seven if you count the time I spend on Sundays planning my week, sketching or doing paperwork," she informed me with a bright smile. "But first I have to make sure Ella is okay."

"She's fine," I assured her.

"How would you know?"

"Because I spent the night with her."

"Oh," she closed her mouth, pressing her lips together into a thin line.

"She memorized my number—when you showed her the note," I accused her, keeping a firm tone. "Those lyrics were just for you, not to show around."

"Well, she got her wish." She stuttered and sucked on her upper lip.

The gesture was simple, but it turned me on. I wanted to drag her body against mine and kiss her tempting mouth slowly.

Deeply.

Claim her as mine.

"Nothing happened between me and Ella," I assured her, hoping that I heard a little jealousy in her tone.

Without wasting time, I explained every detail of what happened between me and her friend.

"You want me to believe that even when she begged, you didn't touch her?" She laughed. "Please, she's beautiful. Everyone wants Ella."

Sadie hugged herself and was again sucking her lip. That habit of hers was driving me insane. If this conversation weren't necessary, I would tease her about her mouth and the things I wanted to do to it. I bet she was fucking amazing in bed and tasted like a goddess. But in order to go from point A to point F, I had to show her that I wasn't an asshole—or a player.

Damn, what was it about this woman that had me tied in a million knots? Or giving a shit about her when she was judging *me* by my appearance and my profession? She looked at me like I was just another junky rock-star dressed in rags, with more tattoos and piercings than common sense.

I usually didn't care about prejudiced people. But I had an inkling that Sadie wasn't judging me, just being cautious. She was a wounded animal who avoided the forest, afraid that a predator would be waiting to attack.

"She's not my type. That's only the tip of the iceberg. She was drunk, and I don't fuck semi-conscious women. That's rape." I showed her one finger and then two. "Second, even if she wasn't drunk, I don't fuck every available female who undresses for me."

Sadie narrowed her gaze not believing me.

"I won't deny that I did it when I was young and stupid," I confessed, showing her three fingers. "Third, I have two daughters. My motto is to treat women with the same respect that I want my girls to be treated with when they grow up. Lastly, she's your friend, and I wouldn't jeopardize what little chance I have of going out with you."

I stepped forward and grabbed her hand, kissing it lightly. She smiled. Her eyes found mine, and we stared at each other for several seconds.

"Thank you for watching out for her." She cupped my cheek and kissed it.

The feel of her skin ignited my entire body. I froze and couldn't think of a single word. My heart beat hard in my chest. Everything around me disappeared. There was only her and the musical notes that surrounded us. A perfect melody for a perfect woman. I wanted to love her, wrap myself around her, and melt with her.

"Give me one date," I said when I finally remembered how to speak.

I held her hand against my cheek, not wanting to let her go. My blood ran hot while powerful lyrics played inside my head.

Sadie pulled her hand back, hugging herself. "I'm sorry for letting her have your number. That was irresponsible on my part."

"And us? What happened to our date?"

"Us?" she chuckled, shaking her head. "If you're looking for a friend, I'm around. That's all I can offer you."

Her mouth said one thing, but I swore her eyes wanted more. She omitted the words and suppressed her feelings, but I could feel the pull of her magnetic personality increasing as the minutes passed. And I saw it. Beneath those beautiful dark pearls, her soul trembled with fear. I had to be careful with my words, and her heart.

"Friendship?" I cleared my throat, trying to calm my pulse.

"Yes, we can be friends. And just because you looked after Ella."

I scratched my temple with my index finger. "See that's something I don't understand. You and Ella being friends."

"We've known each other since we were four, maybe five. She's my person."

More like you're her person. She does whatever she wants with you, I swallowed the words. If I wanted to be close to Sadie, I'd have to play nice with her *person.*

"I could be it for you. Your everything." I dared to offer, because that's exactly what I wanted to be for her. And I wanted her to be my everything.

"My everything?" She crossed her arms, arching an eyebrow.

"You're hot, but I don't just hook up." She shook her head. "Unlike a lot of people, I can't seem to separate sex from feelings. I'm tired of putting myself out there and getting my heart shredded by players who have a menu of women to choose from. And I'm telling you this because you seem like a sensible guy, not to feed your ego."

"You think I'm hot?"

"Seriously? That's all you got from what I just said," she said with a pinch of annoyance.

"You find me attractive," I smirked

"Ugh, my point is that I'm not going to hook up with you."

"No, you said I'm hot and a sensible guy. But you still think that we can be friends."

"Oh, I don't think we can be anything. In fact, I bet you don't even have any female friends."

"I can," I challenged her.

"There's no way you won't try to cross the line within the first couple of days. Which means that even if you accept my offer, we'll go our separate ways almost immediately."

Sadie read people easily. She was right. I was a thirty-three-year-old man who'd never had a single female friend. This friendship would be a test.

"I can be friends with a woman—with you." I accepted because it seemed like it'd be the only way she'd let me near her. "But can you be friends with me?"

I challenged her back, pulling out my phone, powering it back on and starting an email to myself.

Then, I handed it to her. "Why don't you give me your *real* number and your email address? Once I have a new number, we can begin our new relationship."

It'd be something new, and I was positive that it'd be a challenge. But I could try to get to know her. Something inside me told me that I'd be a fool to let her go.

"There's no relationship between us," she said, pulling her wallet out of her purse. "But maybe I can invite you to dinner. A tit for a tat since you took care of Ella."

Oh, I wanted the tit, and after sucking them to ecstasy, I would fuck her a tat. Fucking shit, this friendship thing was going to give me a case of blue balls, but I was up for the challenge.

"Give me a call when you're ready to cash in on that dinner." She gave me a business card.

Hummingbird Flower Designs
Sadie Loza-Bell

"Hummingbird?" I stared at the robin's egg blue card, studying the white silhouette of a bird holding a flower. "A unique name for a flower shop."

The card looked classy, delicate and exceptional. It was the perfect representation of who I thought Sadie was.

"I agree. That's why I chose it," she said, with a satisfied smile. "Everyone uses blooms, or daisies, their last name, and then flower shop."

"But why hummingbird and not another bird?"

"*Nightingale* was in the running since they are my favorite birds. Their singing is beautiful. I love music. It's a big part of me, sets my mood, and calms me. But *hummingbird* made more sense since they only eat nectar and help pollinate flowers. The flower is a gardenia, one of my favorites."

"Music, you love music?"

"You have selective hearing, don't you?" She frowned.

"Music is my life." I traced a finger along my arm. "It's what's inside me, running through my veins."

I stepped closer to her and hummed a part of the melody that had played in my head since we first spoke. "No one has ever inspired me before like you do. I can't wait to finish this song—*your* song."

My lips lingered close to her ear. I wanted to sing to her for an eternity—about meeting the perfect woman and falling deeply in lust from the first sight. I wanted to spend more time with her, to dare to experience what I'd never had before in my life. But I was also afraid that this woman would confirm I wasn't capable of love, or that I was unlovable.

"It's late. I have to open up the shop."

With those words she ran away, leaving her sweet flowery aroma behind, along with many unresolved questions.

Chapter Ten

SADIE

I bolted before I did something stupid. Like kiss him or fall in love, confusing a bunch of pick-up lines for the beginning of a love story. Something about him felt exciting, dangerous, and forbidden. Like a new, dangerous drug that promised to take me to some unimaginable place where dreams come true. The first hit was free.

Once hooked, I'd need more to satiate the craving.

I knew that once the big rush wore off, I'd need more of him. The subsequent shot would be costly. He'd claim my heart, then my soul, and once I had nothing left to pay, he'd discard me broken and desperate for more.

Yet, I didn't take the warning seriously. There was something about that man. His low, rough voice made my heart beat faster every time he spoke. His hypnotizing blue-gray eyes peered down into my soul, trying to possess it. When he was close, I could feel the heat of his body. It made me want to let myself burn with his touch.

Nothing about him made sense. My unusual reactions to him scared me, yet I wanted to be ignited and consumed by his fire.

Was that why there was a constant warmth running through my body?

No. Kaden Hades had no effect on me. I dusted my arms, cleansing myself from his touch. That heat was Ella's second-hand embarrassment. Not my imagination, wondering how his hands and lips would feel when they finally skirted over my naked body.

Because nothing would happen between us. He was sex, sin, and lust. Everything I would want in *bed*. But was he love? I doubted it.

Kaden Hades looked like a bad boy and talked like a smooth operator. I bet he devoured women with just a simple kiss. His proximity alone made me forget myself. What would happen if I let myself taste him just once?

One bite.

To burn the desire growing deep in my core I ran toward my shop, ignoring Ella's "emergency" text. My friend liked to be the center of attention. If Kade rejected her, she'd be whining about it for months— maybe years. I couldn't believe she used the number. The embarrassment and guilt made me sick to my stomach.

Once I arrived at the flower shop, my phone rang. It was Ella. I sent her to voicemail and unlocked the front door. Bending down, I turned on the sensor, and looked around the store to make sure I didn't have to stock the shelves.

I pulled out the bracelets and necklaces from the velvet bags that were in the safe and set them in the display case.

My shop was more than a place to buy flowers. It was a place where people could buy something special for their loved ones to celebrate, commiserate, tell them how much they meant or any other of the many reasons to send a present. I sold greeting cards, frames, stuffed animals, candy, chocolates, books and other knick-knacks for every occasion: from thoughtful husbands to forgetful boyfriends. When young fathers came to buy flowers for their wives, they left with presents for their little ones too.

"Morning, Raven," I called out to my assistant manager who opened the shop on Saturdays so I could have fun on Friday nights.

I never met her expectations though. She anticipated hearing sexy stories about some crazy evening with a rich guy like Christian Grey. But every week I disappointed her.

"Good morning," She greeted me from the back of the store. "Did you do something fun last night?"

"Yes." For the first time in months, I had some sort of answer.

Nothing too sexy, or kinky. Kaden Hades gave me his number, he wanted a date and almost slept with Ella. It sounded like gossip for a tabloid.

"I went to Logan's café. They had an unplugged concert."

"You watched a live performance of Killing Hades!" she screeched like a teenager.

"Who did you sleep with? Kaden or Jax?"

"What?"

"Yes, she banged a rock star!" She clapped and whistled. The noise boomed through the silent store.

"Are the arrangements we have to deliver ready?" I changed the subject.

"Yes, I finished loading the van. If it's okay with you, I'll deliver, and you can take care of the orders we receive starting ... now!" she replied with that game show voice that drove me insane.

"So, what happened during the concert?" Now that tone sounded provocative. "Did you hook up with any of the band members?"

"No."

"A stranger?"

"There was no hookup involved. Zero sex."

"Damn you, Sadie," she protested. "You have to find a man to take care of that itch. Even *I* have sex."

"Of course you have sex. You're married," I reminded her. "I've heard sex is part of the marriage contract, isn't it? And you and your husband have a pretty active sex life."

"Should I remind you about last Saturday when I caught the two of you having sex inside the walk-in fridge?" I made a gagging sound.

She didn't respond, thank God. I was still having nightmares about her and Bill half naked and going hard and fast. My poor innocent flowers witnessed the ordeal too.

"Maybe next Friday I'll find some hot guy, and I'll send you a picture," I offered. "For now, let's get to work."

"Yes, boss."

Before I began working, I dropped my purse inside the tiny room I called my office. There wasn't much to it. A desk, a chair, and a filing cabinet. Everything I needed was in the shop. I walked toward the register, where I had my computer.

As I checked the new orders, my hand flew toward my mouth, and I gasped. "We got a special order!"

I clapped excitedly when I saw that the customer not only ordered an arrangement of jasmine, lilacs and peonies, but also a blossoming gardenia bonsai. This order let me breathe a sigh of relief. The store was only a year old, and though it was profitable, I was still concerned about my future.

Before I gathered the flowers and fixed the bouquet, I pulled out my phone. I opened the music app and chose one of my playlists. I fetched the flowers, some greenery and set them on the working table. Then I went to the storage closet to get a vintage cut glass vase.

"Those flowers are beautiful," Raven approached.

"My favorites." I walked to the stand where I had my bonsais on display.

"Once I finish it, we should take a picture for the scrapbook," I commented, cutting the stems of the flowers.

Since I opened the shop, I'd started a scrapbook with pictures of my designs and notes that were worth keeping because the words were either heartwarming, swoony or touching—or all of the above.

"Where is it going?"

"No idea?" I was too excited about putting it together to read the details. I tilted my head toward the computer. "Why don't you check and print the card?"

Raven walked to the front desk and gasped.

"Oh my God! This guy has a big crush on whoever is getting it. And I have the feeling that the recipient is playing hard to get. Maybe the other guy is married and doesn't want to come out of the closet. Two gay guys and a forbidden love!"

I rolled my eyes at her. "Are we already making up a love story?"

"Of course, that's why I love working for you," she said, sighing while mumbling something under her breath.

"We have to save a copy of this note," she declared with a swoony voice. "This is one of the best we've ever gotten. I swear if she or he doesn't fall for him, I'll divorce Manny and date the guy."

"Your husband's name is Bill," I rolled my eyes, my body shook as I tried to muffle the laughter.

"See, I've already forgotten about him. Just tell my ex to keep our children alive. I'm eloping to Vegas." She hugged herself, moving her hands all over her body, and blew kisses several times.

"When you're done fondling yourself, read it to me," I teased her and continued working on the arrangement.

"I'll take those million moments any way you'll share them with me, and I'll dance to whatever music your heart plays. Your new friend. Kade," Raven sighed after she finished reading the note.

My body froze when I put together the words, *million moments,* and the name, Kade.

"What did you say?" I marched toward the computer to make sure that this Kade wasn't my Kade.

Well, Kade wasn't mine, but the coincidence of the name and similarity of the note to the one he gave me last night was uncanny. And my eyes widened when I realized that the flowers were going to Sadie Loza-Bell. Both the arrangement and the bonsai. The address was my shop.

My pulse accelerated, and my heart melted a little. That damn man with his perfect words had struck again. Apparently, his shenanigans included perfect gestures.

"Those flowers are addressed to you and..." She gasped as she read who they came from. "Is that *the* Kaden Hades?"

Raven traced his name several times. Another example as of why I should stay away from him. Every woman in the world wanted a piece of Kaden Hades. Even my assistant manager, who was happily married, had a crush on him.

"Nice choice to end the drought," she said.

"You're fired," I said, annoyed with her and with Kade.

"Not until you have sex with the rock-God and give me all the deets," she protested. "I want a report that includes everything, even the size of his dick."

She wiggled her eyebrows. "Rumor has it that he has a monster dong."

"Dong?" I chuckled. "Penis, cock, shaft, dick... but don't call it dong."

"Whatever, I just want to know every detail." She walked away and came back carrying my camera. "Maybe take a few pics of his naked, lick-able body."

I tried to ignore her and continue working. But I couldn't stop picturing his taut body. Raven had piqued my curiosity. Should I google Kaden Hades' dick? How big was it?

Would size matter?

"So, what's the story with you and my soon to be husband?"

"There's no story," I clarified while staring at my perfect arrangement and the little bonsai that wanted to come home with me.

"The flowers say something different."

"They're not mine," I insisted.

"Sadie Loza-Bell," Raven read out loud. "That's you. There's no other Sadie at this address."

"Should I fire you?"

"No, you need me, and you'll need me more once you have an active sex life with the hottest man in Seattle."

How do I return them? I'd never accepted presents from a guy I didn't plan on dating. By doing so, I'd give the impression that something more could happen.

I shouldn't allow for anything to happen. Kaden knew the words, but I knew what men like him were capable of. Hurt. They couldn't love. I'd stick to my just one dinner plan.

That was fine until one of his songs played over the speakers. His raspy voice and angst-filled lyrics never failed to make my heart skip. Last night, listening to him sing in person was an out of body experience. We sang every song together. For a moment, I believed he was singing only to me.

My skin tingled remembering his touch, while I wished that his mouth had traced my naked silhouette.

Stop, Sadie. I wanted to kick myself for having those thoughts, and him for making me want him.

"So, that dreamy face has nothing to do with Mr. Rock-God."

"You don't understand, I can't—."

The sensor chimed. I looked up to find Ella entering the store. "Does nine-one-one mean nothing to you?"

"And I thought this would be a bitch free Saturday," Raven mumbled under her breath.

"You didn't have an emergency, Ella," I said exasperatedly.

All the fluttery butterflies that danced in my stomach vanished. They were afraid of Miss Ella De Vil. Her last name was DeVonaire, but some days the former represented her personality to a 't.' Some days it felt like if I weren't around to stop her, she'd be skinning innocent puppies and sucking the blood of innocent children.

"Kaden Hades is gay," she announced.

"Really?" I crossed my arms.

"Do you have pictures of him and a guy—or a video," Raven challenged her. "Because I love watching boy on boy action."

"Well no, of course, I don't." She scrunched her nose in disgust. "Go back to work, nosy bitch."

"Please don't start, Ella," I warned her. "Now, why are you spreading rumors about Kade?"

"I just know." She huffed.

I rolled my eyes and stared at the door, searching for the right words to kick her out. Or wait for Raven who always had fun doing it for me.

"Fine, don't get mad at me but I spent the night with him—naked." She glared at me, then she waved her hands around her body. "He refused to touch this. I was ready for him—I shaved instead of waxing."

I gasped, touching my lips lightly with my fingers. "Shaved?" I mocked her.

"You had to use a *razor*? God, have mercy!" Raven yelled in horror, touching her chest lightly with her left hand and doing the sign of the cross with the right. "Like us mortals."

"Why is *the help* interrupting our conversation?"

"Stop it. I get that you're in a shitty mood but don't take it on

Rae," I advised her with a stern voice. "We can talk about your latest obsession tonight."

When I'm less confused about my own issues with Mr. Hades. Well, they aren't issues. More like doubts about how to react to his smooth words and gestures.

"What's with you today, Sadie?" She walked to the counter, resting her hands and leaning forward. "You're such a selfish bitch. Can you focus on me for a change? This is important. Maybe he's not gay. Though, why do you think he rejected me? I think he's playing hard to get." She smirked slightly. "But I'll get him. You just have to help me."

"First of all, I've told you several times that you shouldn't drink and invite strange men over to your house. You're putting yourself in danger." I paced my hands on my hips. "Second, I'm not helping you get anyone. He's not interested. Leave him alone."

"How do you know I was drunk?"

"He came to see me," I sighed.

"*And* he sent her flowers," Raven marched to where I stood, holding the bouquet.

Ella narrowed her gaze, set her hands on her hips, and huffed. "He's mine. We have an agreement. You promised when we were fifteen."

Raven laughed, holding her stomach. "You always crack me up, Ella." Then she turned to me. "You're not fifteen anymore, are you?"

"Rae, it's delivery time." I tilted my head toward the back door.

The two of them were about to have a catfight if I didn't stop them.

"Fine, I'm leaving, boss." She slumped her shoulders walking away. "But if Plastic Girl is here when I get back, I can't be held responsible for my actions."

"You should fire her," Ella huffed.

"Ella, I have work to do. I'm glad that Kade didn't take advantage of you."

"The fucker swears that he wants you, not me." She fumed, her face turning red.

"Fucking asshole, he thinks you're pure and innocent," she said, bitterness lacing with the words. "But I set him straight about you and told him that you wouldn't fuck his trashy ass."

"You...you what?" My mouth gaped, I was at a loss of words. "After taking care of you, you insulted him? You're unbelievable."

"Well, you wouldn't fuck him, would you?"

"That's none of your business."

I crossed my arms and scanned the flower shop looking for white and pink objects. That exercise calmed my anger and anxiety. It had been a long time since Ella got on my nerves, but she had finally done it. I'd had enough of her. My patience ran thin. In the name of our friendship, I decided to take a break.

"Out," I ordered her. "We need some time apart."

"Not again," she complained, slumping her shoulders and stomping a foot like a five-year-old and not the twenty-eight-year-old woman she was. "I need you, Sadie-Wadie-Woo."

I marched to the door and swung it open. "Out."

Ella straightened her back, lifted her chin and threw her meanest glare my way. "You're going to regret this," she warned me and left.

Chapter Eleven

SADIE

The rest of my working day went off without a hitch. However, Ella's departure left me shaking with anger. As she grew older, her selfish attitude reminded me more and more of my mother. They only cared about themselves and never learned from their mistakes.

The latest incident should have been the beginning of the end. But I was weak. If she dropped by with a big apology, I knew that I'd let her back into my life. My therapist would ask me why I kept repeating the same action and expecting a different result. When in fact, I knew what the outcome would be.

Because I loved her, and we were supposed to see beyond the imperfections of our friends, weren't we?

My friendship with Ella was toxic, mostly for me. Thankfully, after an hour or so I calmed down. Working with flowers relaxed me. This shop was my dream, my therapy, and my entire life. As long as I had the shop, I was happy.

Did I feel lonely?

I looked around, and my eyes landed on the rice milk chai tea latte that was delivered earlier to me. Yet, another present from Kaden Hades. The same drink I had last night, along with a gluten-free cranberry scone—my favorite.

For a few minutes, I allowed myself to believe that he was just a charming man who wanted to woo me. Until another one of his songs began to play on the speakers. Raven's words played inside my head several times.

What do you have to lose if you go out with him?

Before I could answer my question, the chimes of the doorbell rang.

"Sorry, we're closed," I yelled and grabbed my keys.

"Well then, you should turn your sign and lock the front door," the low, raspy voice said.

My heart beat fast. Who could be dropping by at two in the afternoon? No one ever came this late. I held my breath as I saw a tall man turning the open sign around. Hypnotized by his perfect male form, I stared with my mouth agape. Corded arms, broad back. His tight t-shirt showing the sculpted muscles of his back, and for a second, I imagined the front would be as lean and fit.

He turned around and my heart skipped a beat when I recognized him. His bright gray eyes focused on mine.

"Why are you here?" I controlled my tone and ignored the sparks flying around us.

"Can't a friend just drop by to visit?"

A friend, yes. You shouldn't be near me.

"How can I help you, Mr. Hades?"

"Mr. Hades?" He cleared his throat looking around. "Call me Kaden, Kade ... not Mr. Hades. That's too formal. But I liked the way that it sounded coming out of your beautiful mouth." His eyes found mine and he beamed.

I rolled my eyes. *Fight those flirty words, Sadie.*

"Is there something I can do for you? I'm about to close the shop."

"If that's what you're doing, I can help you."

"Cleaning?" I stared at him shocked by the offer. "Don't you have people for that?"

He held his stomach while laughing. "You're funny."

"You're telling me you do the cleaning at home?"

"Maybe I have someone dropping by weekly to make sure my apartment is spotless. But I do most of the *dirty* work." He showed me his big hands. "These babies know their way around a broom and dustpan."

The suggestive tone turned my insides upside down. *Breathe, Sadie. He's just another player trying to get laid.*

I couldn't help but stare at him. My eyes lingered on his body. It was toned, fit. Hard lines delineating each muscle on his chest. And those strong arms ... but it was his hands with those long fingers that made me want to break a few rules.

"Is everything okay?"

My entire body shivered with his thick, low voice. I wanted Kaden to whisper dirty things in my ear, use his hands to touch every inch of my body, to make me come with his touch.

What are you doing, Sadie?

I'm wet and ready for that hunk.

I moved my eyes toward his crotch, there was definitely a package in there. But how big was it?

Stop!

I closed my eyes, mentally slapped myself, and breathed long enough to control the urge.

"Then I hope you don't mind sweeping." I walked to the janitor's closet for the broom. "Do you know how to use this?"

"Yes. I say *Accio Firebolt*, and it'll fly, right?"

"And the guy thinks he's funny." I twist my mouth biting the laugh. "Why don't you start with the front? The dustpan-vacuum is mounted on that wall. Just sweep the trash over there, and it'll suck it. I'll be mopping right behind you."

He saluted me and without hesitation began to work. It took us half the time that it usually would to tidy the place. I grabbed my things, set the alarm, and we left through the back entrance.

"Where are the flowers I sent you?" He stared at my hands.

I smiled. "Raven, my assistant manager, delivered them to my house."

"Did you like them?"

"Yes, I did," I confessed.

I adored them, and I was grateful to him because no one had ever sent me flowers. Or anything for that matter. This guy had studied the book on how to go into battle and conquer. He was good, but I wouldn't let my guard down.

"Thank you for sending them." I hugged myself, avoiding those penetrating eyes.

That gaze hypnotized me. Looking at them was like staring at a magical frozen lake which had a blue fire within. I wanted to get lost in them. My logic won over desire, though. I knew what'd happened after the fire consumed me.

I wouldn't survive.

"You shouldn't have sent them. They're expensive." I said, tilting my head toward my home. "I appreciate the visit and all your presents. Have a nice day."

I began walking away.

"When was the last time someone sent you flowers?" His rough voice slid down my spine, shooting a charge of electricity around my entire body.

I shivered and stopped mid-step. When I turned around, I collided with a sturdy wall of muscle, and my nostrils were hit with his sandalwood and tobacco scent. His hands captured my arms, steading my body. I craned my neck. He bent his. Our noses almost touched, and if I stretched my neck one more inch, I would finally taste him.

"Long ago?" I lied. No one had ever done it before.

"Your eyebrow is twitching," he smiled. "Are you nervous, or upset? Not sure, but those warm eyes are smiling. I bet you don't get angry easily."

"What makes you think that I can't get mad?"

"You might, but it's against your nature."

"My nature?"

"You're made of sunshine, rainbows, and happiness." He caressed my jaw with the back of his finger, his other arm holding me secure against him. "Your bright light is a magnet to my darkness."

I doubted that my make-up included all those, but his darkness did call to me. I wanted to reach inside his soul and evaporate the undeniable pain that he carried with him.

Such a bad idea, Sadie.

How many men have you tried to help that abandoned you, leaving you alone and with a broken heart?

But none of them sent me flowers, helped me clean my shop, or held me like I was precious.

"So, when was the last time someone sent you flowers?"

I shook my head, wanting to run away from him, but I couldn't move. Those eyes hypnotized me. I was at his mercy. "No one has ever sent me anything."

"You deserve to receive them every day."

"Why would you say that?"

"You seem like the kind of person who takes care of everyone and doesn't ask for anything in return. I doubt you have time to care for yourself," he said, brushing away a strand of hair from my face.

A shiver ran through my body. His voice, his *words*, and those strong, safe arms made me want him as my haven.

"What are your plans for the rest of today, *friend?*"

His bedroom eyes and husky voice made the hairs on the back of my head stand on end. I was lost in Kaden Hades, and the scary part was that I wanted to remain there. I took a step backward, leaving his embrace.

In an instant, a rush of coldness ran through my body, missing his protective hold. I hugged myself, rubbing my arms to warm me up, but it wasn't the same.

"Hmm." I tapped my chin thinking of the things I could do to avoid going home so he would leave. "I'm going to the grocery store for food. Maybe the bookstore. There's a gift shop I want to check out that has some jewelry I want to carry."

"What about tonight's concert," he added.

"I'm skipping it." I turned around and resumed walking toward the store. "The next time I leave my house will be Monday morning. Have a good rest of your day," I said, walking away.

Chapter Twelve

SADIE

"Or we can spend more time together." His voice was close, his heat almost burning my skin.

Ignore him, keep walking. But it's so hard.

He followed me all the way to the gift shop.

"Are we spying?" He leaned closer, so close I could feel the warmth of his body.

"Nope. Trying to find out where these beauties come from?"

I touched a beautiful purple necklace with a butterfly charm.

"Owl Creations?" He read the sign. "Why don't you carry this? Not that I understand why you carry so much stuff in a flower shop."

"They're from some exclusive designer. The stores that carry them never reveal much information. There's no website or phone behind it."

I grabbed a yellow and teal bracelet with a bird charm. It was beautiful but almost two hundred dollars. How much of a profit could they be making?

"It looks a lot like your business card."

"That's what I was thinking. It's gorgeous." I put it back, but Kaden took it and went to the register.

I observed him from afar, while he flirted with the cashier. A part of me wanted to stop him—and felt jealous. The other part was curious about this exchange. Was he trying to pry some information out of her? Patiently I waited, until I saw her handing him a small bag. He paid with cash.

"Enjoy," he said and handed me the little bag.

"I can't accept it, but did she tell you where they're from?"

"She said they're exclusive, that the owner handpicks who sells her merchandise."

"It's never going to happen, never in a million years." I frowned, crossing my arms so he couldn't give me the little gift bag he was carrying.

"Why not?" He pulled out his phone.

"What are the chances that the artist would think of me? I own a flower shop."

"There's always a possibility." He tapped his phone, then winked at me.

"Make sure to be at your store next week, though. Just in case someone happens to know said artist." He winked at me again.

"You're a strange man, Mr. Hades."

"So where to next?"

"You're going home. I'm going to the grocery store."

I continued my way down the street to the market and grabbed a shopping basket from the stack. But Kaden, who appeared to be bored and in need of following me, took it from me.

"Any plans for today?" I asked while picking out produce.

"So far just grocery shopping followed by the bookstore." He took my hand and slipped the bracelet over it.

"It looks perfect." Kaden stared at my lips. "You're lucky we're in public."

I stared back at his face speechless. He bought me a bracelet. But I narrowed my gaze. "Why am I lucky?"

"Because I'd be kissing the fuck out of you if we were alone."

"You don't kiss friends." I picked an imaginary piece of lint from my sweater.

"What happens if I do?"

"You'll be banished for life."

"That's harsh."

"No, it's realistic." I grabbed two cartons of rice milk.

"Is the milk a preference?" he asked scrunching his nose.

"No, I'm allergic to dairy, soy, and peanuts. That's why the coffee shop where you played is my favorite. They get their pastries from an allergy-friendly bakery."

"How about ice cream?"

"Allergic to dairy," I repeated and grabbed a bag of frozen blueberries.

"Sorbet?"

"Only if it doesn't have any traces of *dairy*."

"Chocolate?"

"Sometimes I can eat dark chocolate, but it's not my favorite." I scrunched my nose.

"Then I have to cancel the chocolate covered strawberries for Monday."

"Stop sending me things," I said when we stopped by the deli counter.

"That's impossible. I want to make up for the last ..." He started counting with his fingers. "How old are you?"

"How old do you think I am?" I stared at him, sucking on my lower lip.

"You look young, but not that young." He eyed me suspiciously. "Mid-twenties?"

"Maybe," I shrugged.

"Let's say you started dating at sixteen, so between nine and twelve years that I need to make up for," he responded.

"Why do you assume I started dating at sixteen?"

"Guessing, since that's the age my daughters are allowed to start dating."

"Impressive. A father with timelines." I turned around when my number was called.

"What can I do for you, ma'am?"

"Everything is going to be a quarter pound. I need turkey bacon, corned beef, smoked ham, and pastrami."

"Can you give us a pound instead of a quarter, please?" Kaden requested.

The attendant nodded and left.

"Does everyone do everything you say?"

"Sometimes they do, other times they want to kick me out of establishments because they don't like how I look."

"I don't care if you think you can boss me around. You can't change my list. I don't eat that much deli meat."

"But I eat for two—or three. I'm a growing man, you know."

"You're not eating at my house," I said, glaring at him.

"We'll see about that." He walked away toward the bakery.

He came back with a baguette and several pastries. Cookies in case he wanted some during his evening coffee. Who did he think he was?

"*We*, Mr. Hades?" I arched an eyebrow as we walked to the auto check out registers. "You have to go back to first grade and learn your pronouns."

"Pronouns?"

"I." I pointed at me.

"You." I touched his chest lightly. "There's no we."

"*Yet*," he said and began bagging the groceries as I scanned them.

I feigned anger because so far, I had enjoyed his company. Our interaction felt so comfortable. The familiarity between us both scared and excited me. I hated that I enjoyed his company so much. I'd never had so much fun closing the flower shop or going to the grocery store. Once I was finished, I searched for my wallet, but he had already inserted his credit card into the reader. But before he could finish the transaction, I canceled it and replaced his card with mine.

"You're not paying for my groceries."

"But I added things that weren't on your list."

"Well, next time you make your own trip and pay for everything."

"You're stubborn, aren't you?" He smiled.

He turned around, bending to pick up the bags. My mouth opened slightly when his t-shirt pulled slightly giving me a glimpse his muscular stomach. My eyes lifted and looked around us. Everyone was admiring Kaden as if he were on stage.

Something about this guy captivated every person in his proximity.

The simple act of turning around, shoving his longish hair away from his face, and picking up the bags was sexy. His larger-than-life presence, his confidence and determination made him attractive and desired. Or maybe it was something else. I had no idea how to describe it correctly, but he dragged everyone's attention toward him.

"I can take those."

"You paid, I carry." His logic made no sense, but I was still drooling too much over the idea of his abs to fight him. "This way, you can browse around the bookstore freely."

"I think I'm going to skip it."

"We can always go later," he suggested.

No, you have to leave. I don't remember why I don't want you around, but I still have a few functional brain cells that keep reminding me that you're dangerous.

The store wasn't far from my place. When we arrived, I regretted not buying a bottle of wine or beer to offer him. Inviting him for a drink would be the least I could do for him. I'd figure something out. Maybe I should squeeze his oranges. I burst into a loud laugh when I recalled Raven's comment about Kaden's big cock and wondered if his balls were as big as oranges.

Get a grip, Sadie. You need to get laid soon.

It had been too long since the last time I had sex. Lately, I was getting off with the vibrators that Raven gave me for my twenty-seventh birthday, while I watched some quick, dirty video on Tumblr. As turned on as I was, I decided to kick Kaden out and take care of myself with the shower head.

"You can leave the bags on top of the kitchen countertop." I swung the door open.

"Are these the flowers I sent you?" He pointed at the arrangement on top of the table.

"Yes, thank you again, for sending them."

"It was my pleasure." He walked closer to me, lifting my chin.

Our gazes met for a few seconds too long. My skin began to burn under the heat of his lustful look. "You're crossing the lines."

"I wouldn't dare." He broke eye contact and moved away. "But I have to know one thing."

"What?"

"Would you say I delivered the perfect first time?" His eyes crinkled as his grin widened. "Because I plan on giving you the best first, last-time of your life."

My cheeks heated up with that comment, and every logical thought disappeared. I remained standing, staring, blown away by the double meaning of his words.

"Where's the little tree?"

"That's a great question."

Raven had the keys to my apartment for emergencies. Or when I misplaced my keys in the flower shop. I scanned the living-dining room area and then walked into my studio. It was right in the middle of the table.

"Cool room," Kaden stood right behind me. "It's like a reading nook?"

I entered the room and he followed. "It's where I design the wedding arrangements."

He scanned my bookshelves and took one out. "So, there's a college degree for what you do. Flower shop ownery?" He smiled, taking one of my grandma's botanical books.

"That's not a degree," I giggled and cover my mouth because I'm not the kind of woman who giggled.

"Actually, there's landscape design and various botanical degrees. But nothing that's specifically for running a flower shop."

"I was kidding, but that's cool. Which one did you study?"

"Neither," I said, taking the book away from him. "But my grandmother was a botanist, and she taught me everything she knew about plants. We spent a long time in her garden planting seeds, pruning rose bushes ... I knew my way around wildflowers by the time I was five."

I wasn't sure if he was listening to me since he continued browsing my books without acknowledging me. If he was looking for a thriller or some science fiction, I didn't have it in my collection. My shelves were filled with textbooks and biographies. Unlike many, I only read nonfiction books.

"Helping out without Hurting, DBT," he read out loud. "Statistics for Social Workers, Research and Behavior for Effective Social Work."

He frowned touching my old textbooks and reading materials from college and from my other life. "As I said, you care for others."

He turned around and crossed his arms examining me. "I bet you were one of the few good ones in the system." He held my face and stared into my eyes.

"What system?"

"According to your books, you're a social worker." It was a statement, not a question. "I bet you left because you realized the system was corrupt, didn't you?"

"You'd bet wrong. I accept that the system isn't perfect," I paused, studying him.

How did he know? Is that part of the darkness that surrounds his soul? He lost his parents, or they lost him because ...

What's your story, Kaden Hades?

"Nothing is perfect, but I'd like to think that it's better than it was when I was a little girl," I defended what I knew. My truth.

"I wish we had more resources," I continued. "Sometimes we didn't have enough foster parents, and our budget was too slim."

There were times when I had to use my own money to buy clothes for the children that came to us.

"You believe that?" He crooked his thick eyebrow, tilting his head to the side. "Because I bet there are still hundreds, if not thousands of children neglected or abused at home."

"That's a complicated subject. Some parents know how to hide their wrongdoings." I exhaled in frustration. "Like everything that involves humans, you can only help so much. Some days I worked twice as hard without making any progress."

I slumped my shoulders, staring at the wooden flooring. "Many adults only care about themselves, their addictions ... nothing else matters as long as they got their fix and a check from the government."

My mind traveled to the last case I managed, the one I wanted to forget.

"Is that why you quit?" His voice was loud, angry. "Why didn't you just take the children and put them in a safe environment?"

Chapter Thirteen

SADIE

His words felt like a punch to the gut. I did so much, how dare does he judge me?

"I did it!" I couldn't control my voice. He was accusing me. "Twice." I showed him two fingers then I rolled my sleeve, showing him my left arm. "I barely made it out of there."

"What happened?" He gasped and caressed the four-inch-long scar. My heartbeat skipped when he feathered it with kisses.

"She was a meth addict. Her husband was a pimp and a wife beater. The children lived in a good foster home for a couple of years. A part of me wanted to keep them there forever. The other part, the one that had been helping the mom, wanted the family back together. She worked hard to stay sober, got a job. The government provided housing and insurance."

"So, you just gave her the kids back and left?"

"Of course not. I personally didn't hand them over. And we don't just abandoned children. My department continued checking on her. We made sure that she'd kept her job, stayed clean, and didn't neglect the kids. Never told her anything about her ex-husband because he was out of the picture. Well, I assumed that after the beating he gave her, she wouldn't take him back."

"Did you seriously believe that?"

"I wanted to trust her," my voice rose.

"You should have done more."

"Don't you think I did? I used my time and money to keep an eye on them. I paid the neighbors to keep me updated." I paced around the room, calming myself.

"But I bet that the minute the fucker waltzed back into her life, she opened her fucking door, her fucking legs, and snorted everything he gave her," he growled.

Was he blaming me for what had happened? As if this were his own story.

"And you did nothing."

He was blaming me.

"The moment I learned about a guy being at their house, I was ready to ensure the safety of the kids," I defended myself.

"The fucking system hasn't changed." He threw his hands up in the air, glaring at me.

"You can hate the system, but not me. I drove that night to the other side of town to check on the kids, ready to call my supervisor so we could retrieve them if anything was wrong. I never expected to see him," I paused, taking some air. Showing my case before he passed judgment.

"There was a man's jacket on the couch, but there was also some-thing wrong with her. I saw it. The glazed eyes. So, I confronted her. 'Do you want us to take your children away?' I asked her, shaking in rage. Then, I finally noticed. She didn't respond. Her limbs shook. 'Are you high?' I demanded to know, but she stared at the coat closet instead. I grabbed my phone and called my boss, asking him to call the police so they could pick up the kids. That's when the guy jumped out of the closet. 'You bitch,' he yelled pushing me against the couch. 'You won't tear my family apart. I'm going to kill you.' He had a knife. I covered myself with my arm ..."

I broke down, as the fear crept through my body. There I was, lying on a stranger's couch, covering my body with my arms and praying that it wasn't the end. It had been more than a year but as I told the story, the emotional wound opened again.

"I tried so hard."

"It's okay, Sade." Kaden took me in his arms, pressing me hard against him. Protecting me. "You're safe with me."

"I heard the shot. Suddenly he was on top of me. His face bleeding." I rubbed my face, remembering the copper and gunpowder smell. "Sh-she shot him."

I closed my eyes, but all I could see was the blood. His blood, my blood. I pushed him away, he fell to the floor, and I saw her. She pointed the gun at me, yelling that I had ruined her life. It was because of me that she had to kill him. He'd rather die than go to jail.

Take care of the kids, she said. And then... she turned the gun on herself. Her last words before she pulled the trigger haunted me. Her head exploded, blood splattered everywhere, and I couldn't do anything to stop her.

"I wanted her to have a better life," I cried. "But she chose to follow him. She killed herself."

Kade pressed me against him mumbling soothing words, reassuring me that I was okay, that I was with him, that as long as he had me no one would harm me.

"Where were the children?"

"At the neighbors, watching TV because they didn't own one. It had been my idea. I was ready to call the police if I found something suspicious. I just didn't know she was high or that things would turn ... Before she pulled the trigger, she asked me to take care of her kids. But I couldn't," I sobbed.

My body trembled with fear. She could've killed me, and I was just trying to help.

"After that day I couldn't go back to work."

"You're safe. You're with me. What you did was brave, and too dangerous," he said softly.

"Hey, nothing is going to happen to you" he repeated, as tears cascaded down my face. "Let it out. Don't keep anything inside."

His words and the comfort of his arms erased the pain that I had carried with me. I talked about the incident with three different therapists. But no one had held me and let me cry and told me that everything would be okay.

"Sorry," I apologized when I realized that his shirt was soaking wet.

"I'm sorry for being such an asshole to you."

"You were part of the system, weren't you?" He shrugged in response. "Sorry, I don't want to pry or bore you with my stupid stories."

"Hey, they aren't stupid," he said with a terse voice.

"I'm glad you trusted me. That's what friends are for, right?" I nodded in response to his question. "It makes sense that you quit, but why did you decide to open the flower shop?"

"Dad asked me to change careers, arguing that I'd never be safe. He thought I should go back to school." I sighed, going to my room and looking for one of my long t-shirts. "He offered to pay for college. That's him, always thinking of a solution. He never stops to tend the wounds. Honestly, I wasn't planning on going back to work. I couldn't even think beyond the next day, let alone what I'd do with my future.

"Before I quit, I took some time off while I was working through the trauma. I was on administrative paid leave, and their insurance covered my mental health. Every night I had nightmares. Sometimes she shot me everywhere and I gushing blood. Others he beat me ... and in some, I never made it out alive."

I snapped my mouth shut, realizing that I was telling way too much to a man who I barely knew.

"But that doesn't answer why a flower shop."

"Patience is not your strength, is it?"

"Maybe not, but I'm curious."

"Though my father and I don't have a great relationship, he was the one who stayed by my side. He took me into his home. While I lived with him, I spent a lot of time in his backyard. I created a garden and changed the flower beds often. It calmed me more than talking to the therapists. It occurred to me that maybe I could go back to school and study landscape architecture. But then I remembered that grandma once told me that her dream was to open a flower shop. She wanted to deliver joy, congratulations, sympathy, and happiness along with a wide smile. Once I was strong enough to get out of my father's house, I asked him to help me open the shop."

I walked to my bathroom and splashed cold water on my face.

"You deliver all that? I thought your business was flowers." He continued our conversation even when I was out of sight.

"Your business is making people feel through your melodies and lyrics, not just playing," I retorted loudly to ensure that he could hear me.

"I never thought about that, but I guess you're right. Though your job sounds cooler than mine."

"If you ever have free time, you should join me. It's good for your heart." I leaned my face against the wall, trying to find my footing.

"You're good for my heart."

I pressed my lips together when I noticed what I had done. Invited him back for another day in the life of Sadie. Getting rid of him was going to take me longer than I'd imagined.

"Enough about me," I said out loud. I found him sitting on my bed, staring at me with such tenderness I almost melted.

"After all that's happened to you, you still radiate so much light."

"You're blind." I opened my credenza and pulled out one of my favorite extra-large t-shirts. "There's no light around me. Here, change."

"I take you're a fan." He took the shirt, grinning as he read the name of the band. "Killing Hades. No, you're a hardcore fan. This one is from twelve, maybe thirteen years ago."

"Maybe, just maybe, I've been following your band for a few years. Your music isn't half bad."

He took off his shirt, showing his eight-pack and that v that turned me on. I wanted to run the pads of my fingers over his ridges. But I snapped out of the trance once the t-shirt I offered him covered his skin.

"What do you want to do?" He checked the time. "We have a few hours before I have to be at the café."

The smart thing to say would be: *go home, I have things to do*. But I felt vulnerable and didn't want him to leave just yet.

"We could watch a movie or play a board game," I found myself saying without hesitation.

"Board game?" He arched an eyebrow. "I like a good challenge. What do you have?

I walked to the kitchen to put away the groceries. "The games are in my studio. Third bookcase at the bottom."

Once I finished putting everything away and his things inside a reusable bag, I walked toward the living room where he was clearing the coffee table.

"Do you want something to drink?"

"What do you have?"

"I'm afraid just rice milk, water, and juice. Sorry, we don't carry alcohol in this establishment," I tried to joke, figuring a guy like him would think I was lame.

He already knew too much about me. I didn't have to tell him about my mother too.

"Well, that's a good thing since I'm an alcoholic."

He stared at me for several beats. Maybe he was waiting for my reaction.

"Recovering?" I dared to ask. He nodded once. "Mom just got out of rehab a couple of months ago. Since she visits me often, I make sure that there's nothing she can take—by mistake."

"I've been clean for seven years," he confessed, pulling out his phone and showing me a picture of two beautiful girls. The oldest had auburn hair and light brown eyes. The second one had his dark brown hair and the same eyes as her sister. They were adorable. "I do it because I want to be part of their lives."

My heart almost exploded with his words. I'd met plenty of men and women with addictions, and not many had put their children before their vice. I understood it's an illness, something they had all their lives. But some chose to get better and follow treatment, while others couldn't help themselves.

"Should I leave?" He looked at me, then at the door.

"Why? I mean, if you want to."

"I don't want to, but your silence is making me think that you want me to."

"No, I'm just thinking. I've met many people and handled so many cases that involved fathers abandoning their children, mothers only caring about their next fix ... or both doing drugs and putting their children in danger. Not many parents put their children first.

"My parent's divorced when I was six, and after that my mom had a revolving door of men. She was always drunk and neglected me. No one, not even my father, realized it because she knew how to hide it. If she lost custody of me, she'd lose the monthly check my father gave her for child support. Dad couldn't care for a kid. He was too busy with other women and his business." I shrugged.

"You're a rock star who could be more involved in his career and his fans. I don't know much about the lifestyle, but I'm sure you're surrounded by temptation. Yet, you're clean."

"My motives might change your mind. At the beginning, that wasn't my goal. It was just making sure that my ex wouldn't bring danger to the girls."

"Danger?"

"Once we divorced, my ex started bringing other guys to the house. I fought her for custody, but being a drunk and addicted to painkillers lost me my children. The judge granted her full custody until I cleaned up. I couldn't let her win."

"You took a step to recovery, and your motivation was your children."

"It was guilt and fear. This time, I had the power to stop *her*."

"Her?"

"My mother."

"I'm pretty confused, rewind and explain to me how one is related to the other?"

"Alicia, my ex-wife, behaved a lot like my mother."

"What happened?" I walked to where he sat and joined him, taking his hand.

"Dad left when I was one." His attention was set on the coffee table. "He left us for a much younger woman, my sister explained when I was older. Mom couldn't keep a job because she liked her booze and drugs more than she liked to wake up early and work. The men she brought home paid for her alcohol and drug addiction too. She was beautiful, had a great body and knew how to exploit it."

He went quiet, taking several deep breaths.

"Hey, it's okay. You don't need to share, but this is a safe place. I'm safe."

"The men felt entitled, and Mom allowed them to do more than she offered. One time, one of them tried to touch my sister. He beat me because I defended her. After that, my sister and I slept with the door locked. But that didn't stop them when they were too drunk and wanted to beat the shit out of anyone around. Mom didn't care much about our safety. Some of them beat the fuck out of the three of us after they fucked her. I was only ten when I began to drink to forget the shit that was going on at home."

My heart broke for the little boy. I wanted to take him with me and keep him safe. He continued telling me that some winters it was colder inside their home than outside. She barely brought food to the table.

"At some point, her face and body began to change. She became ugly. Not many men found her attractive. When my sister turned sixteen ..." He covered his face with both hands, resting them on his thighs. I drew soothing circles on his back.

"You can stop at any time."

"I had no idea it was going on, I swear." He hits his face. "How didn't I know what they were doing to her?"

"It's not your fault," I told him, turning his torso toward me and hugging him. "You were a kid."

"But I heard her crying at nights. She'd tell me that everything was fine. Two months later she killed herself, and social services took me away from the house. She left a letter describing what Mom was doing. She was afraid that I was going to be next."

"You're safe."

"But she died. Hannah died because of me."

"No, Hannah died because your mother forced her to do things. She died because there weren't any adults to care for her. You were a kid."

"Mom went to jail for ten years. She was charged with child exploitation, child pornography—she was selling pictures of us naked. I had no idea she was doing all that. Possession of drugs and child endangerment."

"And what happened to you?" I couldn't help but kiss his shoulder and hug him tighter.

I hurt for the kid who feared for his safety. They took away his innocence, his loving sister.

"The system," he sighed. "But I was a troubled child—I began drinking Mom's stuff, and by the time I was taken, it was too late. Every night I stole the liquor from their cabinets. Once I robbed a liquor store."

"No one helped you?"

He straightened up and looked me in the eyes. "You weren't there. Not everyone is like you."

I had no idea if that was a line or a compliment, but I felt vulnerable. "You don't know me. I failed many times." I controlled my tone because I didn't want to lose our connection.

"Yet, I know you'd have helped me, saved me from myself." I run a hand through his hair, it's surprisingly soft. He seemed so strong, but the darkness he lived through made him feel powerless.

This guy didn't have a game plan. He had a bruised heart and lots of love to give. It amazed me that as broken as he was, he could be so open and vulnerable. Was he like that with everyone?

The romantic fool inside me wanted to love him, to heal him. But that part of me died long ago, and the shrewd me knew I didn't have anything to give him.

"Not to rain on your parade, but when you were thirteen, I was only seven. Not much I could've done. But what happened to you?"

"I ended up in a group home. By then, I had met Jax, and we started our band. We moved to Seattle when we turned eighteen."

"Where are you from?"

"I grew up in southern California, but not many know that. My mother might or might not live there. I never went back, which makes me a horrible son and human being."

"It doesn't."

"You don't know me," he threw my own words back at me.

"No, I don't, but let me tell you, Mr. Hades, after hearing all that, I know you're a good father, a strong man. And you should be proud of yourself."

"Nah, sobriety is something everyone should do. As I said, I just want to make sure that my ex doesn't bring home trash. That whoever she dates is safe for the girls. So that I can take them away from her if I believe she's not caring for them. I don't want Tess or Hannah to go through the things that my sister, Hannah, and I went through."

"You named your daughter after your sister," I touched my chest, moved by this man who loved his children fearlessly. "Guilt or no guilt, you're a wonderful father, Mr. Hades."

He shook his head.

"How old are they?"

"Hannah is eight, almost nine. Tess just turned thirteen."

"A teenager? Wow, that's a difficult age."

"She's difficult. In fact, your friend Ella reminded me of my Tess. They like to have everything and share nothing. But Hannah, she's sweet."

"Like her dad?"

"You think I'm sweet?"

"I think you hide a lot behind that angry-sexy-hombre façade."

He winked at me, shaking his head. "Come with me tonight?"

"As much as I'd love to go, I rather stay at home and rest," I excused myself. "Monday will be here too soon."

"Fine, I'll take the few hours we have left."

"We don't have anything left, you should leave so I can get comfortable," I pointed to the door. Though, deep inside I wished he'd choose to stay.

"I was promised a game, a drink, perhaps dinner before I leave."

"You're on your own for that. My plan is to order takeout and watch Netflix."

"Homemade meal," he insisted.

"No, today is takeout. It's on the calendar. I might not be very organized, but I have a food schedule to follow."

"Pizza?"

"For the millionth time, I'm allergic to dairy products. But you can always go home and order pizza."

"I have to leave at six-thirty, we should order at five."

"It's three o'clock. Do you know what your children are doing?"

"At their mother's. It's her weekend." He checks his phone. "That means you have me all to yourself this weekend. What do you want to do, beautiful?"

"You're tenacious, Mr. Hades." I threw my hands up in the air, giving up. "Or bored and I'm the only person in Seattle who has nothing to do, like you."

"Maybe that's it." He sent me a grin that made my heart skip a few beats.

A smile pulled at my lips when I realized he wasn't leaving. I was glad because we both had unloaded a lot of heavy stuff. Neither one of us should have been alone. And his company was surprisingly comfortable. The banter between us felt just right.

Chapter Fourteen

KADE

Present

One long week without any news. I should be patient. Every doctor who checks on Sadie tells me when I ask them how she's doing. No one understands what it's like to see the woman I love fighting for her life. She might never wake up. I might never be able to hear her voice again, to tell her that I love her more than anything and anyone. She might never meet our baby, and fuck, I know she wanted that baby more than anything in the world.

And no matter how many times I ask her to forgive me for leaving her, she might never hear what I have to say. I caused her pain, left her homeless...

"Should I just leave you?" I take her hand. "I should have left you that first day? But you opened yourself to me. You listened to me and made me feel like I was worth something. That I wasn't just an excuse of a man who could barely hang onto his sobriety."

She made me feel like a person. Like a regular man who was more than his fame, his failures, and the demons that dragged him to the darkness.

I touch her forehead, caressing her delicate face. "What's on your mind, beautiful?

"Good morning. How is our little one today?"

I turn around to find Aspen Hawkins, and right behind her, Raven. One of Sadie's closest friends and her assistant manager. She glares at me.

"You," Raven points at me. "My name isn't on the list of authorized visitors. Why?"

I flinch, "There's a list?"

"Yes," Aspen confirms, checking on the Little Beanie who is out of the ventilator. The doctors were confident that moving him to Sadie's room was safe for him. "Your people said it was you who suggested the list."

"My people?" I frown wondering if Duncan did something or if it was Pria, my public relations manager, who ordered it.

"Well, you're trying to keep the media away, aren't you?" Raven narrows her gaze.

"While you two catch up, I'm going to check on my patient." Aspen walks toward my Little Beanie. "I heard from the nurses that he's spending too much time with Daddy."

I shrug. "Can you blame me?"

"No, I like that you're giving him just what he needs. Love." She smiles.

"He's so little," Raven marches over to see the baby. "Wake up, boss. You need to meet him."

"Keep your voice down, Rae," I mumble.

She flinches.

"Nothing you say will wake her up. At least not right now. She's still heavily sedated," Aspen informs Raven. "Brynn plans on keeping her that way for another week or until the swelling in the brain goes down."

I tune Aspen out when she begins to explain Sadie's injuries. Nothing new has happened since the surgery. This wait and watch shit is driving me crazy.

"Maybe they'll get out of the hospital at the same time," Raven suggests.

"That's what we're hoping for," Aspen reassures her. "We have to figure out the logistics, but that'll happen later."

"I'm surprised to see you here," Raven saunters closer to the bed. "How did you learn about it?"

"He's listed as her in case of emergency contact," Aspen intervened. "I haven't checked who her next of kin is. Technically, we're breaking protocol. Unless, the administration has done something and I'm out of the loop."

"I'm her next of kin," I assure her.

"That would be her parents, since you two aren't married or together," Raven informs, her voice is calm and her answer right on point.

"Don't call them," I request. "Sadie's father won't come, and her mother might be in rehab."

"No, she got out a month ago," Raven informs me. "This time for good, or so she promised."

"Same thing. She won't care right now. You know her pattern. I'm taking care of Sadie."

"How are the girls?" Raven's passive aggressive hints are wearing on me.

"Fine, I haven't spoken to them. They're on vacation with their mother."

"That explains why you're here. I bet you wouldn't be here if they were in town."

"I'd be here," I protest. "What makes you think otherwise?"

"You walked away from Sadie," she accuses me.

"Raven," I warn her.

"Fine, I'll just be around to hold her when you do it all over again."

I change the subject to something more pressing.

"Hey, did Sadie have names for the baby?"

"Not yet, she was going through a baby book. Nothing seemed to sound right with Bell."

"The baby is Hades," I protest and realize one fucking thing. "She was never going to tell me about him, was she?"

"How would I know?" She twitches her lips, huffing. "Her only focus was the baby. Not to hurt you or anything, but she stopped talking about you a long time ago."

Because Sadie doesn't talk about the things that cause her pain.

"When did she learn about her pregnancy?"

Raven presses her lips together and looks down. That's all I needed to confirm what I've been thinking all along. If the baby's gestation age had been thirty-one weeks and five days, she had been seven or eight weeks pregnant when we broke up. There's no fucking way that *Miss I never miss a period* didn't know about it.

"Fuck, she knew before we broke up." I clamp my lips together.

Suddenly, I connect the flu-like symptoms. She went to the doctor, but I was too busy with the next EP release to even call her. I was trying to have everything set for the wedding.

"But what I don't get is why she didn't tell me."

"It was a surprise. But ..." her voice trails off as does her stare. She concentrates on Sadie. "Look, this is not my call. I'm her friend, not yours. For now, focus on the baby, and once she's better you two have to find closure and a way to co-parent."

Can we find our way back to us? Is that even a possibility?

Why would she want to be with me? I wasn't any different from her father or the fuckers she dated. Once things got complicated, I left. Fuck, I abandoned my pregnant fiancée. Would she forgive me for that?

"How's Tess doing?" Raven asks, touching her head slightly. "Is this something that she'll be able to handle?"

I hold my breath for several beats. How am I going to break the news of the baby?

"She doesn't have to handle anything," I respond with conviction. "Tess and Hannah have a brother. He's mine."

I look at my broken Sadie. "Until Sadie is strong, I'm all he has."

And in some way, he's really all I have. The only person who might give me some unconditional love. My daughter's innocence was shattered by their mother, and in exchange for some of their love, I have to meet a lot of conditions.

My alarm sounds. Call time.

"Hey, can you stay with them for a minute? I have to make a call."

"At the moment I'm not available, but please leave a message," Alicia's voicemail picks up immediately.

I hate that I have to call her. Why didn't she let the kids take their phones with them?

"It's time for my daily call. Text when you're ready for it. And about your email, the answer is no. I gave them enough money for their personal expenses."

Fucking bitch. She's a piece of work. I should call my lawyer and fight her for full custody. But with Sadie and the baby ... what am I supposed to do now?

Alicia: The girls had a long day. Call tomorrow.

Kaden: We have an agreement.

Alicia: Did we? You promised to provide for them, and yet, during their time of need you're turning them down. Send money.

Kaden: Have them call me tomorrow. I won't send you another cent.

Alicia: By the way, there's a rumor that you're dating a new skank. You need to start thinking more about your daughters and a little less about your fucking dick. Tess's mental health comes first.

There are no rumors. Alicia is the one who calls the tabloids to sell them fake news. She gets paid and then uses them against me. I regret the day I met Alicia. My daughters mean the world to me, and I shouldn't think that way. But other than Hannah and Tess, everything related to Alicia is toxic waste. To think I tried to make things work with her in the name of *family*. Maybe it's me. I'm not meant to be happy or loved.

Everything and everyone I touch ends up hurt.

I turn around toward the hallway that takes me to Sadie's room and second guess my next step. Neither Sadie nor the baby need me, or my problems. I should go home. Take my drama with me.

"Relationships between two people are complicated," she once told me. *"Families even more so. Not everyone is the same. Each member of the family is unique and important. You learn to love them and make everything work in the name of love. You don't give up. You fight together."*

That's why I didn't give up on Tess or Hannah. Alicia will always be a part of them, and that's why I deal with her. After what happened to Tess, we should all have fought. But I let one member of our special family go. I never fought for her. My lungs collapse because the fear of losing Tess made me listen to Alicia. For a few seconds, the same fear almost made me leave and give up again.

Will she still love me when she wakes up?

I trace the seven letters tattooed on my right wrist.

Forever.

It's part of a couples tattoo we have that was inspired by Lily and Snape. The woman who didn't like fiction absorbed my love for the *Harry Potter* books once I began reading them to her. And then, we created our own version.

We'll be together forever, no matter space, or time or ... I take off, running to her side. For the first time, I don't give a shit about washing my hands or changing my scrubs.

Holding her hand, I look at her wrist. *Together.*

I press them against each other for a second and breathe out.

"The flame of our souls fused a long time ago, and it can't be separated. It's forever and always," I whisper in her ear. "I'm sorry for giving up so easily, but we're a family, and you taught me that we should fight together."

I look at her unmoving body. The only way I know she's still with me is when I see her chest rise and fall. I brush the strands of hair from her face and kiss her nose and then her cheek.

"Meet me in your dreams. Hold my hand. Don't let go, baby. We have years ahead of us. Our son is waiting for you. I can't lose my best friend and the love of my life. We will fight together."

Carefully, I hug her and press my forehead to hers. "For the next hundred years, even after this life, we'll be together. I promise."

Chapter Fifteen

KADEN

Three Years Ago

"Do you ever sleep?" Sadie yawned as she opened the door of her apartment.

Fuck me. My jaw dropped when I drank in her entire body at once. She wore a pair of shorts and a tank top. Her sleepy eyes made me harder, and fuck! That mouth was created to be kissed—by me. If only ... but I'm not going to act. Nope, I made a promise.

"A few hours a night." I handed her the chai tea I brought her.

"Tea?" she frowned at it. "Thank you, but you didn't have to."

"Well, you said yesterday that this is your favorite drink." I entered without being invited. "What's your poison?"

"Poison?"

"Favorite breakfast food," I responded, going to the kitchen. "Eggs, omelet, frittata, pancakes—"

"Either, all... I don't know." She followed me into the kitchen and whispered. "Why are you here?"

"Why are we whispering?"

"Maybe I have a night visitor who's still in bed." She smirked, walking to the fridge and pulling out a bottle of orange juice. "Or just because I don't want to fully wake up so I can go back to bed once you disappear. Waking up at six in the morning on a Sunday is a crime."

"Crime?" I looked around her cupboards and found the all-purpose flour, a waffle maker, and almost all the ingredients to prepare waffles from scratch. I checked her refrigerator and pulled out the milk I bought yesterday. "Do you have any whipped cream?"

"I'm allergic to dairy," she reminded me.

"Right." I put the milk back and grabbed the rice milk. "At least you have berries."

"You're making breakfast and then leaving, right?"

"No. On a day like today, staying at home would be the crime. That's why we're spending the day at an awesome event." I squatted, searching for a bowl. "Do you cook?"

"Yes, why do you ask?"

"You don't have pots, or... where are the bowls?"

She grinned and went to the coat closet. "Not everything fits in this small kitchen."

"A whisk and measuring cup?" I scratched my head wondering if I should go to the bathroom or her studio.

"My bathroom?" She laughed, but she pulled open a long drawer where most of the spatulas, wooden spoons and utensils were stored. "Sorry, I couldn't help it. Your face was priceless."

"Vanilla?"

"Are you asking if I like it or if I own it?" She smirked and gave me a side glance. "Or if I like only vanilla sex? Because I like it with a little cinnamon, you know, spiced with kink."

My pulse spiked. Fuck, I wanted to drag her to her room. No, take her here in the kitchen. Lift her petite body and place her on top of the counter. I'd pull her little shorts down and eat her pussy for breakfast. Afterwards, I'd feed her my cock while she made herself come with her fingers.

"But you shouldn't ask me that. *Friends* don't discuss sex." Her eyes sparkled with lust.

God help me, this friendship was going to be the death of me.

"They don't?" I swallow hard.

"Nope, Mr. Hades. It blurs the lines."

Baby, I would erase them if that meant you'd let me touch you just once. One time would annihilate the craving for that fucking luscious body.

"Now that we've established a new rule, keep your eyes to yourself and explain what this amazing event is that you'll be going to while I stay home sleeping for a few more hours."

"*Friend,* would you mind getting dressed?" I requested. "We are going to a canine foster/adoption event. I promised to be there as a sponsor."

"We get to see puppies?" Her eyes brightened.

"All kinds of dogs."

She narrowed her gaze. "You play dirty, Mr. Hades."

"You have no idea, Miss Loza-Bell."

"Just Bell," she corrected me. "Mom insisted on hyphenating my last name, but it's a pain. And while growing up, I liked Sadie Bell a lot more. It sounded like Tinkerbell. Though, now that Disney came up with more fairies I prefer to be Rossetta or Iridessa, garden and light fairy respectively."

My mouth opened because she knew her fairies well. I did because of Hannah. "How do you know all about them?"

"It's part of my job."

"You're fucking adorable, do you know that?"

"No, it's really part of what I do. When kids come over to the flower shop, it's my duty to entertain them sometimes." She winked at me. "That convinces the parents to buy them books or whatever I talk about. Also, they come back because I made them feel like family. It's part of my service. If you plan on having a kid's party, you don't think flowers. But I have everything to cater it. Balloons, decorations, numbers to rent bounce houses, tables, you name it. I can plan and deliver. Therefore, you'll hire me instead of some creepy clown."

I made a mental note to hire her for the next party I had to organize. This year it was Alicia's turn to organize Hannah's ninth birthday, but maybe next year Sadie could help me.

"Go change," I insisted. "We have many, many things to do."

"Make a note that I'm changing because I was promised waffles, puppies, and lunch."

"Lunch?"

She nodded, leaving her scent lingering after her departure.

☆ ☆ ☆ ☆

"So...you're the spokesperson?"

"Something like that," I answered. "I'm donating my time to the cause."

"Well, there's a good crowd, and every time you say, 'I like this dog,' someone adopts it." She pets a Labradoodle that's been following us around. He's in love with her. But she can't adopt him because he's too big for her apartment.

"You should get him," I insisted.

"Me?" She shook her head. "Nope, but I'll find him a home. Why don't you take off your shirt, so we can attract a bigger audience?"

"There are children around."

"The kids won't notice. But *they* will." She pointed at a group of women that had been watching us from afar.

"No. They told me to keep it kid friendly, remember?"

"I can make balloon animals while you try to find forever homes for your canine friends... while showing your abs. See? Kid friendly."

"You know how to make balloon animals?"

"No, but I'm sure that I can learn after I watch a YouTube video —or five."

"What if we give the wrong dog to the wrong person?"

She slumped her shoulders. "Fine. I just want to find a home for all of them." She pulled out the sunblock, squirted some on my hand, and then applied more to her own arms and legs.

"You should take him."

"He's too big for my apartment." She squatted and rubbed his ears. "But you're such an adorable guy. I should find you a place. Hmm, you know what? I think I know where he should go."

She pulled out her phone. "Hey, are you guys busy?" She nodded, made some sounds. "Well, I have a friend who wants to meet you. No, not that kind. What's in it for you?"

Sadie looked around the area and her eyes found mine. "I'll introduce you to Kaden Hades, but only if you bring your children and meet my other friend. Sounds like a plan. I'll text you the address."

"Who was that?"

"My assistant manager, she's been talking about adopting a dog for the past couple of months. But her husband is allergic to them. However," She pointed at the puppy. "This boy is hypoallergenic. And doesn't cost an arm and a leg. Wait, don't you have children?"

"I'm not adopting a dog," I stopped her because I could see where her mind was headed.

"But you'd make your kids happy."

"The last pet I bought them died accidentally while they were visiting their mother," I explained. "My ex is a bitch. The kind that would boil a bunny if she wanted to get rid of a pet."

"She boiled a bunny?"

"No, but she let the hamsters escape and then called the exterminator and said she had a mouse infestation."

"Alicia and Ella could be twins," she chortles. "No, but seriously, that's what she did?"

"Yes, she called it an accident. The girls were broken hearted, and I gave up buying them pets."

"I'm assuming you have more horror stories?"

"Your assumption would be correct; there are too many to remember."

"Why did you marry her?" Her eyebrows furrowed as she wrinkled her nose.

"I knocked her up."

"Not the best reason to offer forever, Mr. Hades."

"I learned my lesson. I won't marry anyone just because there's a kid. In fact, I'm debating having a vasectomy."

A girl around Hannah's age and a younger boy charged toward where we were standing. "Aunt Sadie!"

They hugged her tight, almost pushing her down to the ground, but I caught her just in time. I loved the kids. They gave me an excuse to hold her again.

The couple approached, and the woman with light brown hair and pink sunglasses gawked at Sadie. "Sunday morning and you're out of the house?"

"All in the name of these puppies," Sadie responded, and thankfully, she hadn't pushed me away, yet.

"Raven," she pushed up her sunglasses. "My ex-husband, Benny, and your new children."

"Seriously, Raven?" Sadie protested. "His name is William, we call him Bill, not Benny. And I found the perfect dog for you."

"Don't take her too seriously," her husband told me, laughing at his wife. "She's harmless—most of the time."

"I can hear you." His wife bent to pet the dog that her kids were already hugging.

"I take it you're the famous Kaden Hades," he extended his hand. "William James, everyone calls me Bill. That's my wife Raven, my daughter Leah, and my son Lucas."

"No relation to Star Wars," Raven informed me. "We're regular citizens who have never watched sci-fi movies."

But I laughed when I saw their Star Wars t-shirts.

"Hey, I'm going to look around while you set this guy up with his new family. Is that okay?" I saluted them.

"Yes, I'm totally fine." Sadie waved me away. "Actually, I can drive back with them."

"Oh no, we're having lunch together, and then we're going home for a movie marathon."

"We'll make sure she sticks around until you come back." Raven stood straightening herself. "Find her a puppy, or a hypoallergenic cat though."

"Hypoallergenic cat?"

"She's allergic to cats, but she adores them."

"Good to know. I think we're going to be good friends, Raven." Bill cleared his throat and stared at me. "And you too, Bill, of course."

☆ ☆ ☆ ☆

"Are you allergic to dogs?"

"No, just cats and bunnies. Wool." She fake-sneezed. "Maybe you."

"There's medicine for that," I reached out for her hand and kissed it.

"What did we say about kissing friends?"

"You have too many rules," I complained. "Are you ready for sorbet?"

"Not yet. I feel like I just ate two minutes ago." She patted her stomach. "You had a successful day."

"I just showed my face."

"No. You talked to a lot of families, worked your way around, and survived Raven."

"What's her story?"

"Bored housewife," she responded. "Thank God, because the first three months she worked for free. Her husband is a computer geek. She used to work on Wall Street. When they moved here, she had a baby and decided to focus on motherhood. But she's an overachiever, and once the little ones were in school full time, she found me."

"They seemed cool."

"They are great, except when I find them fucking around my store."

"Are you serious?"

"Yep, and she wasn't serious about leaving her husband. Though, she does have a little crush on you. Like every living woman in the world."

"Except you."

"Except me." She grinned. "So how are your girls?"

"Hannah is doing well, but Tess was busy doing homework." I pushed away my phone since I just called to check on them. "That, or she's at some party on a school night, and Alicia knows I'm not going to be happy."

"You're the bad cop in the relationship? That's unfortunate. You should work together. Not against each other."

"There's no relationship."

"The first step to healing as a family is accepting your reality. She's not your wife, but you'll always have a relationship with her because of the girls. Like it or not, you need to learn how to deal with her and vice versa. Become partners. Just because you don't love each other anymore doesn't mean you don't both love your girls. For their sake, you have to find some middle ground and co-parent. You can't be enemies trying to persuade the girls to take sides."

"Honestly, I wish I could take them away from her. But I have to work to support them. Music is my only source of income. If I could take them with me on the road, I would, but they have to go to school and have a normal life."

"Why don't you talk to her? See what you two can work out. Family therapy might be helpful."

"She's going to think that I want us to get back together."

"And that's not happening?"

"I can't stand her. She's uncaring, selfish, demanding, and greedy. But I'm just as bad as her."

"That's where you're wrong. You are a good father and an incredible human being. Don't let anyone tell you otherwise."

Sadie surprised me every second with her light humor, her banter, and her sincere advice. She made me feel worthy of more. And as much as I was attracted to her, I didn't want to lose what we were building. In fact, all I wanted was to spend every single moment with her.

"When you asked what time I opened the store, did you mean something like, 'What time shall I begin making your life miserable?'"

"No, I wanted to walk with you," I said.

"I'm sure you have work to do. You mentioned something like that yesterday."

"Almost everything is done. Composed an entire song, picked up Hannah from her mother's and drove her to school."

"Tess?" She put on her coat. "Thank you for the tea."

"She spent the night with a friend."

"Uh-oh. How did that go?"

"I'll talk to Tess. The next time she has a party, the answer is no."

"Well, I'm glad you're almost done with your day. Now, if you'll excuse me, I'm going to start mine."

I took her big tote bag and followed behind her.

"You remember inviting me to work with you, don't you?"

"It was a suggestion, not an invitation. Go back to your life. The weekend is over. You passed your 'let's be friends with a female' test."

"What's gotten into you today?"

"Hmm?"

"You're a little grumpy, like someone tried to douse your flame."

"Mom's back in rehab. Dad called me an irresponsible daughter."

"What happened?"

"I wasn't at home yesterday to receive my drunk mother, and she decided to visit my father instead." She gave me a hard glare. "While he was entertaining important people. Needless to say, he forced her into rehab."

"He can't do that."

"Oh, but he did. Which means that Mom's going to come out again and lose her shit within months. Because I bet he made her believe that he still loves her."

"It's not your fault," I took her empty hand and kissed it. "Your parents are adults. Everything they do is their own fucking responsibility."

"Yeah, but that doesn't make it less painful. I swear Mom has a punch card at the rehab center. Next one is free. It's just ... what if one day she doesn't look both ways when she's crossing the street or does something stupid?"

"You can't worry about things that are out of your control. That's not something you can fix, sweetheart. Let's concentrate on today's deliveries. I might have a surprise for you."

"What kind of surprise? Are you performing a disappearing act?"

"I won't disappear, but I'm leaving at two."

"What are you up to afterward?"

"Dad duty, which includes picking up children and driving them to numerous activities," I responded. "And while Hannah is at ballet and Tess at acting lessons, I'm going to be recording with Jax."

"You three are pretty artsy. That sounds like fun." She opened the door of the shop and disarmed the alarm.

"Where's Raven?"

"Mommy duties and cross fit," she said, turning on the light in her office. "She usually arrives around ten and leaves at two."

"Do you have someone working with you during the evenings?"

"No, I can manage alright by myself. Mornings are our busiest time."

"What do you need me to do?"

"Are you serious?" She stopped and directed her attention toward me.

"Yes, I'm yours from now until two o'clock. What would you like me to do?"

She exhaled and stared at me for a few beats. "What's your motive, Mr. Hades."

"I love when you call me Mr. Hades," I winked at her. "I can't wait for you to scream it when I make you come."

Her tanned skinned darkened slightly, her mouth opened, but no sound came out.

"You're imagining it too, aren't you?"

"You want to get fired on your first day, don't you?"

"I'm hired?"

She tossed her hands up in the air and rolled her eyes. "You're impossible."

"Where do I start," I paused, "Boss?"

It didn't take long for her to set up her working table. She had me printing the orders, and then the cards that went along with them.

"Not a single note worth saving," she complained when she had me read them. "No hall of famers."

"What's that?"

"My scrapbook. That's where I put a copy of the good ones along with photos of the custom-made arrangements." Sadie sighed, pulling rolls of ribbon out of boxes, her gaze wandering around the flower shop. "There's a story behind every new order, and sometimes there's a special note with such deep meaning that you have to save it."

I never sent flowers. Sadie was my first, and when I got to the screen where it asked me what I wanted my note to say, I froze for several beats. It couldn't be something ordinary. *Your eyes are beautiful* felt like another cheesy line from a teenager. In less than 400 characters I wanted to convey everything, yet sound different.

"Did mine make it into the hall of fame?"

"I'm still debating." She twisted her lips, checked the list she printed, and walked toward the roses. "The picture of the flowers is in the binder, but the note ..." She shrugged.

"What about it?"

Was it because it was something for just the two of us?

"You write lyrics for a living," she spoke slowly, her attention on the stems of the flowers she was cutting with a knife. "It's easy for you to throw together a few words, weave them into a line, and make people fall for you."

"Only when it comes to music."

She placed the knife on top of the table and her eyes found mine. "How many times have you sent women flowers?"

"You're my first, Miss Bell. The first woman I wrote a note to—twice."

"Do you want to be in the hall of fame?"

"Nope, I only care about being in your life," I confessed, feeling vulnerable, but safe.

There was no logic to the emotional state I lived in from the moment I set eyes on her. We shared something when I sang, and we looked at each other. Something inside me shifted. Different notes played inside my head, along with the words. She got one thing right, I know how to weave words, but only when I have the right melody. After Sadie though, I could scribble a thousand love poems with a single glance at her.

"You're persistent, Mr. Hades." She smiled and moved her gaze toward the flowers.

I had no idea what I was doing, but I didn't plan on quitting anytime soon.

☆ ☆ ☆ ☆

"I was promised emotion, joy ..." I stopped to remember the exact words she said when she described her job but couldn't remember them all. "Gratification?"

"You're not a patient man, are you, Mr. Hades?"

"Stop calling me that, Sadie Bell. It makes me horny." I glance quickly to her side. "You don't want me horny while driving."

"Why did I agree to bring you along?"

"I promised to drive while you worked on your bridal proposal."

"That reminds me, stay quiet, sir."

"So, how many deliveries do you have on average?" I asked while waiting for the green light.

She tapped her chin with the green mechanical pencil she was using. "Monday is our busiest day of the week."

"Have you thought about hiring someone else?"

"Not yet. I'm trying to keep my costs low. So far, I've managed to handle everything with one part-time employee. But if you want the job, you're hired ..." she paused, and I wished I could take my eyes off the road because I could feel some teasing or bantering remark coming my way. "With no pay or breaks."

"At some point, I'll figure out some kind of payment." I came to a light and turned to her. "You can pay me in kind."

"Ooh, you went almost two hours without flirting. You were doing so great, Mr. Hades." My last name coming out of her mouth was my favorite thing. It was music, sex, passion and some other emotions I had never experienced before. "We should have a sexual innuendo jar and charge you a twenty every time you say something inappropriate."

"Babe, I never bet on anything I know I'm incapable of winning, so no. There's not going to be a swear jar, teasing jar, or any of that fucked up shit. This is what you get."

I remained silent for the rest of the ride. That prevented me from flirting or saying something stupid shit like, 'the van is big enough to fuck in the back.' I liked her company too much to cross the line. A couple of days ago, I didn't care much about staying within the lines. But now, every warning and rule had become important. If I fucked up, she'd disappear. I wasn't ready to let go.

As a matter of fact, I wanted to stay right beside her, watching the radiance every time she smiled. Feeling the warmth in my heart as she beamed with magic. I planned on sticking around as long as I could. At least, until she allowed it.

I needed to absorb just a little more of her light before I recoiled back into darkness.

"Ready for the next delivery, boss?" I parked the van and turned my attention toward her.

Sadie put away her sketchbook and pulled out her iPad, checking the list. "Hmm." She pressed her lips together while reading. "I don't like this one."

"Why not?" I raised an eyebrow.

"I think he cheated over the weekend. He called to order my biggest bouquet of red roses. He paid extra to have it delivered before noon."

She climbed down from the van and shut the door hard. I guessed she didn't like cheaters.

"Why do you assume that?"

"The card says, *I'm sorry. I won't do it again*," she said opening the back of the van.

I picked up the arrangement and followed her wondering if flowers could make up for something like cheating. Maybe not the best way to patch up things after screwing other women?

"Hmm, never thought about sending flowers when I cheated."

Sadie came to a complete stop and glared at me. "You've cheated?"

Those eyes stared at me with disappointment, and I could hear the silent, *I knew it, he's an asshole.*

"Would it make it better if I said that Alicia did it first—with one of my bandmates?"

"Nope." She shook her head. "If you don't love someone, you call it quits before you hurt them. Taking the eye for an eye defense doesn't make it any better."

"It wasn't like that. I assumed we were over and started doing my own thing." I rang the bell.

"How did that work out for you?" She shot me a glare that I couldn't understand.

"That's when the divorce and the custody battle began." I breathed harshly, looking down at the welcome mat.

I wasn't proud of my behavior. Sadie was right. I should've called it quits instead of assuming, and before I hurt Alicia. Fuck, I shouldn't have married her in the first place. We hurt each other with words and our behavior. She used the girls as weapons. After two years and a lot of money, I got joint physical custody of the girls.

The woman who opened the door was in her mid-forties. She was dressed in yoga pants, a loose sweatshirt, and flip-flops. Her face was made up, but not overdone and her long blonde hair was pulled back into a messy bun.

She stared at the flowers, then at me. Her green eyes were narrowed, rigid, and hard. "You can tell him to shove the flowers up his ass. If he needs to talk to me, he can contact my lawyer."

"The flowers aren't to blame for whatever happened," I suggested, using the same voice I used when my daughters were distraught.

"*You* should accept them then, they'll brighten your day," Sadie suggested.

"I promise to refund his money. They'll be a present from me instead," I added.

The woman raised an eyebrow and studied me for several seconds. Then, she turned her attention to Sadie.

"Is this a joke?" she glanced outside her door toward the van, and then looked up street and down the street. "Where are the cameras?"

"Cameras?" I arched an eyebrow.

"This is a show, isn't it? You bring a celebrity to deliver flowers and—"

"There's no show, ma'am," Sadie glared at me.

"He's gifting me these flowers that I bet cost a lot."

"He likes to give things away. If I were you I'd say yes, or he'll keep coming around," Sadie said.

"But you're Kaden Hades, aren't you?" She narrowed her eyes, studying me.

"Nope," Sadie denied my identity. "He's my new driver. Do you think a rock star would be spending his free time delivering flowers?" Sadie sighed. "That'd be insane, he'd have to be a little crazy if you ask me." She smirked with an air of satisfaction.

"Well no, I guess you're right, but he could be his twin."

"He could, but this one doesn't have an ego the size of Texas."

"Yeah, I heard Hades' package is pretty big." The woman stared at me below the belt.

"I was talking about his *ego*, but whatever." Sadie's eyes moved to my crotch for a few seconds and her skin darkened. "Anyway, keep the flowers."

The lady sighed. "They are beautiful, but if I accept them, my husband is going to think that his behavior is okay. He bought a new car without consulting me. A mid-life crisis kind of car and you know what's next?"

"He didn't cheat?" Sadie arched an eyebrow.

"No, of course not. I would've shot him in the dick if he dared to even think about cheating."

"How about if I leave the flowers out here. Try to talk this through. Sometimes it's all about communication," Sadie said, taking the arrangement away from me and handing them to her. "You two can share the car, talk about what he wants, grow together—not apart. But ultimately, of course, that's up to you."

"Do you mind if I take a picture with you?" The woman hadn't moved her eyes away from me.

"Sorry, I'm not who you think I am." I hid the sneer and sent a silent plea to Sadie.

Get me out of here.

"Well, thank you for choosing Hummingbird Flower Design. Have a nice day," she rushed the words.

Sadie waved at her, grabbed my hand and pulled me toward the van. "Let's go, baby."

"Baby?" I tilted my head, once I climbed in the truck. "We're already using terms of endearment for each other, Pumpkin Bread."

"Just trying out some of them, Sugar Plum."

"That's a girl's name."

"Awe, is Snuggle Bunny upset because he didn't get something manly?"

"No, Honey Bunny. Me and my big ego are fine with a girl's nickname." I laughed when I noticed her chewing on her lip and looking outside. "The rumors are true. It's huge."

"I don't want to know, Poopsy Doodle."

"Poopsy Doodle?" I threw a quick glance at her. "I have to draw the line right there, Muffin Bun. But seriously, that back there was a little crazy, wasn't it?"

"Kicking him out and filing for divorce because of a car?" She shrugged. "I wouldn't know, but I guess if you're going to make such a large purchase you have to discuss it with your partner. How did you handle it with your ex?"

"I've never bought anything big. So, I wouldn't know."

"You don't have a big house, a private jet, luxury cars?"

"I don't splurge. Almost every penny I receive goes to my investment accounts. My goal is to save money because one day I might not be able to play, and I want my kids to be covered. I don't want to be old and poor."

"Really, people swear that you live in a big ass mansion."

"Nope, I live in a three-bedroom apartment. You already saw my truck which is five years old, and my expenses are pretty basic."

"Your wife?"

"Ex-wife," I corrected her. "Alicia lives in the first and only house we bought. A three-bedroom home in Capitol Hill."

"At least she was conscientious with your hard-earned money."

"Not exactly," I disclosed. "Alicia never learned how much money I made back then, or now."

I didn't trust my ex. She had no idea of my net worth. Once I began to earn enough to save, I kept my expenses to a minimum and put the rest into investment accounts. Her lawyer was too stupid to check my assets, and my lawyer didn't offer anything.

"Honestly, I have no idea how I'd handle it with Alicia. At least back when we were married. But it's a *car*, I don't see why she lawyered up."

"Marriages are hard. We don't know what's going on behind closed doors." Sadie sighed.

The silence between us lasted for several blocks. I was about to change the subject, but she spoke first. "Counseling. Did you think about that before the divorce?"

"We hated each other. I don't think a counselor would've helped us at that point."

"That makes sense," she agreed with me, which made me feel like less of an asshole for cheating on Alicia.

While we delivered the flowers, I kept thinking about the way I handled my marriage and the divorce. It was a clusterfuck. We both made mistakes. The first one was marrying a woman I didn't even know.

"When I get married, I'm going to suggest that we have couples counseling at least twice a year. Just to tune things up, you know."

"Tune it up?"

"Yes, relationships need adjustments. People change. They grow. And when they are in a relationship, they have to also learn to accept the changes and growth of their partners."

"That's deep, Muffin. So, you're going to put the marriage in someone else's hands and subject it to their opinion, Shnookums?"

"At least once a year to make sure everything is working well, Sugar Booger."

"Fine. Add it to the rules, Sexy Ass. We'll go to a counselor to make sure we're in tune."

"We don't talk about asses or how sexy they are, Babycakes."

Before I parked at our next stop, I realized something. "You're also a good listener, aren't you?"

"What?"

"You gave her a few relationship tips."

"A simple suggestion, that's all I did back there."

"This delivery shit isn't so bad, I'm going to make sure that I can fit it into my daily schedule."

"Or not, Sugar Puss."

"Cuddles, stop it right there. I'm not the one with the pussy. That's you."

"You're crossing lines, Doodle Bun."

"It's hard not to, Sadie Bell."

"Fine, Love-Cicle, but we have to agree that I won this round."

"That's a confusing nickname, and what makes you say that?" I parked the car at our next stop.

"Because I think I won, don't you?" She turned her body toward me, her smile wide and bright.

"You're adorable, Little Fairy." I leaned forward and kissed her forehead. "Thank you for letting me spend some time with you."

Chapter Seventeen

KADE

Knocking up a girl at twenty didn't give me room to decide if I ever wanted to get married or have children. I stepped into the role of a father, and accepted it knowing I wasn't going to be like mine. I promised myself that Tess and Hannah would have a present father. But I had no idea how to keep that promise when I never had a good example.

Nonetheless, I tried my best. At times I felt like a failure, and others, I just tried not to screw up. Some days I wondered if not taking my daughters away from Alicia was fucking up, and if I should do something. There weren't any signs of abuse. The girls loved her. They never complained about her and went back to her house happily.

But the shit Alicia pulled sometimes was unacceptable. Following the signs was different from following my gut. Something told me that Alicia both neglected and spoiled my children when I wasn't watching. Today wasn't an exception; her actions never failed to infuriate me. And when they affected my girls, it enraged me to the point of wanting to call the lawyer and fight her for full custody.

"That's a flower shop," Hannah pointed the big sign that read *Hummingbird Flower Designs*.

She crossed her arms and came to a complete stop.

"Trust me, Pumpkin," I opened the door and directed her inside. "Is anyone home?"

"You promised to take me somewhere fun where they'll organize my party," Hannah pouted and stomped her feet. "This is just a boring flower shop."

Her frustration didn't allow her to listen to reason. It wasn't her fault. Her mother had failed her. Since that woman always poisoned the girls against me, I had no doubt that Hannah didn't expect much from me. But I always came through with my promises.

"Sweetheart, I get that you're upset about what happened, but give *me* a chance."

"Nothing is boring in this shop, young lady," Raven said as she walked toward the counter. "We have books, toys, fun things to color, puzzles, and coming next week, kits to make your own jewelry."

"Kits to make your own jewelry?" Hannah gave Raven her full attention.

"I see you guys are carrying new jewerly." I pointed toward the big owl logo on top of the table.

"Yep. Owl Creations came by. The artist suggested the kits along with a few pieces."

"Thea came through?"

Thea was the wife of a good friend of mine. A former child actress who, after living in front of the cameras for so long, preferred to keep herself out of the public eye. When I told her about the flower shop and its originality, she agreed to visit and see if she'd sell some of her stuff in here.

"Yep, she's actually giving some exclusives to the store thanks to a mysterious referral." She smiled at me. "Sadie is over the moon."

I looked around the shop searching for the little fairy. "Where is she?"

"Delivering the last bouquets of the day. She got her daily chai tea. Do you know something about that?"

"I might."

"Who is Sadie?" Hannah frowned. Her light brown eyes stared at me suspiciously.

"She owns this place, and my sources tell me that she also organizes parties."

"I don't want flowers." Hannah clamped her mouth.

"You would if you wanted a fairy party," Raven said, opening a binder.

"Fairy party?" Once again, Hannah offered her undivided attention to Raven. "You have those?"

"We have pictures of some of the parties we've organized. If you're interested, I can show them to you." Raven walked into the office and came back carrying a binder. "When is this party?"

"Next Saturday," I bit the anger.

I had one week to come up with a birthday party for thirty-some kids. Which included her school friends and the girls from her ballet class. Alicia swore she had everything under control. But yesterday she announced that the next weekend she was backing out. She hadn't had time to organize Hannah's birthday party.

You're kidding, Raven mouthed.

I shook my head.

"Sadie won't be long," Raven said, searching around the counter and under it. "Let me call her, see where she's at."

"Rae, you never texted me back, and I didn't pick up lunch." I heard her voice coming from the back room. "We should order something or call Mr. Fudge Nuggets who spoiled me these past couple of weeks."

"We have a customer, *boss.* They want us to organize a party—for next Saturday."

"Oh, that's interesting." Sadie came to a halt, her wide eyes staring at Hannah. "I assume you're the customer looking for a party."

Hannah pressed her lips together and crossed her arms again.

"My name is Sadie, and I will be happy to serve you." She took off the baseball cap, letting her hair flow around her shoulders.

I counted by twos when she took off her jacket revealing a light pink tank top that showed her perky boobs. Thank fuck Hannah was with us or I'd be dragging her to the freezer.

"How can I help you?" She rested her forearms on the counter, bending forward and staring at Hannah.

"You can't," Hannah dismissed her. "This is a flower shop."

"It's not your regular flower shop, if that's what you think," Sadie said gleefully, fighting Hannah's surly attitude. "We do a lot of things here, even magic."

Sadie winked at Hannah. "I can even guess your name."

"You can't." My daughter's voice came out too harsh.

"Pumpkin, simmer down. Cut the attitude."

"Let me try." Sadie drummed her fingers on top of her mouth. "Hannah?"

She gasped. "How did you know?"

"Fairy powers," Sadie responded. "What can I do for you?"

"I want a party. A big party." Hannah extended her arms to either side, her eyes opened wide, and her smile followed. "With unicorns and a unicorn cake."

Then she slumped her shoulders. "But my mom said that unicorns aren't real and that my friends canceled. But Daddy promised to fix it. He said that it was a misunderstanding."

"This sounds serious, but like something we can fix."

"You can't. This isn't a party store," Hannah explained, her voice trembled with anger. "This is a flower shop."

Hannah pointed at the sign. "You design flowers."

"No, I design bouquets. The arrangements go to different places. Hotels, weddings, parties of all kinds. But I also have balloons and know people who make the best cakes and can rent me bouncy castles."

"Tess says that bouncy castles are for little kids."

"We have all types of different things, even ponies," Sadie salvaged the moment. "We should start with the details. When is the big day?"

"Next Saturday," I sighed.

"Oh wow, that's..." Sadie closed her mouth tight. "In seven days."

"More or less," I looked at her, my eyes begging her to do something.

My desperation knew no limits. I'd pay rush-charges and do her laundry for a month.

"Raven, can you take our customer to the table? I have a few things that I need to bring over." Sadie turned to me. "Would you mind helping me Mr. F—Hades."

I grinned because Fudge Nuggets was coming out of her mouth.

"What the fuck?" She asked when she closed the door of the fridge behind me.

My jaw dropped the moment I heard her cussing. Sadie had a whole live, love, laugh mentality. When she got angry, it was because someone had fucked up royally. In the three weeks since I'd met her, I'd never even seen her upset, let alone dropping f-bombs.

"Sorry, I didn't know where else to go." I rubbed my neck, flabbergasted by her tone and the flare coming out of her eyes. What did I do to her? "I thought ... but if you can't?"

"Oh, I can! I am just raging because of your ex." Her hands became two tight fists. "If only I could punch her, or at least give her a piece of my mind."

"You're not mad at me."

"I'd be punching you in the gut if I were," she joked, smiling a bit. "What happened?"

"She never organized the party," I said, leaning my body against the door. "Poor Hannah is heartbroken thinking that her friends didn't want to come."

"Your ex is a bitch."

"How refreshing. Your mouth is showing me its naughty side," I smirked. "Are you sweet on the outside and naughty on the inside?"

"Wouldn't you like to know?"

"I'm dying to find out how naughty you are, Miss Bell," I grabbed her hand and brought it to my mouth, pressing a soft kiss on her knuckles. "I'm going to lick the sweet cover and find out how to get to the center."

Sadie snatched her hand. "Your daughter is only a few feet away, Mr. Hades," she chided me.

"One day, I'll be pushing you up against the wall of this fridge and fucking you hard while you scream, '*More, Mr. Hades.*'"

Sadie glanced over at me but continued to walk around. "Party details, Kaden." She snapped her fingers. "You said next Saturday, but what time?"

"Early, late, I don't fucking know. Any time would work for me. I'm lost." I grabbed her shoulders, stopping her from pacing back and forth. "You were the first person I thought of when I got the news. But you don't have to do anything. If you can just—"

"Hey, Mr. Fudge Nuggets, I'm here for you, okay?" She cupped my cheeks, and I wanted to hold her in my arms and capture her mouth. Bury myself deep inside her and forget about Alicia for a few minutes.

"I'm glad you came to me," she whispered. "This can be done. We just need to power through it and make it perfect—for her."

Her words, her voice, everything calmed me. I lifted my hand, caressed her beautiful face with the back of my finger. "You're incredible."

"Stop it, Hades." She pushed me lightly. "Before I go see what I can do for her, I need a budget."

"Don't worry about the cost."

"I won't splurge, but I'm warning you. This won't be cheap." She grabbed a basket, placed a few flowers in it and handed it to me. "Let me go to the office to grab all my binders. You might want to get us some tea and soda. We have a lot to get through."

Per Sadie's request, I swung by the coffee shop to buy a smoothie for Hannah, coffee for Raven, and another chai tea for her. For an hour I was invisible to Sadie and Hannah. Everything revolved around my daughter and what she wanted for her birthday.

I couldn't remember when Alicia had ever dedicated that much time to either one of our daughters. A stranger treated Hannah as if she were the only kid in the world and her wishes mattered more than anything else.

My sometimes-inflexible daughter, who didn't take well to strangers allowed for a switch from unicorns to ponies. The theme was *enchanted forest*, and one of the activities would be to build your own fairy wings.

"We still need a garden," Raven said, setting the phone on the counter. "Everything is booked for next week."

"That's it." Sadie exhaled and grabbed her phone. "I'm going to have to make the call."

"Not the call," Raven gasped, then turned to me. "Are you going to let her make the call?"

"It's our last resort, Rae," Sadie said dramatically, touching her chest before she pressed send. "There's nothing he can do."

All eyes were on her, as she took a deep breath. "Hey, Daddy," she said with a chirpy tone.

I arched an eyebrow, waiting for more.

"How are you?" She rolled her eyes and smiled. "I'm glad that you closed the deal. Oh well, that's perfect." Sadie looked at her nails. "That's incredible. I hope you and Angelique enjoy the trip. What?" She shook her head. "You broke up with Angelique. Ah, that's nice that you met someone new. I'll be happy to meet her. Well, since you're going out of town, would you mind renting me your garden and the pool house for a party?

"No, it's not for me, it's for a customer. Yes, I trust them, Dad. You will? Well that's pretty generous of you. Oh, that's my birthday present."

Her shoulders slumped, and I wanted to ask when her birthday was. But I couldn't interrupt the call.

"Well, thank you for your generosity. Of course, I'll be fine, Dad. I'm going to be twenty-eight. You said she'll be there for six months this time. Well, there's not much I can do, she's a grown woman, isn't she? Yes, Daddy, I'll make sure the guests don't go into the main house. Thank you so much."

She hung up and high fived Raven. "We got it, but I'm going to have to endure dinner with him before he goes out of town."

"It can't be that bad," I suggested. "Spending time with your father must be fun."

I'd hate it if my daughters didn't want to spend any time with me when they get older.

"He's bringing his new girlfriend. I doubt she's over twenty-two, and he'll be on the phone," Sadie explained. "Not as fun as you might think."

Then she turned to Hannah, "We have the best garden in all of Bellevue. It's magical." She whispered the last two words.

"All you have to do now is give us the list of your guests, and we'll have the invitations ready by tomorrow."

"Tomorrow is Sunday," I reminded her.

"Well, the party is next Saturday, and she needs to deliver those invites by Monday."

"Do you think it will be cool enough that all the kids in my class will want to come?"

"Hey, it's about having a cool party," Sadie says, "But they're also coming because they love you."

Hannah hugged herself, her chin dropped to her chest. "Mom said that nobody wanted to come to my party."

"Maybe the invitations got lost, and that's why they didn't RSVP, Hannah." Sadie took her hand, squeezing it.

"This time, we'll make sure everyone receives it. Maybe your dad can hand-deliver the invitations to your teacher?"

"That's a great idea," I agreed.

"Can you get the list to Miss Tinkerbelle, Dad?"

"Sadie Bell," I corrected her. "Miss Sadie is more like Rosetta or Iridessa."

"Rosetta!" Hannah gasped.

Then she clapped with enough enthusiasm to make me want to jump from my seat.

"She's the flower fairy," Hannah concluded and smiled at Sadie.

"I hate to break up the celebration party, but we have two more arrangements in the queue," Raven announced, checking her watch. "Do you want me to stay?"

"No, I'll do them." Sadie closed the binders and her notebook. "I can come back afterwards and close the store. Go home. You have plans with your family."

"Hey, Hannah. Do you mind if we stay to help Miss Sadie?"

"Can we?" Hannah asked, her face illuminated with awe.

"You don't have to," Sadie insisted. "Go home, I have everything under control."

"Please, it's the least I can do."

I needed to be by her side. It had been hard not seeing her today, but after the way she treated Hannah, I wanted to hug her, kiss her. Thank you wasn't enough. Words weren't enough when it came to Sadie.

"Okay," she agreed.

It didn't take us long to pull the material for the arrangement. After working with Sadie for a couple of weeks, I knew pretty much where everything was stored. Hannah helped her with the flowers while I cleaned the front of the store. When they were done, Sadie and I straightened the working table and swept the floors before leaving. I put the arrangements in my Suburban. It was easier to use my car since I had a car seat for Hannah. We made two stops, and Hannah joined Sadie for the second one.

"I got a cookie," Hannah declared holding the treat with one hand.

"But we agreed that you can't eat it until your dad says it's okay."

Hannah, who wasn't patient, handed me the cookie and gave me a sharp nod. Sadie impressed me. She was a pro at handling both last-minute emergencies and children. I wanted to kiss her badly, but with Hannah in the car, I wasn't going to cross any line.

This was the first time I'd introduced my kid to a woman, but until Sadie and I had something substantial, I would keep things on the down low.

"You made my kid happy,"

"No, *she* made someone happy, that's why she's smiling."

"Ah the Sadie-Belle-mantra, how could I forget it." I turn on the engine. "Where to?"

"Home. It's been a long Saturday."

"Your birthday's coming up?"

"Maybe," she shrugged. "That reminds me. The garden is free."

"How much does he usually charge for it?"

"Three grand. It's worth it though, but I don't ask for it unless it's my last resort. Dad's always around scaring away my clients. Thankfully, he's going to be out of town."

I didn't say anything, but I planned on paying her. For the little I could hear during her phone conversation, the use of the garden was her birthday present. If I gave my daughters a gift, it was because I wanted them to enjoy it. Not to pass it on to someone else.

When I dropped Sadie off, I wanted to stay with her for the rest of the evening. But Hannah was with me, and I wasn't ready to share Sadie with anyone else. Our time together was mine—for now.

"Send me the list to prepare those invitations. If you send me your address, I can drop them by tomorrow."

"I'll text it to you when I get home, call me if you need anything else from me."

"It was nice to meet you, Hannah."

"She's nice," Hannah said, after Sadie entered her apartment building. "Can we go get a magical outfit for my party?"

"Where do we get those?"

She shrugged. "Why don't you ask Sadie? She might know."

I didn't waste time. My daughter just gave me the best excuse to spend more time with Sadie.

"Yeah?" Sadie answered her phone.

"We need help."

"With what?"

"A party outfit, do you have some time to go shopping with us?"

She remained quiet for several seconds. I checked the phone to verify that she was still on the line. "Sade?"

"I shouldn't, Kade," her voice was severe, dry.

"Why not?" My heart beat fast. Did she have a date?

"Because I'm getting used to being around you ... too much. It's not healthy, not for me."

What did that mean? Was she finally confirming that there was indeed some magnetic pull between us? I wanted to run toward her apartment and finally kiss her.

"Those lines are getting pretty blurred, Kaden."

If she let me, I would erase them all, and demolish all the walls in an instant as well.

"What's going on, Daddy?"

But I had to think about everyone, including my daughters. Tess, Hannah, and Sadie. Even Alicia. If she learned I was going out with someone, she'd go batshit crazy.

"Please," I begged her. "This is a serious matter. We have to find the perfect outfit."

"Please, Sadie!" Hannah didn't know the reason for her hesitation though.

"On one condition," Sadie said.

"What?"

"We don't see each other until next Saturday."

My lungs collapsed, my heart stopped.

"Sadie," I closed my eyes, recovering my breathing.

It had been hard enough to go through a Saturday morning without her. I knew we wouldn't see each other this weekend, but now that I had a reason to be with her, I didn't want to waste it. She couldn't take away my week. Soon I'd be taking off for New York, and I'd miss her like crazy.

"This is a bad idea," she mumbled.

"Sorry, but *I need you*."

"Somehow, I don't believe that you're actually sorry, Mr. Hades. But I'll be downstairs in a few minutes."

"Is she coming with us, Dad?"

"Yeah, she is."

Chapter Eighteen

KADE

Kade: I'm not going to be at work today.

Hummingbird: For the last time, you don't work for me.

Kade: I work for your customers. They pay me with cookies and candy.

Hummingbird: I'll let them know that they can save their sweets and put away their cameras.

Kade: You're going to miss me, right?

Hummingbird: Nope. I'm glad you finally found something else to do with your time.

Kade: Hannah is sick, but once she's better I'll come back to work.

Hummingbird: I'm so sorry to hear that she's not feeling well. She didn't look well Saturday night. Do you need me to bring you something?

Kade: You know what, I have an idea. And on your way, can you pick up crackers? We're out of those.

Hummingbird: I'll bring crackers and chicken soup.

I didn't reply to her text but pulled out my computer to order flowers for Hannah. She told me on Saturday that she'd love to receive flowers one day. It seemed like a sick girl could use some cheering up in the form of daisies.

"How are you feeling, baby?"

Hannah shook her head and rested it back on the pillow. I grabbed the thermometer and moved her legs cautiously before I rose from the couch. Gently, I tugged on her ear, pulling it back. Inserted the thermometer into the ear canal, turned it on and removed it as soon as it beeped. I kissed her right after.

"Ninety-nine-point-nine," I read out loud. "The fever is finally going down, pumpkin."

I alternated between two different medicines to keep her fever down. The doctor told me to worry if it rose higher than one-hundred-and-two. After Alicia dropped her at my apartment, Dr. Hawkins came to visit and diagnosed her with a viral bug.

"How are you feeling?"

"Okay." Her little voice was barely audible.

"Do you want more seltzer?"

Hannah nodded. "Am I going to go back to Mom's in the evening?"

"No, Pumpkin. You're staying with me until you feel better. You know I love to take care of you."

Alicia hated to care for the girls when they were sick. When I was out of town, she sent them to her parents. Though I loved to care for my girls, they didn't need to know that their mother had zero interest in nursing them back to health.

"Will I be okay for my party?"

"Yes, and the invitations were delivered earlier," I assured her because she was still afraid that no one would come to her party. "Jax handed them to your teacher, and he'll drop by the academy later today to give them to your ballet teacher."

When I called Jax to cancel our practice and explained to him about the party, he offered to deliver the invites. He knew that I couldn't trust Alicia.

While Hannah watched television and took a nap, I emailed back and forth with Duncan, the band's manager. We were working on the schedule for the upcoming tour. I remained by my kid's side until the bell rang.

When I opened the door, the most beautiful woman in the world was standing right in front of me. My heart beat faster whenever she was around.

"Hey, beautiful," I leaned forward, kissing her cheek and grabbing the tote bags she carried. "I was wondering if you'd be showing up with my order."

"Because we didn't charge your card?"

"Sort of." I moved away from the entrance so she could step inside. "It's been several hours since I placed my order, and there hadn't been any text from my bank that I had a new charge. Nor a call to ask about my request."

"Today's delivery is free," she said, showing me a bouquet of balloons. "We aren't delivering what you requested."

"I can see that."

"Hannah prefers balloons."

"You remembered." My heart pounded hard against my ribcage. Not only was she beautiful, but she was also thoughtful and sweet.

"You brought more than the crackers." I shot up an eyebrow staring at the bags I held.

"Yes, and be careful with the yellow bag," she warned me as she handed me the bags. "The soup is still hot, and I don't trust the containers I used. It might spill."

"You had time to make soup?"

"Yes, we closed early so I went home to make some chicken soup."

"Thank you," I bent over to kiss her cheek, but she ducked before I reached her and walked toward the living room.

"Let me say hi to Hannah, and then I'll help you serve the food."

I marched to the kitchen and set everything on the counter.

"She looks so sad," Sadie entered the kitchen.

"Understatement of the year."

"She said that her mom brought her last night."

"Alicia doesn't like sick kids," I stated, focusing on the groceries Sadie brought and not the anger boiling in my veins.

Sadie opened the cupboards. "Where are your bowls?"

"The cupboards right next to the stove." I turned around and counted two bowls. "You're not eating here?"

"I ..." She gripped the countertop taking a deep breath.

"What happened, Little Fairy?"

"Mom called," she breathed the last word.

"Wasn't she supposed to be in rehab?" I stopped putting the stuff away and concentrated on her.

I wasn't a stranger to rehab or getting clean. For the first thirty days, I had no contact with the outside world.

"Yeah, she *was*," Sadie slouched.

My heart stuttered as her body radiated sadness. There was this spinning down feeling dragging me closer to her. A need to fix her day, to make her smile.

"What can I do?"

"I'm concerned about her. I'm sure she went into rehab in hopes that Dad would be around for her once she got out."

She tilted her head slightly, looking at me. "It worries me."

"Why?"

"Because I think she still loves him. No matter how long it's been since the divorce, or how many boyfriends and husbands she's had. Mom still loves Dad. Once she learns about the new girlfriend ..." Her shoulders sagged, her voice trailed.

"She's going to drink more," I finished the sentence.

"And use more painkillers to numb herself." She turned to look at me. "I shouldn't care. She's an adult. But I can't help myself."

I grabbed her hand and pulled her toward me. "Lean on me, Sadie. It must be hard to see her sick and unable to help her."

"How hard is it for you?"

"The craving is there, but I remind myself of what matters. The people I might lose if I let the sickness win."

"I'm proud of you," she mumbled.

My heart exploded inside my chest. No one had ever been proud of me, or supportive. At that moment, I was falling for her.

It was so obvious. She never left my mind. She was never far—mentally if not physically. Sadie was becoming my one stable force. My one support in a world filled with chaos. I so desperately needed that in my life—her. And I couldn't believe I'd only just realized it.

"But I think I hate you," she murmured, breathing deeply, her hands grabbing my t-shirt tightly.

"Somehow, I don't believe you. Why do you think you hate me?" I kissed the top of her head.

"Because you're making me care about you," she paused, her head rested on my chest. Her body fit perfectly against mine.

I held my breath and waited to hear more about her ambivalent feelings for me. She remained silent for a long time, her eyes were closed. I wanted to capture her mouth and kiss her until all her doubts disappeared.

"So, you care about me."

"Maybe I do. But I keep wondering what's going to happen to me when you leave."

Her doubts pinched my heart. I experienced the pain of my sister leaving. My mother neglected us for years. The abandonment and the loss scarred me. The wounds were so deep that I couldn't let anyone into my world or my heart. Except for this woman.

But what would I do if she left?

The answer came to me immediately, I would never let her go. I wouldn't abandon her either.

"Not everybody leaves, Sadie," I whispered in her ear, pulling her tighter against my body.

"Sometimes I'm the one who has to leave because the other person is hurting me."

Those words coupled with her broken voice felt like an arrow through my heart. I wanted to keep her close to me and promise her that no one would hurt her again.

"Who hurt you, love?"

"It doesn't matter."

"You can't believe that when you wear the scars in your heart. They matter, and I am here to hear about those battles you lost, the ones you won."

At that moment, I came to the realization that she was broken like me. But my new antidote was her. She made me feel complete. Whole. I wanted to be the one who would complete her. I stared at her lips and debated if I should kiss her, but I remembered Hannah was there with us. Thank fuck there were a few walls of separation between the kitchen and the living room.

Until Sadie and I had something solid, I didn't want to say anything to my girls. Everything was new to me. Too new. I hadn't had a serious relationship with another woman since their mother. How would my girls react? I stopped worrying because in my gut I knew that Sadie wasn't ready for *us* yet.

"Correct me if I'm wrong, but I believe that you need time."

"Time?" She pushed herself away from my hold.

"To come to terms with your past, and hopefully give me a chance."

"You and I being in a relationship is such a bad idea, but I accept the invitation to have dinner with you and Hannah."

"Hannah, come over. Dinner is ready."

I kissed Sadie's cheek again, aware that it might be the last time she'd let me do it. My gut told me that she was about to raise those walls and draw a thicker, more permanent line between us.

Chapter Nineteen

KADE

Present

    It started with just one look
    A simple hello
    Ever since, my heart wouldn't let you go
    Your beautiful face, sweet smile, silky voice
    I just couldn't get you out of my head
    I was speechless. There are words that I can't speak
    My heart started to race on that day

———

But how could I fall for an angel
    My dark secrets hide in the ocean deep
    It's only you I want to seek and keep
    Forever be mine

———

I never said them before
    Never felt them before

Love, is that it?
I'm falling, don't stop me

———

But how could I fall for an angel
  My dark secrets hide in the ocean deep
  It's only you I want to seek and keep
  Forever be mine

———

In my dreams there is you and me
  If that sweet dream turns into reality
  It'll be forever
  Just you and me

———

But how could I fall for an angel
  There are things that I always kept
  My dark secrets hide in the ocean deep
  It's only you I want to seek and keep
  But would you love me in the dark? I need your light. Please, don't leave me now. Forever be mine.

"That's the very first song I wrote for your mama, Little Bean," I put the guitar back in the case and go back to the sink to wash and change my scrubs before taking him in my arms.

"She loved when I sang for her before bed," I say, marching toward him. "I'll teach you how to play as soon as you can hold a guitar. That woman lives through music. She'll love watching us play together."

I carefully maneuver the tubes connected to my baby and hold him close to my chest. "How are you this morning?" He wiggles his body closer to mine. "I heard they're planning on introducing you to formula. Though, not before they check to see if you're allergic to milk or soy, like your mom."

Little Bean opens his eyes, staring at me. He's starting to become more aware of his surroundings and that's making my heart grow.

"I'm Dad," I say softly.

He focuses his dark blue eyes on me. The little guy probably wonders who I am, while I bet he's missing *her*. I hate that I missed the pregnancy. This time it was supposed to be different. We were going to share everything from the beginning. Morning sickness, first heartbeat and—I suck in air and freeze.

Fuck, I'm such an idiot. We did share the morning sickness for a couple of days before our breakup. Sadie had been puking for three days straight.

"It's nothing," she said. It was everything. It was our baby. This Little Bean who needed me back then. Fuck, *she* needed me. *"You don't have to worry about me anymore."*

If I felt like an asshole and a failure when I left her. Today I feel even worse. How could I not know? Because I've never been around a woman with morning sickness.

If I know her well, which I do, I bet she talked to him every day. From the moment she woke up until she went to sleep.

"You miss her voice, don't you, baby boy?" I kiss his forehead. "I do too. So much."

I cradle him and sing to him softly as I ponder our future. So far, I haven't thought much about it. What are we going to do when Sadie is ready to go home? Should I buy a house like we had planned? I don't understand why she's living at her father's place. Raven insists that the flower shop continues to grow. There are so many things I missed.

But before I can think of the future, I have to wait. There's a chance that she might not wake up. My entire world threatens to fall apart and yet, I have to find the strength to be everything for our son.

"Did she tell you that we've wanted you for a long time?"

His eyes remain closed, his breathing is deep. He's comfortable in my arms. If I could, I'd keep him with me all the time. Every time I set him back into the crib, my arms feel cold and he fusses. We need each other, and we've been forging a bond that I don't want to lose. Ever.

Whenever Sadie and I mentioned having a family, I wanted to experience everything. I didn't want to miss a single moment. Listening to his heartbeat, being there during the delivery, the late-night feedings. I wanted to experience it all with Sadie.

"If you'd have told me, I'd have been there for you from the beginning," I say out loud.

Sadie doesn't answer. She remains asleep, but I know that she can hear me. That's what it says in every article I've read about patients in a coma like hers.

"Are you too tired to meet me in your dreams, Little Fairy?" I lift my gaze and watch her.

These are the moments when I wish I could see her in my dreams. During the few hours of sleep that I get at night, I haven't seen her. We used to dream about each other, with each other. She swore that she came to me in my dreams. No matter how far or near we were from each other, we found one another.

There haven't been any changes. The bruises on her face are healing, her condition continues to be stable. I understand that she needs to recover. But I'm desperate. This state of limbo where I wait, having zero guarantees, is infuriating.

"You know what mama would say?"

My little boy doesn't make a sound. It's only the machines and my voice filling the silence.

"She'd say, 'just have faith and be patient, Kade. Things happen at the right time. You can't rush perfection.'" I kiss his little hand. "That's what we're going to do. Have faith and wait."

Sadie did everything on her own time. I need to have faith that she'll wake up when she's ready. In the meantime, I have to figure out how to be a father to a newborn, find us a home, and figure out how I'm going to break the news to my daughters. Would they care that Sadie was in an accident?

Hannah would, she adores Sadie. But Tess...I exhale harshly. For now, I'll have to focus on learning how to care for a newborn. My daughters will have to deal. There's someone as important as them now who needs me more than anyone else in this world.

"Are you up to the task of being my little helper, Little Bean? We have a lot to do. Soon I'll introduce you to your sisters. They're going to love you."

I hope.

The uncertainty is weighing on me. Yet, even when my heart breaks at the sight of Sadie, it also beats with happiness because I have him. The ambivalence makes no sense. I'm ecstatic and can't hide the joy that I feel because of him. Yet, my insides are crumbling because Sadie is in a coma, and I have no fucking idea if I'll ever see her soul shine again.

"When you wake up, you'll be surprised with my new parenting skills, love," I say out loud, hoping that Sadie can hear me. "You'll have to catch up with me. We agreed to do this as a team, remember?"

"How would you rate my services so far, Little Bean?" He remains still, looking peaceful. This little man reminds me so much of Sadie when she would fall asleep in my arms. "You know what, we should play you a video of her, so you can listen to her voice."

Instead of maneuvering him back to the incubator and grabbing my laptop, I take out my phone and go through the videos I've stored from Sadie. I go back to New Year's, but I skip it since I remember that we left the phone on while I made love to her that night. I found the one where I had to play the weekend after Thanksgiving in Madison Square Garden, and she couldn't come with me.

"Hey, cuddle bunny, good morning. I'm not sure if you've landed yet, but I wanted to say hi and thank you for the rose you left on the pillow ..." she trails her eyes around. *"And breakfast."*

She blows me a kiss. *"I miss you already, even when I just saw you in my dream."*

She sips some of her coffee. *"I wanted to wish you good luck on your interviews and the next thirty concerts. You're going to rock their world. Have I told you lately that I love you? No? Well, I do. I love you from here to the next universe and back. You're the most wonderful man in the entire galaxy—and I'm happy because you're mine. Remember that no matter how far we are from each other, we'll be together in our dreams—every night. Have a great tour, Kay."*

Sadie looks around, her face closing in on the phone. *"Let's Facetime tonight, Mr. Hades. I'll be naked, wet, and ready for you."*

"And you didn't need to hear that last part." My gaze moves toward our Little Beanie whose eyes are open and whose legs kick around.

"Yes, that's Mama. I knew you were going to like hearing her voice."

I rewind the video enough to repeat the part where she says, 'I love you,' and play it several times for us. My heart beats fast as I remember the way she loved me. She didn't open her heart immediately. But when she loved, she loved fiercely.

She is fierce, strong, and loving. She isn't perfect, but she was proud of her flaws. She's honest, unstoppable. But she knows fear and sometimes Sadie doesn't fight until she's ready for battle, and strong enough to slay the beasts that threaten her mind.

That's how I know that she'll wake up sooner or later. What I don't know is if we have a future.

Are we over?

"We can't be over," I warn her. "You can't separate two soulmates. It's just impossible, Hummingbird."

"She'll come back to us soon. And she'll be telling you how much she loves you. I can picture her, holding you in her arms as she reads you endless stories and tells you that you're the most handsome boy in the world."

He opens his eyes, stares at me and I swear this kid wants to talk. There's something important he wants to say, or maybe he wants to tell me everything he and his mother did while I was away.

Since I have the phone, I text Raven to check on her and the store. Yesterday she said she had everything under control. That Sadie had hired a couple of employees to help them during her maternity leave.

Raven: Everything is fine, but if you want to take a shift you're more than welcome.

Kaden: That'd mean leaving the hospital. I can't.

Raven: You should get out for a few hours. Going to the coffee shop across the street isn't enough. Are you sleeping?

Kaden: A few hours when there's someone around to keep them company.

Raven: Think about resting more. Once they're out of the

hospital, they are going to need you. And your children will be back soon.

Kaden: I'll be ready.

Raven: Before I forget, Sadie's Mom called. She left a voice-mail. I won't call her back but if she drops by, I'm going to have to tell her. Are you prepared to deal with her?

Kaden: She's not on the list.

Raven: Wake up and smell the roses, Kaden. You're not family. If either one of her parents wants to, they can kick you out her room.

Kaden: They don't give a fuck about her. Only I do.

Raven: You've been gone for too long. Sadie has been living in Andrew's pool house since she moved out of your place. It won't be long before he notices that his daughter isn't home, don't you think?

I huff, because if that's the case, he should have noticed days ago. He's proving me right. The fucker doesn't care enough about her.

Andrew Bell might learn about Sadie in a couple of months. He'll send her some expensive present and give her the news that he has a new woman in his life.

Kaden: I'll deal with them if they ever show up.

Sadie and her father have a strange relationship. He loves her, but he doesn't know what to do with her. She's not a car he can store in his big garage, or a property, or an expensive piece of art. Andrew Bell can only hold a relationship for so long, and Sadie is a permanent fixture in his life. A living, thinking, talking human who has her own ideals and doesn't like to follow his.

And he hates me. I am everything he despises—a fucking uneducated musician, and a high school dropout. The one good thing he has going for him in his life is his daughter. I tried my best to be cordial with him, but there were times when I couldn't keep my shit together. He can try to kick me out, but he's too busy to follow through with his threats. Andrew likes to create chaos between Sadie and me. But since the beginning, he's only managed to bring us closer together.

Chapter Twenty

KADE

Three Years Ago

For a change, Alicia took care of the girls during the afternoon. Only because they were spending the evening with her parents. They wanted to celebrate Hannah's birthday a few days early. I debated between dropping by the flower shop or going to the studio to play. In the end, I decided to spend my evening composing a new song—for Sadie—at home. But my muse dropped by my house, changing all my plans.

From the moment I set my eyes on her, I couldn't let her out of my sight. She wore a little black dress, high heels, makeup, and her hair was pinned up in a bun hiding her colorful highlights.

The little bunny dressed as a fox tonight. Blood rushed to my groin, my hands itched to grab her, and my mouth wanted to claim hers. I closed my eyes for a second trying to come up with mundane thoughts unrelated to sex.

"Hey," her silky voice greeted me.

My mouth salivated. After several deep breaths, I finally controlled my lust.

"How many boundaries would I cross if I said you look fucking hot, and I want to pin you against the door and fuck you thoroughly?"

"Hello to you too, Mr. Hades." She reached inside of her handbag, pulling out a white envelope.

"You left this at the shop. I texted you earlier about the invoices, but you never answered. I need the money to pay for the ponies and the cake."

"Fuck!"

That cooled me down. If we didn't pay those two in full, we won't have a party this coming Saturday.

"I totally forgot. Sorry."

"It's okay. You seemed a bit distracted today."

"You are my only distraction," I responded.

My mind only had two settings. Worry about my mundane life, and thinking about Sadie. I salivated all day long. And wanted to kiss her every single second. I needed a little taste of those luscious lips. Like today, I just couldn't get my mind off her and planned on bringing up our situation. However, I'd been too busy to even take a break.

Hummingbird Flower Design was growing rapidly. There was a rumor that the flower shop had a driver who looked just like Kaden Hades. After three weeks of working with her, it was bound to happen. We didn't have much time to hang out or chat like we usually did. At noon I left with ten arrangements, and never went back to the store.

"Why don't you come in? I can cook you something. We can talk about how gorgeous you look or—"

"Enough flirting, Hades. I have to go." She rolled her eyes, wiggling her fingers.

"Dinner plans?"

She nodded twice and checked her watch. I noticed the pearl necklace, the matching earrings, and the makeup she was wearing. There was something about her that didn't feel natural. She seemed off tonight.

"You okay?"

"For now. Not looking forward to my date."

"Cancel. Stay with me," I suggested, opening the door wider.

The fuck she was going out with someone else.

"I have dinner plans," she repeated.

"Why don't *I* take you to dinner?"

"That selective hearing, Kade."

"If I recall, you owe me a dinner, Little Minx."

"I could invite you to come along, Hotshot," she proposed.

There was a catch behind the invitation. My gut told me to stay at home and wave goodbye, but my heart wanted to be with her.

"Tell me more. I'm interested." I tapped my chin, narrowing my gaze.

"There's not much to say. I'm going to dinner. You're welcome to join me, and it's at a fancy restaurant only a few blocks from here."

"We're having a formal dinner," I smirked, eyeing her again. "You and me."

I leaned forward, my lips scheming along the sweep of her cheek.

"I'd call that progress, Miss Bell."

"Keep your lips to yourself, Hades." She pushed me lightly.

"There's no progress. This is an invitation to join my father, his new bimbo, and me for dinner."

"You want me to meet your father, Honey Buns?" My body tensed, and I took a step backward.

Alicia's parents hated me; even though I was the father of their granddaughters. There was no way Sadie's father would like me.

"No, Melon Belly. I don't want you to meet my father."

I pulled my shirt up slightly and patted my stomach. "There's no fat in here, Sugar Tush. But tell me, do I get to meet your dad or not?"

"Yes, but not the way you think."

"You know what I'm thinking?" I crossed my arms and arch an eyebrow. "I doubt it because if you knew you'd be complaining about the lines I've crossed and walls I'm tearing down. Mostly, you'd be criticizing my terrible friendship etiquette."

"You're so irritating sometimes."

"Am I?"

A crooked smile touched her lips, her cheeks darkened slightly.

"Me thinks you're flustered because you want the same thing I do."

"You're a nightmare." She rolled her eyes.

"I'm not. To prove it, I'll go with you and be on my best behavior. I'll be perfect for Princess Aurora."

"Look Prince Charming, if you're going to call me a princess, I'd choose anyone but *Sleeping Beauty*. And if you're joining me, you have to hurry up and change."

"Change?"

"It's one of those no jacket, no service kinds of restaurants."

"You want me to dress for the occasion?"

"Unless you can't, then I'll be on my way."

"I can, but you're going to owe me."

"If we're charging for favors, you owe me your first born after what I had to pull this week for Hannah."

"I'm not sure Tess would be willing to go with you, but we can have a baby together if you want."

"Thank you, but I'm not in the market to get knocked up, Mr. Hades."

"One day, you'll be begging for one," I smirked at her.

And fuck if I wasn't whipped. The image of a little girl with her long hair and eyes appeared out of nowhere. Or a boy, our son. *Stop it, you're done with children and commitments. You suck at those.*

I turned around and march toward my room.

☆ ☆ ☆ ☆

Stars lit the sky like snowflakes in the night. Sadie smiled, and the wind blew her hair into a tousled mane. Once we left the restaurant, she undid the tight bun and the weight she carried on her shoulders disappeared. My girl was back and the evening became everything.

"See those." She pointed at the sky. "The constellations. They've witnessed everything that happens, during a night, a year, even a millennia. They watch and record every tiny moment. How many stories do you think they'd tell?"

"You like stories?"

"Yes, all kinds of stories, real stories—biographies. I got that from Dad, I think."

"I didn't like him." I grabbed her delicate hand and kissed her wrist.

When Sadie and I walked toward the entrance of the restaurant, her father arrived. Once he spotted me, he handed me a twenty-dollar bill and his car keys. He asked me to look after his baby, or I'd be jobless the next day.

"However, I'll be happy to take care of his baby." I handed over the money her father had given me.

"You think that twenty is enough to care for me?" She laughed.

The sound of her laughter rushed in and around me. I loved everything about it. The sweetness. The soulful clatter that resonated through my heart, making it beat faster.

"Your safekeeping is priceless." I opened the passenger door of my truck. "I'd give all my money to keep you safe. But then again, I would take care of you myself."

"Dad meant his car," she said once I climbed into the driver seat.

Your dad's a fucking asshole.

"How can you stand the man?"

"Dad's an acquired taste," Sadie said kissing my jaw before I pulled out of the parking spot. "You have no idea how much I appreciate you coming with me."

I kissed her knuckles and stroked her bare arm with my fingers while holding the wheel with my left hand.

"Next time I might bail or give him a piece of my mind."

"Thank you for controlling yourself."

"It was fucking hard," I mumbled between clenched teeth. "He's an asshole, but I admired the way you put him in his place."

"He's used to people doing everything he says and wants. But that's something I refuse to do for him. No one can make him happy. Why even try?" she said with resignation.

"Thank you for getting us his garden. Now I understand why Raven told me to stop you."

"Rae likes to exaggerate. It was a pleasure, and I did it for Hannah. If I'd had more time, I would've gotten something else. But I can handle my father."

"I can't believe that someone so sweet can be related to that asshole."

"We can't choose our parents, but at least I know what I don't want with my own children."

"Is that something you can choose?"

"I want to believe so," she shared, leaning closer like she was about to tell me a secret.

The closeness of her body made me want to pull her into my lap, but I kept driving and controlled my urge.

"Wouldn't it be great to have a family where everyone loves and respects each other?" She questioned, animatedly. "I'm not saying there wouldn't be arguments, but I want to be a parent and a friend, the person they go to when they need an adult and not the one they hide from because they're afraid of my reaction."

"Have my children," I offered.

"You already have children, and from what I've witnessed so far, you've done a great job. Hannah is charming and kind."

"She happened to like you too." I parked in front of her apartment building. "I've never introduced anyone to my daughters."

I never saw myself with anyone, but every minute I spent with Sadie was unique. We worked perfectly together. The way she treated my kid and how patient she was with everyone, drew me closer to her. Her judgmental father tried to put her down several times. Not once did she let him, and every time she used her sweetness to keep him in check.

"I'm flattered you trusted me with her birthday, and for letting me spend time with you two." She continued looking toward the entrance to her apartment building. "Thank you, for everything."

"Sounds like you want to cut tonight short."

"I have to be up early tomorrow morning."

"Me too, I have to pick up your tea before work."

"You don't have to do that."

"But I love to do it, just like I love to spend time with you. Come home with me, we can watch movies and just hang out."

"Maybe another day. Tonight I have to be home."

"Can I invite myself in?"

"You can, but we shouldn't."

"We are friends who happen to like spending time together. Why do you keep fighting me?"

"Because I know how it'll end."

"You don't, but I'll give you time."

"Why are you so insistent?"

I'm not sure. My soul knows, my heart too. My head is the one that's figuring it out, but while that happens, I don't want to let you go.

Chapter Twenty-One

KADE

The suburbs didn't hold any appeal to me. Many of my friends lived in Seattle, a few other on the islands. It never occurred to me that deep in Bellevue there was another world. Sadie's father lived in an urban retreat only thirty minutes from the city. Last week I realized he had more money than brain cells, but fuck me, he was loaded. No wonder he behaved like the world was his.

"He owns a palace," I mumbled under my breath as I parked the car in front of the estate home.

"Is this where we're having my party?" Hannah bounced in her seat.

"Ugh, can you stop it?" Tess snapped at her little sister.

"Tess, be nice," I warned her.

"This is a kid's party. I don't understand why you had to drag me along," she pouted.

"Because it's your sister's birthday, and we're family."

I refused to give her the biggest reason because her lousy attitude would worsen. Her mother was out of town, and there was no adult to supervise her. At thirteen, she was too young to stay at home for hours without someone to care for her, especially when I was almost forty minutes away.

"Look, Daddy! There's Sadie!" Hannah squealed.

"Who's Sadie?"

"Daddy's friend."

"You have a friend?" Tess glared at me suspiciously.

"Several. You've met them."

"But none of them are *girls*."

"She's a woman, and she happened to know all the right people to help us get this party together."

"Is she like a groupie?"

I tried to keep my daughters away from groupies, alcohol, and drugs. But when I took them with me, it was hard to avoid some of that stuff.

"No, she's someone I met at a coffee shop."

"She's pretty and nice," Hannah said. "She brought me chicken soup when I was sick, and balloons."

"Are you planning on dating her?" Tess's entire body slumped. "Please don't. You're too old for that, and you have Mom."

I massaged my temples. "Sweetheart, we already talked about it. Your mother and I are over. We divorced a long time ago.

"Parents." She rolled her eyes. "They don't realize what's right in front of them. I'll just wait until you decide to come back home."

Tess shut the door and bolted out of the car.

Teenagers. They liked to make my life miserable.

"Is she right?"

"About, Hannah?"

"You and Mom getting back together," Hannah mumbled.

"No sweetheart, that's never going to happen. But we love you both, a lot."

"You love me more than Mom."

"That's silly, honey. Let's go down and see what Sadie needs from us."

"Our guest of honor has arrived," Sadie said, unloading her van.

"And I brought the birthday girl too."

"I was talking about her, but if it makes you feel better, you can be our guest of honor number forty-nine."

"How many guests do we have?"

"Forty." She smirked.

"You never miss a chance to make me feel welcome."

"It's my specialty." She stopped loading stuff onto the golf cart and looked at Tess. "You must be Tess. Your dad has told me a lot about you."

"Well, he's never mentioned you."

"I'm glad because that means he doesn't have any complaints about the party or my shop." Sadie smiled at her, disregarding the rude comment coming from my mouthy teenager. "There's nothing worse than having an unsatisfied customer. Do you mind helping me with the bags of balloons, please?"

"Why?" Tess took a step back, her eyes wide and her mouth open just as big.

"Because I need a grown up helping me, Tess," Sadie explained. "Since this is a last-minute party, I don't have many helpers. And you don't seem like the kind of person who'd enjoy a ... kid's party," she mumbled the last words close to Tess. "I'm guessing you'll be perfect to be my game coordinator."

"I want to be a game coordinator," Hannah raised her hand and jumped up and down.

"Pick me!" my youngest daughter begged.

"You're the birthday girl. Your job is to enjoy the party." She turned her attention toward Tess. "What do you think? I'll pay you for the hours you work."

Tess crossed her arms. "I might be interested. Keep talking."

Sadie laughed. "You are your father's daughter. I'll pay you ten dollars an hour. If you stay to clean up with us, I'll give you five more."

"Not bad. I think I'll take it."

"Great! Start hauling things to the pool house." She handed her a bag of balloons. "Just go around this house, and you'll see it right away."

"How can I help, Sadie Bell?"

"Well, you're the birthday girl, and you're not supposed to do anything. But if you insist, why don't you go to the next car and check with Raven?"

"The pool is closed, and everything's secured. I made sure of that last night."

"I could've come with you," I stated.

"You had a concert. How was it?"

"I released a new song. I wish you'd have been there," I mentioned casually.

"You can play it some other day, or I'll buy the song once it's available."

"We're not releasing it soon, and I won't see you after today."

"Finally, I got rid of you." She joked, but those eyes didn't seem to happy.

"Sorry to break it to you, but that's never going to happen, my Sugar Plum Fairy."

"Then why won't I see you?"

"I'm leaving for New York. We're recording a live album and doing a few presentations for late night shows."

"I'm getting rid of you for a few months?" she squealed.

"Only for a couple of weeks."

Her body stiffened, and her expression switched slightly. I saw a glimpse of sadness in her beautiful eyes, but it disappeared almost immediately. It reminded me of last Sunday when we had dinner with her father. There were moments when her expression switched to sadness or frustration, but it disappeared within seconds.

"Before I forget, this is for you." She handed me a gift bag. "Here, you're going to need this."

"It's not my birthday." I stared at the present, then looked at her.

"You're the dad, it's your day too. Thirteen years of being an amazing father should be celebrated."

"I wouldn't say that I've been amazing or count it as thirteen years —I didn't do much for the first five."

"I'm sure you changed a diaper or two."

"Never. I was out of town, or just ... I wasn't that great at the beginning." I combed my hair with my free hand. "You could say I was a lousy asshole."

"Don't beat yourself up. That's all in the past. You changed, and those girls look happy."

"You're very thoughtful," I said while opening my present.

It was a professional camera. "This is amazing, but I have my phone."

"But this takes better pictures and records longer videos without having to worry about storage. I'm giving Hannah a scrapbook. You two can do a lot with it together."

My heart stopped at the significance of the present. She was giving me a chance to bond with my child. There was something about her that kept pulling me into her world. Sadie was an open book, and yet as strange as the deep blue sea. She was starlight with a hint of darkness. A beautiful chaos that drew me into her world. And even if I wanted to stop it, my heart kept falling deeper and deeper in love with her.

"You didn't have to," I stared at the camera. "It looks expensive."

"Well, someone paid me extra. I used some of that to pay for it."

"Just when I thought you couldn't be more perfect," I brushed a strand of hair away from her face.

"I'm not perfect, and never forget that. Don't put me on a pedestal because I'll fall."

"You're on the highest one, and you'd never fall. I'd be close enough to catch you every time and put you back." I reached for her hand, but she stepped away from me.

"Like they say when you're about to ride a rollercoaster, keep your arms and legs inside the vehicle at all times. Or just...keep your hands to yourself, Hades."

"Do you think I can?"

"It should be easy."

"Too fucking complicated because every fucking day you make me feel ... I don't fucking know how to describe it."

"You can always write a song, call it *Sadie My Obsession*. It could be your next hit."

"Your suggestion comes a little late when there are already seven songs about you included on my next album."

"Seven?"

"Yes. The band only allowed me to add seven, and I had to delete four of the ones we planned on recording."

"Seven?" Her voice lowers. "About me?"

"Should I point out that no other woman has ever inspired me?" I leaned closer, our mouths almost touching when I heard the little voice.

"Dad!"

"Behave, my Silky Roll," Sadie said, stretching her neck. "Nobody saw your little display. But like I said, keep your hands to yourself."

"You're going to start with the nicknames again, Poochie Doo?"

"Daddy, you need see my cake." Hannah grabbed my hand. "You have to come with me. It's a unicorn, and it has fairies flying around it."

"Go. Take pictures of her around the garden and with the cake before the guests arrive."

The cake was just the way Hannah wanted it. Tess loved the cake and asked if she could have a cool cake like that for her next birthday. I wasn't sure what that meant, when every day her mood changed, along with what she liked or hated. No one warned me about the teenage years. Some days I missed my little girl, the one who adored me and smiled all the time.

Before the party began, I joined Sadie in the main house. It was as impressive as it was on the outside. Maybe more. Marble floors in the foyer, high ceilings and open windows all through the living room and dining area.

"This house is impressive."

"I love it," Sadie continued her way into the kitchen. "It was different when I was younger."

"You lived here while you were growing up?"

"No, this was my grandparents' home. Dad inherited it after grandma died." Sadie opened a big pantry. "His siblings got the other properties."

She came out of the pantry with two big trays and handed them to me. "But I did visit often and spent a lot of summers here learning about flowers."

"The garden is beautiful."

"It's all me," she responded with a wide smile and a hint of pride. "It was my project while I was between jobs. Grandma would love it.

Someday, I want a house like this and a greenhouse where I can grow food and orchids and ... it's just a dream of course."

"It could happen."

"No, it can't because I'd need a lot of money," she challenged, presenting a fact.

"But it seems like you're rich."

"Dad's rich. I'm getting by with a flower shop that's just starting." She looked around the house, and then back at me. "We're done with the house for today. No one can enter. Not even the Queen of England."

She closed the door behind us, locked it, and pulled a small box from her pocket. "If you'll all excuse me."

Sadie walked away toward Hannah, she bent down and gifted her the box. My girl jumped up and down, and then opened the box. When I reached them, I spotted a beautiful necklace with a unicorn charm.

"Thank you! It's beautiful!" Hannah hugged her tight.

"Do you want me to help you put it on?"

Hannah nodded once. Sadie unclasped the chain and placed it around Hannah's neck being careful with her long dark hair. "Happy birthday, sweetheart."

"Thank you." Hannah pressed both hands on her necklace. "This is the best present ever."

"You shouldn't have," I said.

"It's her birthday. She deserves a unicorn." Sadie winked at me. "Follow me. The caterer needs those trays."

☆ ☆ ☆ ☆

"Thank you. You made all her wishes come true."

"She looks exhausted."

"They're both exhausted. I'm still blown away by the way you handled Tess."

"She's a teenager," she said as if that explained everything. "They want to belong everywhere, yet they feel as if they don't belong anywhere at all. If you help them find something that they enjoy, it's hard for them to be broody."

Tess spent hours bossing kids around, organizing games, giving away prizes, and helping Hannah open the presents. She let Sadie give her instructions without snapping or talking back.

"I gave the thank you notes to Hannah. Tess has the list. Tomorrow you three can spend the day signing them."

"For being so disorganized, you seemed to have your shit together."

Her lips pressed together, her eyes smiled. "That's between you and me."

Our gazes remained connected. The fact that we shared something special, a secret that only the two of us knew, blew me away. I wanted to hug her, kiss her, and say goodbye properly. But the girls were watching. "Your secret is safe with me, Gummy Bear."

"Goodbye, Sugar Puff."

"Can I drop by your house later tonight?" I could order pizza for dinner and leave Tess in charge of Hannah for a couple of hours.

"I'm not going back home."

"Why?"

"I want to work in the garden tomorrow morning."

"We could come over," I suggested.

Give me a few more hours before I have to leave you for two long weeks.

"Thank you, but that's something I like to do by myself."

"It might be better if you have people helping."

"No, it wouldn't because it's my therapy, and I rather do it alone. Thank you for the offer, though."

"Do you realize that I won't see you for two weeks?"

"You keep saying that as if I should be sad, but I'm having an internal party as we speak."

"You're cruel."

"You should go." She waved at the girls.

"Sadie?"

"Goodbye, Kaden Hades," she whispered my name. "For what's worth it I enjoyed these couple of weeks. See you around."

Kaden: *I feel like you just kicked me out of your life.*

She never answered my text, and I felt like I'd lost a part of myself.

Chapter Twenty-Two

KADEN

Sadie never responded to my texts. I called her daily, but I only got her voicemail. She never returned my calls as I requested. After seven days of not seeing her, I couldn't wait any longer. Breaking my routine, I flew back home. That woman thought we were through, and I had just started. Armed with what I hoped was the most powerful weapon to break through to her, I drove to her shop as soon as I landed.

"Where is she?" I looked around the shop.

"I knew you wouldn't fail me," Raven grinned.

"What are you talking about?"

"You don't know, do you?"

"Know what?

"Why are you here?'

"Because she's not returning my fucking calls or my texts," I explained, running a hand through my hair as I tried to push away my frustration. "I miss her, and she thinks we're over. But she's wrong."

"Good enough reason."

"Is there another one?"

"Yours is better. Sadie went home to avoid her mother."

"Then that's where I'm heading. Thank you, Rae."

I snatched a daisy from the bunch she had on the working table.

Instead of driving to her place, I left my car where I parked it, close to the shop, and walked toward Sadie's house. As I approached her apartment building, the light rain that began when I left the shop became a downpour. The droplets were the size of almonds, they smashed their way down my body. I ran fast to reach my destination. Thankfully someone was coming out of the building when I arrived.

"Where are you going?"

"To visit Sadie Bell."

"The girl from 4C? She's a sweetheart," the woman said walking away but leaving the door open for me.

I took the stairs, but the weight of the wet denim slowed me down. Once I reached her floor, I spotted Sadie. Her back facing the stairs. She was wearing a pair of colorful leggings and a long dress. Her feet were bare, and her hair was tied into a braid.

"Just the woman I wanted to see."

She turned around and smiled at me. Her gaze took hold of me. She searched my body up and down like I'd just appeared out of nowhere, like a dream or a mirage.

"Hades," she whispered.

"Hi, Little Minx. You seem a bit preoccupied."

"Something tells me you are the mastermind behind these boxes." Sadie stared at the soaking flower I brought. Her eyes widen, and her mouth opened. "What did she do to you?"

"I didn't think about the rain when I decided to run with it."

"You don't run with flowers," she bickered, placing her hands on her waist. "Have I taught you nothing?"

"I don't recall having a lesson on what not to do when you're in a hurry."

"Poor thing, you annihilated it," her eyes moved from the flower I held, traveling slowly along my body until they found my own. "You're soaking. Why are you here?"

"Where's your phone?" I replied taking a step closer to her.

"In my pocket ...," she answered cautiously, turning to the carrier I had with me. "You came all the way from New York to check on my phone?"

"I called you several times."

"I noticed."

"You didn't answer."

"The messages said, 'Call me when you can.' That gives me leeway."

"You're mad at me."

"Why would I be mad at you?" She turned to the boxes. "Well, other than having all these packages outside my house for no reason."

Her back tensed, and slowly she veered, looking back at me. "Why is your bag squeaking?"

"Invite me in, and you'll see."

"Nah, I have some stuff to do."

"Like go back inside and watch Netflix?"

"Eat popcorn with chocolate chips."

"How can I forget the ritual?" I slammed the heel of my palm on my forehead.

"What's in that bag," she insisted and walked toward me.

"You have a cat in there? I'm allergic." She scrunched her nose staring at the carrier. "Come back when you don't have a weapon to kill me."

"Aren't we exaggerating a little?" I followed behind her.

"Here, take this." I handed her the carrier. "Don't open it until I get all the boxes inside."

She stepped into her apartment, opening the door wider for me. It didn't take me long to pull the boxes in and open them. Food, a bed, a tree, litter, and the litter box had arrived earlier as I requested.

I marched toward her, kissed her cheek.

"Hey," I whispered and nuzzled her hair, putting my arms around her while I took in her sweet aroma of jasmine, gardenia, and peach. Home. "I missed you."

"You shouldn't," she mumbled, her hands wrapped around my neck. "We need some time apart."

"After seven days without you, I'd have to disagree." I pressed her closer, not caring about the fucking lines. "You were right from the beginning. We can't be just friends. And I've discovered that I can't be without you."

Our eyes locked. She could deny that there was something between us, but the lust burning in her gaze disagreed with her words. Something was growing between us, I dared to call it love. The kind that I wrote about but never dreamt that I could feel myself.

"*Meow.*"

Sadie moved her gaze toward the carrier, releasing my neck.

"Why do you have a cat in that bag?"

"Because you need a furry friend." Hesitantly, I released her body feeling empty when I lost her warmth.

"She's a demanding girl."

"*He* is vocal," I corrected her and opened the bag taking out a small furball.

"Oh my God, he's adorable," she clapped lightly, leaning in closer. "You're precious, handsome boy."

"He's a Bengal cat," I explained. "Hypoallergenic, active, and he's only ten weeks old."

"A kitty?" she switched her attention from the cat to me several times.

"He's ready to be loved and to take over your apartment."

"You're making this hard."

"What's *this?*"

"Keeping my distance from you."

"Why do you fight it?"

"Because it doesn't feel safe for my heart. You're a great friend, but …"

"But I'm a famous asshole, a playboy with a failed marriage, and incapable of love. You believe that if you take the leap, I'll hurt you when we're done." I shrugged.

"You can love." She stared at the little cat and bit her lip. "Though, you're confirming my point. You don't want to be with someone for the long haul. To fall so deeply that you don't know where you end or begin."

"Weeks ago, I'd have said you were right, that there was no way I could fall for a woman. However, you've proved me wrong. I accepted your challenge, and we're friends—but there's something about you that I never even knew I wanted or needed. If you give me more time to figure it out, we can discover more—together."

"You make it sound like an experiment. Do you want me to put myself on the line while you research? As if I were the guinea pig?"

"You're a tiny little bird, not a rodent," I corrected her. "Maybe a kitten ... like this one."

I changed the subject because I wasn't ready to disclose more. I needed more time to understand what we had and make sure I didn't fuck it up.

"He's handsome. Thank you so much for the gift." She hugged him against her chest.

"But he needs a name." She sat on the couch, setting him on her lap.

"It's your job to name him."

"The blue-eyed guy reminds me of ..." she turned to look at me and smiled. "Your eyes are too clear in comparison to his. Hmm."

She tapped her chin. "Frank Sinatra."

"I thought you'd go for something like Snowball."

"That's perfect. Sinatra Snowball Bell"

"No, he should be Hades. Frank Sinatra Snowball Killian Hades."

"Killian Hades sounds great. Like your band." She twisted her mouth to the side. "You should save that one for a human child, not a furry child."

"I already have my quota of children."

"That's right, you have two beautiful girls. But I didn't know there was a quota."

"It is two too many. I'm not the best person to be having children. Look at me. I suck as a parent. The wisest thing to do is quit while I'm ahead."

"You're a great father. Tess and Hannah are lucky to have you."

"Every day I feel like a failure," I confessed. "I wished I could be around them a lot more. That I'd done more when they were babies."

"The fact that every day you try to be a better man says a lot about you," she reached for my hand and squeezed it. "You are a wonderful father. I've seen you. Never doubt that, but you can keep improving."

"Then we put Killian Hades away from the cat list."

"Up to you."

"Wait, we can't name a kid Killian. The nickname would be Kill." I snickered. "Kill Hades"

"That didn't occur to me. But I'm sure there's another name out there that would go great with Hades."

"Do you realize that my children are doomed?"

"Nah, it's a cool last name. But you have to create a good list of names for children before you have any more."

"You think I should have a list of names before I meet my son?"

"Well, yeah. The name needs to match the last name *and* his personality. What if you name him Cameron and he looks like a George?"

"I hate those names."

"Calm down, it's just an example," she said, hiding a smirk. "You can buy a book or browse baby names online."

"We buy a book then," I suggested, caressing the kitten's chin.

"To name the cat, Snooker Boo?" She whipped her head around.

"No, I'm talking about *our* children, Puddin' Knickers."

"I have to stop you right at Puddin' Knickers, Pookie Bear. That's the worst nickname," she protested. "Now, let's go back to children. There are no children on my horizon."

"Not in the immediate future," I corrected. "But there's always the possibility."

"Well, first, I'd need a boyfriend. I think we'd need a couple of years to get to know each other. Maybe move in together. He could propose, and by the third year, we'd get married. We'd have two kids or three, and when they were older, we could also become foster parents."

"Slow down, Hummingbird."

"What did you call me?"

"Hummingbird," I repeated.

"Hmm," she closed her eyes for a second and when she opened them she granted me a bright smile. "I actually like that one."

"I figured, but let's get back to the fostering more children. We'd need a big house."

"Well, by the time I'm ready for that step, I hope that my shops are bringing in enough revenue for a big house, and to support them."

"Shops?"

"I'm planning to open at least two more flower shops, but they'll be in the suburbs." She grinned.

"That'll happen. I have faith in you. But if your husband has the money to afford a big house and support a lot of kids, why do you have to work?"

"For me, because I won't lose my identity or myself. I'm not going to be only *mom* or *wife*. I'll be Sadie Bell. The husband and I are supposed to complement each other, to make each other succeed, not lose who I am because I decide to marry."

"Who's going to take care of the kids?

"Both of us. Feedings, diapers, waking up late is for both, not just me. Same when it comes to working."

"But just two children?"

"Three if possible with a two to three-year age difference in between. Growing up as an only child isn't fun."

"Having siblings doesn't guarantee closeness. Look at my girls."

"That's a unique case." She shut her mouth fast, opening her eyes wide.

"What are you not saying?"

"Nothing," she mumbled, moving her gaze to the cat.

"I think I'm starting to learn your subtle gestures. That little eyebrow-lift you do along with the clamped mouth." I traced her eyebrow with my index finger. "It means that you're hiding something, Sweet Cheeks. What are you not telling me?"

She shrugged.

"Spill the beans. You don't like my girls or something."

"Tess and Hannah are adorable," she said genuinely.

"But?" I arched an eyebrow.

"In my opinion, being close to your sibling depends on the parents."

"How so?"

I couldn't understand what she meant. Was she calling me a bad parent?

"You teach your children to love their siblings, to respect them, to be friends. To count on each other," she stated. "You set the foundation of their relationship where they build a bond between them, make them partners in crime. Them against the world—even against the parents."

"I can't imagine Tess and Hannah being that close," I declared and thought about my children. "They are so different. I always tell Tess to be nice to her sister."

"There's *be good to your sister* and teaching her that they can be friends. You teach them that from a young age."

"If that's scientifically proven, we can try with the next generation. But does it work?"

"Actually, I helped a mom and her girls get out of a bad situation. They stayed with me for a week while I found a safe place for them."

Leave it to Sadie to harbor people in danger and put herself at risk in the process.

"Where are they now?"

"They live in South Carolina. The mom hit the restart button and started over from zero, but they made it. I receive a Christmas card every year with an update. But we're getting off track, Mushy Gushy Tushy. Frank Sinatra Kieran Snowflake Bell doesn't need another name."

"Frank Sinatra Benjamin Snowflake Hades-Bell"

"Nope, we don't hyphenate."

"Then Frank Sinatra Benjamin Snowflake Hades."

"Frank Sinatra Kieran Bell Hades, we call him Sinatra. Sin when he's not behaving," she offered.

"Bell as a middle name?"

"Yeah. I'm compromising for the sake of the kid, but don't expect this from me ever again."

"But Kieran Hades could be a good name for our boy," I suggested.

"And Grady Hades sounds cool," she proposed. "Greyson Hades if he has your eyes."

"Angus Hades."

"Sounds like meat approval. Angus Beef Hades, USDA Choice. Nope." She frowned.

"Anders?"

"Maybe. There's Atlas and Rocco. If you have another girl, you should think about Isabella."

"Belle Hades?"

"No, Isabella, don't shorten her name."

"Gail Hades?

"Aubrey or Blossom."

"Mia?"

"For a man who doesn't plan on having more children you're too excited about naming them."

"What did you say the other day?"

"I say too many things every single day, Licky Sticky Poo."

"About nothing being permanent and finding my own shit."

"I'm sure that's not what I said."

"The gist of it."

"Nothing is guaranteed or permanent. Life is ever changing, nothing set in stone or promised to us. The world doesn't owe you anything, nor you to the world. To receive, you have to give, but yet never expect. You have to find your own path and change it as many times as needed. Adapting, accepting, and learning that you aren't guaranteed happiness or love. But the more love and happiness you give, the more will come back to you. Trust the journey. Always trust your heart."

"What if I find love, and I want what she wants?"

"Who is she?"

"The woman I fall in love with."

"Then go for it."

"Just like that. I go for it."

"Somehow, I'm lost in this conversation," Sadie said with an uncertain tone. "We were talking about my cat's name."

"Our kitten has a name," I corrected her. "He's our furry kid. And haven't you paid attention? His name is Sinatra?"

"Frank Sinatra Snowflake Kieran Bell Hades?" She tilts her head to one side and presses her lips together.

"Leave Kieran for our boy."

"What boy?" She touches the base of her neck. "I'm lost."

"Our—"

"Sadie, open the door." A female voice came from the other side of the door and knocked.

Sadie's eyes opened wide.

She's here, she mouthed.

"Come on birthday girl, I want to see you." The slurred, choppy words were barely understandable.

Sadie jetted out of the living room, holding the kitten.

"Who is that?"

"My mom," she whispered. "Let's hope she can't find her keys. I don't want to see her today."

"It's your birthday?"

She shrugged, disregarding that it was the most important day of the year.

"Communication, love. You need to tell me when your fucking birthday is. I can't guess shit like that."

"What?" she squeaked.

"I almost missed your birthday. Is that why you were upset with me?"

"Slow down. Keep your anger at bay." She whisper-yelled. "What are you talking about? I'm not upset at you."

"Last weekend, when I told you I wasn't going to be here," I explained. She was just like Alicia, playing games and making me feel edgy because I couldn't guess what they wanted. "That's why you didn't answer my calls."

She chuckled. "My birthday was the last thing I had on my mind."

"Then why did you pull away from me?"

"I ... I already explained that to you."

"Sadie, open the door. I didn't bring my keys." The voice became louder, desperate.

"What's the deal with your mom?"

"It's what Mom does every year." She sighed.

"She's here to invite me to dinner. She probably made reservations at some fancy restaurant. Mom will order a salad and some juice mixed with the best vodka they have. After several drinks and criticizing that I don't have a life, she'll leave me with the check."

My gut churned as I stared at those brown eyes filled with sadness. No wonder she avoided her mother.

"What do you want to do today, love?" I moved a strand of hair away from her face, caressing her jaw with the back of my index finger.

"Nothing. I usually spend it alone."

"That's before me. Today, I want it to be the best day of your life."

"He's the best present I've ever received on my birthday," she smiled at me.

Sadie marched right in front of me and kissed me on the corner of my mouth. Her lips were so close to mine that I was tempted to move and capture them. But I behaved.

"Thank you for the kitty and for being here. Your presence is more than enough," she breathed.

My heart hammered hard and fast against my chest. I swallowed hard, reading her posture, those sweet loving eyes. As much as I wanted to kiss her, I wanted to do it when she was ready.

Give me a sign.

"Sadie!"

"Are you going to open for your mother?" I asked, trying my best to remain civil.

We were in her room. There was a bed only feet away, and I was hungry for her.

"Nope," she said sounding genuine.

Sadie placed her index finger on her lips. "If we stay here really, really quiet, she'll leave soon."

"Sometimes I worry that my girls are going to end up like you, avoiding their parents."

"Just keep building a relationship with them." She lifted one shoulder and shrugged. "I can't talk about your ex-wife, but if you keep doing what you've done so far, I guarantee that they'll be happy when you call them or invite them to dinner."

"Will they be okay with the babies?"

"That depends on how you and your new wife handle things."

"I trust you," I said, leaning forward and capturing her lips.

Chapter Twenty-Three

SADIE

I was five when grandma threw me a My Little Pony birthday party. It was the best birthday. Between the concept and that being the last year my parents were happy together, I believed that nothing would top that day. But Kaden Hades showed me that birthdays can be magical and sweet at twenty-eight. He brought me a kitten.

The man surprised me every time he was around. After following his career so closely, I thought I knew everything about him. But knowing his music career was nothing like knowing the real Kaden Hades.

Some facts printed in the media were right. He was famous, talented, handsome, and wealthy. But spending time with him, I learned who he really was. What he ached for, his dreams, and how his heart beat.

We kissed tentatively, passionately, and then tenderly. I felt little sparks of static electricity dancing over my skin. I wanted to fight him, his big hands and his mouth. That mouth I thought about kissing more times that I wanted to admit. His hands cupped my face as his mouth fidgeted with my lower lip. His fingers trailed down my neck, toward the small of my back. Heat radiated from his body, and I melted in his arms.

The heat of his kiss set my heart aflame, consuming me. Everything was quiet, except the crackling sound of the fire that surrounded us. Yet, his kisses were sweet. Like cotton candy or strawberries. They were succulent, sticky, and a little tangy. They tasted like love and sin.

Those hands continued caressing me with a feather-like caress. I squirmed and moaned as his tongue slid against mine. My heart dipped with his words. *I trust you.* At that point, I had no idea what I had done to win his trust, but my mind couldn't think of anything as his lips came down on mine.

I wrecked them. The titanium walls I built to keep Kaden away melted with his passion. I opened myself. My heart let him through. Everything inside me changed.

My world shifted.

My heart finally understood the meaning of love.

The fear I harbored in my heart for so long disappeared as our kiss deepened. His strong arms healed my broken soul. His kisses melted the doubts in my mind.

"Sade," he said, with a velvety voice filled with lust.

His lips strayed as he spoke, but I felt them moving against mine. "You taste like peaches, heaven, and magic. I think I have a new addiction."

"Addiction?"

I was stunned by the kiss. My brain had a hard time understanding his words because every cell in my body wanted more of him, of his kisses. He lured me with his lips. His eyes baited me, those strong arms trapped me, and he entangled my heart with his.

"You, Little Fairy."

"We just crossed the lines." I rested my head on his chest.

"Do you regret it?" His voice deflated. It lost the power it had only seconds ago.

"No, I just don't know where we go from here. And though I'm excited, I'm also afraid of what can happen."

Where were we supposed to go from here?

He had a career, two adorable children, and a life entirely different from mine. I didn't see myself fitting into his world. In fact, I never fitted into anyone's world.

"Come with me to New York. I have to be there for another week."

"I'd love to accompany you, but I can't."

He proved my point. Kaden would be gone for another week. I'd never traveled in my life.

"Why not?" He narrowed his gaze.

"I have a flower shop to run and a new kitty."

"The children are already slowing us down, aren't they?"

"We have children?"

"Not yet, but we just talked about it and agreed on having two or three."

"You have to slow down. This is too much, too soon."

"But I can't," he lifted my chin with his calloused finger. "I've never felt the way you make me feel. Ever. I didn't know it would be possible, but with you, I want everything. We'll get married someday and have babies. A boy named Kieran and a girl named Aubrey."

I blinked a couple of times as I stared at his handsome face. His eyes radiated the purest happiness I'd ever seen. But his words accelerated my breathing. We'd just met a few weeks back, and he was already naming our children. *Ours.*

"It's okay, Hummingbird," he said, cradling me in his arms.

I shivered as his lips brushed against my ear. "This isn't a race, Precious Vixen, but a marathon where we wait and make things happen slowly. At your pace."

"What is this?"

"Honestly, I'm not sure," he responded, caressing my arms.

"*Meow.*" Our kitten purred.

I turned around. Sinatra was on top of my bed, watching his surroundings.

"But before we figure it out, I have to set up this little guy's litter box."

"You stay with him while I set up everything. Just guide me since this is your place."

☆ ☆ ☆ ☆

Despite the time we'd spent together as friends, my stomach was tied into knots at the thought of dinner with Kaden. As a couple. *We're a couple.*

There wasn't an exact definition for our relationship. Except he'd said earlier, "I'm taking my woman for dinner, to celebrate her birthday."

My heart fluttered. I was that woman. We're going for dinner. At Sushi Ronin. The guy snapped his fingers, made a few calls, and got us into the one restaurant I'd been dying to go to. He asked me to wear the same little black dress I wore when we had dinner with Dad and my tall boots for the occasion.

"Are you okay?"

"Yeah."

"You're shivering."

"It's the breeze," I lied.

He didn't need to know that it had been years since my last date. Or that I was still thinking about our kiss. His lips. The lust growing inside me, spreading like wildfires in the middle of July.

"You clean up well," I tried to sound casual, but I sounded like a dork.

You clean up well... I needed to practice my social skills before going out with this rock god. I was rusty, unused in all possible ways. But with him I wanted to be used, fucked hard against the wall.

My cheeks heated up. Where did that come from?

I should stop watching porn to get myself off.

He grabbed my hand, entwined our fingers and brushed my knuckles with his lips, creating a spark that that ignited my body, making me feel alive. Every glance, every kiss and touch made me feel alive.

My thoughts couldn't line up. Every time he was around they scattered everywhere in my head. Being close to him gave me sharp palpitations.

"I even got a jacket." He winked at me, his gaze traveled over me, making me quiver with need.

"It's a different look, but it fits you."

He'd dressed in a button-down shirt, a pair of distressed jeans, and a sports coat. His longish hair was tied into a ponytail. His gray eyes were shining like the moonlight at night. He was handsome, but that's not what had me jittery. It was the way he spoke to me, the way he cared for everyone even when he had the look of a man who didn't give a fuck.

"You look gorgeous tonight," he said, opening the door of the restaurant and releasing my hand. "After you, my lady."

Inside the front door was a lobby where a hostess stood by herself behind a wooden podium.

"Our reservation is under Sadie Bell."

"Right, you asked for our private room. Take the elevator to the second floor."

While we walked through the tables on the main floor dining room, I admired the place. It had a Japanese vibe with soothing tones and contemporary Japanese art along the walls. There was a wrap-around bar in the middle of the room, and above it, hanging sculptures that simulated a flock of cranes.

The place was beautiful, the food perfect, and the company excellent. Our conversation ran naturally. Like two friends who were sharing a meal but stole caresses and a few kisses in between bites. It didn't take long for me to realize that I was having a good time. The best time I'd had in many years.

We talked about his first concerts. How for most of his songs, life was his inspiration. His surroundings and his demons. When it came to romantic or heartbreaking ballads, it was different. He took ideas from his friends who always had tragic stories. Or sometimes he watched romantic movies with his bandmates.

"You watch romcoms?" I couldn't hide the laughter.

"There's nothing wrong with getting in touch with my feminine side and getting some inspiration."

"So, you create songs by the day."

"You'd think, but that's not the case. It's easy to come up with the melody. Lyrics can take me weeks."

"Why is that?"

"They have to be a sequence of feelings. If I've never fallen, how can I create a story within a song?"

"Each song is a story?"

"Yes, but once I have a solid one, the lyrics flow."

"I need times," I perked up with curiosity.

"Times?" He drummed his fingers against the table.

A tic he had when he was thinking. He tapped a surface, or if there was nothing close to him, he touched his leg or his chest.

"The longest took me almost a year. I had the music, a few lines, and an idea but nothing that called to me." He leaned forward.

"Rewrite our Story." He mentioned one of his biggest hits.

"Seriously, that one took you that long?"

He nodded once, his eyes scanned the room. "It was a hit, but man that thing was longer than a pregnancy."

"What's the shortest one?"

"A day," he answered without hesitation. "And only because I couldn't touch my guitar for twelve hours."

"Which one is it?"

"We haven't released it yet. I have my guitar in the car. If you want, I can play it for you when I drop you off."

"Mr. Hades, I'm impressed. A kitten, dinner, and you'll serenade me."

He grabbed my hand. "I just want to make you happy. And it's not a line, love. Your smile brightens my day. You're the sun. I'm a sunflower who follows you along."

"Lines, lines that make me fall deeper because I've discovered that they come from your heart. You could be a poet. If you could do something else, what would it be?"

He stared at me for several beats. Those fingers drumming on top of my hand. His lips pressed together tightly, and his eyes brightened when he had an answer.

"I love what I do. Composing, playing. I'm not a poet. I'm a musician who gives pieces of himself through lyrics and melodies."

"You're a passionate man."

"You have no idea," he mumbled, kissing the back of my hand and nipping it.

"Stop," I said harshly, fighting the heat climbing into my cheeks.

"Somehow, I think you want me to continue." He traced my brow. "I can tell. Let's go home."

He lifted his arm, snapped his fingers, and the waiter entered the room. Within minutes we received the check, and Kaden paid. I rose from my chair, and he grabbed my coat. His eyes darken as he helped me put it on. I swallowed hard as the unmistakable glare of desire promised a night of pleasure. Scarlet heat warmed my cheeks.

One question cut through the thick fog of lust inside my head. *Was I ready for him?*

Chapter Twenty-Four

SADIE

As soon as we arrived at my apartment, Kaden shut the door behind us. I opened my mouth to speak, but before any words came out, he pushed me against the wall.

His eyes flared with lust as he crushed his mouth to mine. Our bodies pressed against each other, and the temperature of his body was hot enough that I felt like I was melting. I was dissolving into him.

His kiss was slow but possessive.

He devoured me while making love to my mouth.

It was a raw kiss that I returned with equal intensity.

Though it wasn't just a kiss, but an act of passion, possession, and discovery.

He grabbed the back of my hair, yanked it, and traced his opened mouth down my neck, sucking on the sensitive skin. An electric jolt shot down my spine landing right in the center of my core. My legs shook, but he steadied me.

"I need you," he groaned. "I need to feel you in every way."

"Don't stop," I begged him, taking his lips.

He tasted amazing. Like vanilla frosting, tobacco, and magic. His lips became a fervent flame that lit every cell in my body turning me into a wildfire. Our tongues swirled together. My toes curl, and my hands held onto his shirt.

"Let's go into your bedroom," he panted out, placing his hands under my ass and lifting me off the ground.

I hooked my legs around his waist and continued kissing him. We kissed for several minutes with urgency. The lust building, my core throbbing with need. I ached with desire.

"Sade," he mumbled my name as he unzipped my dress.

Kade pulled down my dress, his roughed and callused fingers running along with the fabric, baring my body to him. His hands traveled down peeling off my lacey panties. My pussy ached for him, his touch. I needed him inside me. Those long fingers skimmed along my skin, sliding up my inner thigh. His hand cupped my crotch, his long finger dipping inside and then he licked his finger.

"Delicious," he said with a throaty voice. "I'm going to taste every inch of your beautiful skin."

I was a pool of desire. My skin wanted his touch. My heart hammered faster as he drove me toward the bed. I rested the weight of my body on my forearms as I watched him unbutton his shirt, leaving his gloriously ripped and inked chest exposed. He unbuckled his belt, opening his jeans.

No underwear, I thought as his gorgeous dick sprang to life.

My heart thundered in my chest as I gazed at his perfect body. He was perfect. Hard in all the right places with broad freckled and inked shoulders and ripped abs.

I gasped and stopped as I stared at his massive erect cock. He was thick and long making me salivate. A blowjob wouldn't be easy, but I'd be up for the challenge.

"You're beautiful," I said as I licked my lips.

He smirked, pulling his wallet out of his jeans pocket and pulling a condom out of it. He dropped it right next to me and watched me with predator's eyes.

"That's my line, Little Vixen." He lowered himself pushing my knees open.

☆ ☆ ☆ ☆

Kade

Sadie was a vision. The most beautiful woman in the world was spread open for me. I dropped myself beside her taking her mouth. My new favorite thing was kissing Sadie. My hands touched her hardening nipples.

She whimpered as I interrupted our kiss, and moaned when my mouth trailed down her jaw, her neck and eventually pulled and bit on her hardened nipples. Fuck, her tits were perfect. Full, round, and tasted like flowers and peaches. Her back arched, and I moved her hands away from her pussy as she tried to touch herself.

"I'll want to watch you get off any another day, but not tonight, love. Tonight, I'm the one who makes you come."

Slowly, I went down on her, kissing every inch of her body until I arrived at her core. The scent of her arousal hit my groin. I couldn't think of anything but tasting her warm, tender, beautiful pussy. I slid my tongue through her folds, sliding one finger inside of her.

"You taste delicious," I mumbled against her sweet pear, blowing on it.

She grunted, pushing her hips to my mouth, grabbing my hair when I thrusted a second finger inside and nipped her rosy bud.

"Harder," she ordered. "Fuck me harder!"

"Stop," I commanded. "We like to top, don't we, Vixen?"

She chewed her lip, her eyes locked on mine.

"Not tonight. You have to be patient because I'm planning on taking it real slow. I want to taste you. Devour you slowly. Not just push you over the edge and fuck you."

I stood up, pushing her back onto the bed, kissing her hard and teasing her entrance with my dick.

"You want this?"

"Please," she whimpered when I thrust a finger between her sweet labia.

"Taste yourself," I said and placed my finger on her lips.

She wrapped her lips around it, swallowing it deep. Sucking it. Her chocolate eyes filled with craving, and she stared at me needy. The fire within was melting her brown-eyed gaze I couldn't wait to be inside her. I kissed her one more time.

"I'm falling in love with this scent," I panted as her fingers touched my shaft.

"Not yet. If you touch me one more time, I'm not going to last."

Kissing my way down her slicked torso, I went back to her core. Slowly, I stroke her with my tongue, brushing it against her wanting, quivering pussy. She whimpered as I strummed my fingers over her swollen clit, but she didn't move. Oh fuck, her obedience increased my hunger. I couldn't wait, I inserted three fingers and continued finger fucking her while my mouth consumed her. It happened faster than I wanted. Her inner muscles contracted, squeezing my fingers tight. She was about to explode, I stared at her heaving chest and looked at her beautiful face. Eyes closed, mouth open, and the moment fueled me with desire.

I pressed my tongue against her tender bulb as her spasms increased and her legs trembled.

"Hades, Hades!" She screamed my name, and it was the most exhilarating sound.

"Please," she begged. "Fuck me!"

"Are you sure about this?" I whispered, watching her eyes burn with desire.

"I want you," she said, desperately. "All of you."

Carefully, I climbed back in between her legs, picking up the condom I had pulled out of my wallet, and rolled it on my dick. I placed the head of my cock at her entrance before sliding into her. Her eyes met mine. She was holding her breath as I pushed myself slowly until I was deep inside her. She was tight and warm and fuck if I didn't want to lose myself inside her forever.

She was perfect. We fit just right as if she had been made just for me. Mine. I leaned forward, slammed my mouth against hers, and kissed her deeply as I thrust in and out of her. Pleasure, craving, and lust dripped from every pore of my body as I claimed her. Our tongues moved against each other the same way our bodies did.

It was a perfect symphony. The edge of the tempo crept up as the friction between us ignited a fire as hot as a deep inferno. Too soon, we reached the edge. We were at the peak of the mountain, touching heaven, and about to fall into each other. A shock of electricity zinged from the base of my spine all the way to my groin, exploding into a billion notes playing inside my head. She milked me dry with her pussy. All too soon it was over.

"I love you," I confessed, releasing the three words I had never told a woman.

"Kade," she whispered, her arms wrapped around my back. "You don't have to say that."

"But I mean it," I nuzzled her hair. "I knew from the moment I set eyes on you that you were special. That I had to get to know you. I've fallen in love with my best friend."

Moisture wet my cheeks. I lifted my head, and she was crying.

"What did I do?" My heart stopped beating. "Did I hurt you?"

"No, you love me," she said, silently. "I thought I was falling alone."

"Never, baby. We'll always fall together."

"I love you," she said, fusing her mouth with mine.

Her words broke me into a million particles that her heart assimilated. We didn't just make love, we fused our souls and became *us*.

Chapter Twenty-Five

SADIE

The sound of the acoustic guitar and Kaden's low voice woke me up. The sight of his naked chest reminded me of last night, making my heart flutter. The sun filtered through the closed curtains as I watched him strumming his guitar, singing with his eyes closed. It was a song I hadn't heard before, but the melody enveloped me into a warm cocoon, rocking me gently as the lyrics took my breath away.

> *She had the appearance of a quiet soul*
> *But inside her, there was something wild*
> *It's dormant, waiting for her soulmate to arrive*
> *But she's a wildflower*
> *Wildflowers can't be controlled.*

———

> *She's all I need to believe*
> *She's a sunflower during the day*
> *A bright star during the night*
> *She's water and air*
> *She's all that I need to save me from myself*
> *When we touched something inside her began to brew*

Bubbling up until it exploded
She spread her wildfire
Melting my heart and my soul to hers
Now I exist only with her
In her dreams

"That's beautiful." I propped myself up on my elbow. "I don't think I've listened to it before."

"It might be because I just wrote it." He leaned his guitar against the wall.

"Just now?" I arched an eyebrow. "What happened to it takes at least twelve hours to write a song?"

"You inspire me, Sade." He rose from the chair and walked toward me.

I rubbed my eyes with my hands and looked back at the guitar one more time. "Where did you get the guitar from?"

"My truck. It's always with me." He winked. "How are you this morning, Pixie?"

"Great, but ... you're leaving."

I hated sounding like a needy woman, but I wasn't ready for him to go away.

The bed deepened when he sat down next to me. His fingers caressed my face.

He looked at his phone and smacked his lips.

"In a couple of hours." He exhaled harshly. "Come with me to New York."

"Why don't you stay with me?" I whispered.

For a few seconds, I closed my eyes because I didn't like to ask for anything. I always gave freely.

But I didn't want him to leave so soon. Not after last night. Not ever.

I wanted him to fill me up again and again.

I wanted him to make love to me.

To have raw, hard sex and the sweetest, softest touches.

I needed him to fill me in the dirtiest, grittiest way.

I desired his gentleness and his unapologetic appetite too.

He was the only one who could quench my soul's thirst.

But he was leaving, and it would be too long before he came back to my side and into my bed.

"If it were possible, I'd stay with you in this bed, forever," he said with conviction.

"Not tomorrow, but next Monday, I'll be here with you. I promise not to leave the bed unless you have to go to work."

Kade leaned in and bit my shoulder lightly. He feathered kisses along my neck, his hands latched onto my breasts. His fingers pulled and pinched my nipples into hard beads. I gasped, and my back arched.

"You have to leave soon," I reminded him, hating that he had to leave. "You have to be in New York tonight."

"Take a shower with me." He sprang out of bed, grabbing my hand. "I want to get you dirty before I leave."

"Four times, Mr. Hades," I reminded him. "And you still want more?"

"Miss Bell, I'll always want more when it comes to you."

He pulled me toward him, giving me one of those *searing, curl your soul, fall in love with me* kisses. We stepped into the shower unable to keep our hands off each other.

"Seems that you're ready, Mr. Hades."

"With this body, it would be a sin to not be aroused at the sight of you."

He lathered me with foam. His hands slid up and down my body. Kaden's hands circled around my nipples, then he glided his hands between my thighs, teasing my core. I took his cock in my hands, stroked it, and rubbed his swollen crown. I wanted so bad to kneel down and take him in my mouth, but it was so big, thick that I doubted it would fit.

"Not today," he said.

Kaden tore the square foil, rolling the condom down his big cock. He lifted me. "Hug me with your legs," he ordered.

I did, and he lowered me down, filling every inch of me. He's buried himself deep inside me. His hands grabbed me by the ass; my arms held onto his broad back.

"More! Faster!" I screamed with pleasure when he pushed me

against the tile and began pumping himself in and out of me at a quick pace.

I bit his shoulder to stifle the screams.

"Fuck! I love it when your pussy swallows my hard cock." He thrust his long, thick cock in and out faster and harder.

Kaden kissed me roughly and hungrily. Like he was eating his last meal. I took everything he gave me, and he brought me back to life. He consumed me with his heat. The energy between us, mixed with the magic we created, became a storm that grew more and more ferocious. And when we reach our climax, we both exploded, spiraling out of control.

"I'm going to fucking miss you, Hummingbird," he panted. His forehead rested on my shoulder. "After today, I don't think I'll be able to live without you."

"Only seven days," I sighed, as I recovered my breath. "Be patient, my Nightingale. There's always phone sex."

"I'm counting on that, Little Vixen."

Chapter Twenty-Six

SADIE

Present

It's a dream, I mumble.

We're back at Paradise Park. This place is one of my favorite places in the spring, and I only share it with him. It's perfect. The breathtaking view of Mt. Rainer and the meadow that's like a magical wildflower sanctuary bring me peace.

The meadow is a glorious area of grass dotted with petite, fragrant flowers that rustle gently in the breeze. There's a narrow brook that flows through it. Tall water-mint with pale lilac flowers, like dozens of tiny bells, grow at the edge of the stream.

I'm aware that I'm dreaming, and that I should wake up now. But I can't snap out of it. Nor do I want to. Not yet. I want to see him, speak to him. Feel the safety of his arms around me.

It's been a long time since I've allowed myself to dream of him. Too long. I know in my heart that the moment I wake up pain will run through my veins for days. There's no way I can stop loving him when we share the same heart and soul.

It's hard to let go of what we had when my biggest wish is to have him by my side.

"You finally came," he says, in a miserable tone that almost breaks my heart.

"Why are you so sad?" I walk toward him.

"You look beautiful, Hummingbird," he breathes lifting his hand to grab mine. "I miss you."

"I look down to my belly." My heart stops when I realize it's flat, my hands cover it and I stare in horror because I've lost my baby.

It takes me a couple of seconds before I can remember that this is only a dream. When I wake up, my little baby will still be with me.

"He's with me," Kaden says, a soft smile plays on his lips. "Safe and growing."

"Who?"

"Our baby boy. The Little Bean."

"I wish it were true, that you were here with us. But ..." I trail my voice and my gaze staring at Mt. Rainer. "You have your family."

"You and our boy are my family too."

"The girls." I hate my voice. It comes out bitter, angry.

But it's hard not to be upset when I chose them over my own happiness. I want my baby to have a father because Kade is the best father. It'll break his heart to have to choose between his two worlds. I'm upset because as hard as we tried, we couldn't fuse our lives.

"Wait, did you say boy?" I laugh. "You still think that our first child will be a boy?"

"I know for a fact that he's a boy."

"*Kieran* if we have a boy," I say softly.

"Kieran Griffin Bell Hades?"

"Because you want him to be a part of Gryffindor," I joke.

"*Griffin* means strong lord. I think the name suits him since he's a fighter, like his mother."

The name would be perfect, but only in my dreams. The whole world seems to be moving in slow motion. Everything's becoming hazy. The baby won't be a Hades. My shoulders slump because I haven't yet dared to tell Kade about our baby.

My latest excuse was that he's on tour. I'll find something else once he's back in Seattle. It'll give him five minutes of joy and then will turn to dread at being a father to a newborn while caring for his own children. I wouldn't do that to my baby. He needs a father who will be with him all the time, not a part time father who will only see him when it's convenient.

"Don't cry," he breathes the words as he scoops up me into his arms, cradling me by his side. "Fuck, I miss you so much, love. Come back to us?"

I look into his gray, gloomy eyes that appear lifeless. I'm terrified of their darkness. My heart beats fast when he releases me and begins to fade into the fog. The meadow dries, and the air becomes chilly.

"Don't leave me," I beg him. "Kade, stay! I don't want to be alone in here."

"Find your way back, Little Fairy," he says, as he disappears and so does my light.

Chapter Twenty-Seven

KADE

Present

It's been a long time since I dreamed of Sadie, and this was different from every dream I've shared with her. This time I had a flashback of our first kiss. Then, we were in her favorite meadow. But the end terrified me because she was slipping away from me. I tried to hold onto her, but I couldn't keep her by my side.

I hold my breath. My stomach feels like a ton of lead bricks. "What if she's gone?"

Petrified by the thought of losing her, I bolt out of bed and run to the room next to mine. Aspen is with the baby, while Brynn is with Sadie.

My eyes dart to the machines that continue to beep. Air comes rushing back. My heart restarts. She's still with me.

Sadie will be back when she's ready.

"Who is chasing you?" Aspen, who is scribbling on Little Beanie's chart, asks.

Kieran.

"Kieran," I say it out loud. "His name is Kieran Griffin Hades."

"That's a beautiful name," Brynn says gently, arranging Sadie's left arm.

"We chose it years ago." I march to Sadie's side.

Taking her hand, I lower myself and whisper, "you're not alone. I'm right here."

I study her face which isn't swollen anymore. Her facial expression remains the same, motionless. But I can't help to remember the fear harbored in those beautiful brown eyes during my dream.

Is she as scared now as she was in her dream?

I squeeze her hand, kiss her cheek, and brush her lips lightly with mine.

"Take your time," I press my mouth to the inside of her wrist. "I know you'll come back to me."

"We're doing a CT scan tomorrow. The team is getting together to decide when we'll take her out of the induced coma."

"Okay." I swallow hard.

"We've tried to accommodate you the best we could." Her voice is cautious, my pulse spikes. "But it's time to call her next of kin."

"I am her next of kin."

"No, you're her ex-fiancé, Kade," Aspen interrupts. Her tone is dry. "We know how much you love her, and that you'd give your life for her. But there are rules. Her parents have to be notified."

I look around the room and then stare at Sadie. Andrew and Catherine are unpredictable.

"Her parents aren't reliable," I inform them. "What if they don't show?"

"It would be up to the legal department and social service to decide the course of treatment if her parents don't show," Brynn responded.

"If they come and want to kick me out, can they?"

"They could since you two don't have any legal relationship," Aspen responds. "But you do have an ace under your sleeve. This handsome boy."

"Yes," Brynn nods. "But we need proof that he's yours."

"He's mine," I groan, filled with anger.

"We don't doubt it, but his grandparents can't kick you out from his side if you have documentation that supports the claim."

"Are you suggesting I get a paternity test?"

"That's the best way to establish a legal bind to the baby—and

Sadie. It guarantees that you'll take him with you when he's ready to go home."

"But she's going to wake up," I insist.

"You have to have a backup plan. Kieran is reaching his milestones at a fast pace. He might be ready to go home before Mom wakes up."

A paternity test feels like betraying Sadie. She's going to think that I doubted her. I know in my heart that he's our boy. Ours. *Use your head, not your heart.*

"Let's do it today."

☆☆ ☆ ☆

It only took a day for the lab to deliver the results. There was no doubt that Kieran's mine. But with proof, I was able to fill out the hospital paperwork to obtain his birth certificate. Duncan found me the best lawyer who can represent me in case I have to fight for custody with Sadie's parents.

He told me that I don't have any legal rights to her. However, if her parents try to pull her off life support, I could file for custody. A fight I wouldn't win, but that would give her time to recover. A legal battle like that could take anywhere from months to years. The lawyer knew how to work the system in my favor if it ever came to that.

"Everything will be fine," I assure Kieran who's staring at me. "You're growing bigger and stronger every day. The hospital is giving us a few more days before they call your grandparents."

The CT scan showed that the swelling is almost gone. In a week the doctors are going to wind down the sedatives.

"'*Give it time*,' is their favorite phrase," I say annoyed with the situation. "That along with, '*Wait. You have to be patient.*'"

I can be patient, but I feel like I'm running out of time. My instincts tell me to take my family out of here and hide. I've been in the middle of a legal battle. It took me two years to win joint custody of my girls. For two years, I had to have supervised visits every other weekend.

"They won't do that to us," I promise Kieran. "We're in this together, buddy. No matter what, I'm going to be with you—and with your mom."

My phone buzzes several times. It's either ringing or someone's sending multiple texts. Any other day I'd ignore it, but what if the girls are stranded in some city in Europe because their mother forgot them?

The screen is filled with missed calls from Jax, Kevin, and Duncan. I slide my thumb through the screen and check Duncan's first.

Jax: Dude answer your phone.

Jax: Where are you?

Jax: Answer your fucking phone, we have an emergency.

Hades: I'm at the hospital with Sadie and Kieran.

Jax: Finally. I'm on my way. We have a problem.

Hades: Sadie and the baby are in the hospital. Fix whatever you need to fix.

Jax: That's the problem.

Hades: What do you mean?

Jax: See you in a few minutes. Meet me outside their room.

"Let me see what this man wants." I kiss Kieran's forehead and place him back in the plastic crib. "Promise to make it back before feeding time."

Unfortunately, he's allergic to milk and soy like Sadie. However, there's a formula that's made for babies like him. And Kieran loves it.

This little man has me wrapped around his finger. Leaving him alone breaks me inside, but I head outside to the hall where I find Jax already waiting.

"What's going on?"

"Shit's been going down," he explains. "I know your girl and your kid are in the hospital. I tried to take care of everything, but you have to be ready."

He hands me his phone. I gasp when I see the picture of a pick-up truck smashed against the flower shop's van. Scrolling with my finger, I read the headline. *Kaden Hades is in jail. Sources close to the rock star say he's hired the best legal team in the city to represent him. His fiancée, whose name hasn't yet been released, was killed during the accident. She, along with the couple's newborn baby, are fighting for their lives in the hospital.*

"What the fuck?" I look at him and he shrugs. "These are lies."

I scroll down more and find an old mugshot of me.

"Where's this one from?"

"The time they arrested us in Houston for starting a fight."

"That was ten years ago," I protest.

"Thirteen," he corrects me. "That's why the image was trimmed. They cut off the county and date."

"I'm suing," I say, massaging my temples. "Can you get me a lawyer?"

"The PR and legal teams are working on it already. They're suing all the media sources that are spreading fake news about the accident and your whereabouts."

I sigh with relief. "Then it'll be taken care of?"

But the calm only lasts a few beats. I rub my neck and stare at Jax. "How viral is this?"

"Wide. We have fans from all over the world messaging us about this. Twitter, Facebook... you name it."

I pace around the room. The week I thought I had is gone. No matter where Sadie's parents are, they're going to find out about this soon. My daughters too. Alicia's going to find a way to make this about her. How did the press get ahold of the story?

"Who leaked this?"

"They're investigating the hospital personnel." He pinches his lips together, staring at the door. "The band, our friends, and the few people who knew about it wouldn't talk. We're just as protective of your private life as we are of our own."

"I know. I wouldn't accuse any of you."

"It says that I killed Sadie and my newborn child is fighting for his life. That's messed up." My voice echoes against the walls. "Does this mean that the police are coming to interrogate me? I can't leave the hospital to clear my name."

"Dude, calm down." He pats my shoulder.

"The team is working on this. I came to see you because you need to know what's going on. We distributed a press release and uploaded it to the website. I tweeted it from my account and the band's account. We posted it on Facebook too."

I pull out my phone and check the band's Twitter.

The Killing Hades family appreciates your concern for our bandmate. We ask for your prayers in these difficult moments. Kaden was in California when the unfortunate accident occurred, but he's currently by his fiancée's side and caring for his newborn.

I browse through the messages sending love, prayers, and support.

"It's not as bad as I thought," I breathe the words with some relief. "But what about the police?"

"Dude, when I said that I'd take care of everything, I meant it. The other driver died at the scene of the accident. He had a heart attack."

"What?"

"It was a freak accident—wrong place, wrong time—fucked up shit."

"What about the press?"

"Unfortunately, they're parked outside the hospital."

"Fuck!" I groan.

"Daddy!"

My heart stops when I hear Hannah's voice. I turn around and find my daughters making their way toward me.

"What are you doing here?" I arch an eyebrow, crossing my arms.

I frown, looking at my two girls dressed casually in jeans and sweat-shirts. They were in Europe less than twenty-four hours ago.

"How long since the news broke?" I ask Jax.

"Yesterday, why?"

"Why are you here?" I ask the girls again.

"She wanted to come," Tess sneers, staring at Hannah. "The accident was all over the news. I called your manager, and he said that you were here at the hospital with *her*."

"I wanted to see you, Dad." Hannah hugs me. "Are you okay?"

"It says on his webpage that he's fine *and* he's with *them*," Tess says.

The venom she spits makes my heart hurt.

"Is it true?" Hannah stares at me. "We have a little sister?"

Before I answer their questions, I have some of my own. I spoke to them less than twenty-four hours ago. They were in Barcelona and going to Portugal. "When did you arrive?"

Hannah gasps, covering her mouth. Her face is red and her eyes downcast.

"Where is your mother?"

Tess rolls her eyes. "France, Spain ... I can't remember her itinerary."

"But you're here."

"She didn't take us with her." Hannah's words rush out, as she watches her sister. "We've been with grandma and grandpa since she left."

I run a hand through my hair. *You've got to be fucking kidding me.* Alicia abandoned our daughters with her parents while she's on vacation.

Before I explode, Jax places a hand on my shoulder and shakes his head. "Cool it. It's not their fault."

"What am I supposed to do now?" I bite back the anger.

I paid for a trip to Europe, and yet, they never went. I should've taken them with me on tour. But I couldn't. It was too fast paced for them to accompany me. I feel like a big failure because I have no fucking idea what I'm going to do. The girls are here. I'm the one who should be with them, not their grandparents. I turn to the room where Sadie and my baby are waiting for me. My head explodes.

"You've been lying to me," I force myself to control the anger. Though the words come out tight and harsh.

"Mom told us—"

"Hannah, stop, or you're going to get us in trouble. I told you this was a bad idea."

"But I wanted to see if Dad was okay, and ... Sadie. They said she died." Her chin quivers and her eyes water. "Is she okay?"

I close my eyes, taking several deep breaths.

"Sadie's in a coma."

"So, she's going to die," Tess looks at her hand, admiring her nails. "See, Hannah, he's fine. We can go now."

"Can I see her?" Hannah requests.

"Hannah, we need to go."

"You don't like her, I get it," Hannah fumes. "But I love her. She loves us."

Hannah touches the unicorn necklace that Sadie gave her when she turned nine. "Can I please see her?"

"I'm sure Sadie would be happy to hear your voice," I assure her.

Sadie adores my girls. She forged a strong bond with Hannah from the beginning. The way she looked after my girls made me love Sadie even more.

"Follow me, Pumpkin."

I hand her the scrubs, show her where to wash her hands, and give her instructions.

"Who is that?" Hannah points at the crib.

"His name is Kieran," I whisper. "He's your baby brother."

Hannah approaches the crib and smiles at him. "Why does he have that tube up his nose?"

"To help him breathe. He was born a few weeks too early."

When I turn around, I spot Tess standing at the corner of the bed staring at Sadie. Her eyes are closed, and shoulders slumped. I don't understand if she's angry, sad, or just desperate to get out of here. Our relationship shifted after she tried to kill herself. She's a closed book. She seeks attention but pushes me away when I get too close.

The day she tried to kill herself, I lost my little girl, my fiancée, and the chance to have a family. With all the people I love in one room, I wonder if we can heal or if I'm going to have to split myself in half for the rest of my life.

"Did she tell you about the baby?" Tess asks, turning her back to me.

"No, I had no idea."

"What would you have done if she did?"

"That question makes no sense, Tess. I won't dwell on the past."

"Mom said you wouldn't want us anymore," Tess confesses. "That once you had a new family, you'd forget us."

"She lied to you, Tess."

"Mom said that I only had one chance to end it before you left us. But Sadie's back."

"What are you talking about Tess?"

"Nothing." She turns toward Sadie.

"Dad, is Sadie going to die?" Hannah holds my hand, tears pouring down her cheeks.

"What will happen to the baby if she dies?" Tess bites her lip. "He's going to be all alone. You're always busy with us. Will you send him to a foster home like they did with you?"

"You wouldn't give him away, Dad, would you?" Hannah sobs even harder.

"Of course not. Tess, Kieran is your brother. He's my son. He's going to be a big part of your life. I won't leave him."

"But if she survives you'll leave them alone."

"Tess, I love you, and I won't leave you. No matter how much you push me, I won't leave you."

"But you'll stay with them," she says, glaring at me. "Do you know what this is going to do to Mom?"

"What do you mean?"

"Never mind." She leaves the room.

"What happened?" I stare at the door for several seconds.

"Hormones," Hannah responds. "At least that's what Grandpa says when she doesn't make sense.

"Your grandpa should be looking into the problem, honey." I kiss Hannah's head. "Not just saying chauvinistic nonsense."

"Grandpa is old. We have to understand his ways."

She needs to stay away from those fucking prejudiced assholes, but how can I take them when I can't care for them?

"You've been spending your summer with your grandfather and lying to me?"

"When you put it that way, it sounds bad."

"It's bad, Pumpkin. Your mother ..." I sigh because I hate talking shit about her in front of the girls. "She knows better than leave you with your grandparents without notifying me."

I'm at a loss. Alicia shouldn't leave the girls with her parents for that long without consulting me. The girls lied to me under her orders. They've been playing me. I shove my hands into my pockets and stare at Sadie.

Babe, wake up. We have a fucking mess on our hands.

Chapter Twenty-Eight

KADE

Six months too late, I'm asking Sadie, who is unconscious, to guide me. If she were awake, she'd know what to do. She always did or at least helped me process it. If only I had done that before we broke up. My biggest regret comes back to face me head-on in one of the hardest moments of my life. I should've handled it differently. Sadie and I were a couple. We said *forever* years ago. The stupid marriage certificate didn't matter. What mattered was that we stayed together.

But the fear of losing Tess the same way that I lost my sister blinded me. Alicia's threats to take away my daughters made me react. It was all too real. The images of Hannah, my sister, laying on the floor lifeless played repeatedly in my head. This time it was Tess's face, and her dead eyes staring at me. The note next to her saying that she couldn't do it anymore. Details of how my mother pimped her printed in her handwriting. Tears were pouring down my cheeks because I'd lost the only person who loved me.

I couldn't go through the same thing with Tess. Yet, I'm sitting by Sadie's side waiting for a miracle. It's like I can't keep those I love with me.

No matter how many times I visit the chapel or pray, I'm wasting away by the minute. The woman of my dreams, the love of my life, may never come back to me. Nothing I say or do will fix the past. Holding onto a future that might never exist is tearing me apart inside.

"If only I had stayed with you, Hummingbird."

☆ ☆ ☆ ☆

Six Months Ago

"Thank you," I kissed Sadie when I arrived home after dropping my daughters at their mother's place.

"For?" She wrapped her arms around my neck and stared at me.

I could never get enough of that loving gaze. The woman brought me to my knees just with three words—*I love you*—and that look.

"Taking the girls out after the dress fitting," I said, grabbing her ass and lifting her off the floor.

I stared at the cluttered hallway and took a deep breath. The new bookshelves were a bad idea. Avoiding them while I tried to seduce my fiancée wasn't easy.

"We need a new place," I complained.

"We already talked about it, Mr. Hades," she reminded me. "A five-bedroom home so it can fit your daughters and our little ones too. As for our outing of the day, it's my pleasure. The bridesmaids' dresses are gorgeous. They're going to look adorable."

"Will I get to see this white dress you keep talking about?"

"You're so insistent."

"Because I can't wait to see you, or to marry you." I kissed her neck. "I'd marry you right now. I just want to spend the rest of my life with you."

"Patience, Hades," she sighed, burying her face in the crook of my neck.

"What's with the sad voice?"

"Hannah," she exhaled, caressing my neck with her breath. "She was fine today, but I feel like we lost our link. That friendship I tried to forge with her."

"She adores you. I'm sure it's just a phase."

I wanted to believe it was temporary. Hannah had accepted Sadie from the beginning. They bonded right away and understood each other. If my kid had a problem at school, she'd ask Sadie for help. My fiancée was the center of her universe. Until a couple of months back when she began to change. It wasn't the brooding teenager act, more like an act of rebellion against me and her target was Sadie.

"Today she behaved like the old Hannah. You know, when she told me about her week and hung out with me at the shop. Tess was *friendly*."

"Maybe she's back to her old self, and Tess understands that you're here to stay," I said confidently.

It made my heart swell to know that my family was finally coming together. At the beginning of the relationship, Tess didn't care, but a few months later when Sadie moved in with me, she became a different person. Some days she'd be sweet and social, while others she'd be rude, spoiled, and hurtful toward Sadie.

I understood that the changes affected them. I suggested family therapy. However, Alicia disagreed with me. The shitty part of having joint custody was that we had to make decisions together. She said that I just had to get over the obsession with Sadie and pay more attention to my daughters. Of course, my ex wasn't happy about my fiancée or my upcoming nuptials. Thankfully, Sadie understood the transition wouldn't be smooth, and she kept trying for my sake.

"So, what is the amazing news you have to share with me?" I changed the subject.

"After dinner, Mr. Hades. It's a surprise."

"Will I like this surprise?"

"I think you're going to love it."

"Is it a new tattoo?"

"Patience isn't your strong suit, Mr. Hades," she said, nibbling my neck.

I shivered, craning my neck. "Stop, Little Minx, and tell me what this big surprise is."

"I won't tell you, and we have to leave soon."

"Do we have time before we head out to dinner?" I rubbed my hard cock against her pelvis.

"You always make time." She grinned. "If not, I'd beg you. I need you, Mr. Hades."

"You know I love it when you beg."

"Please, I need you, Mr. Hades." She used her sultry voice.

My phone rang several times, but I ignored it as I kissed my woman. We only had thirty minutes to get ready before we had to meet our friends for dinner.

"You have to answer," Sadie broke the kiss. "Whoever is on the other line is not letting up."

"I'll just turn it off," I said, but froze when I saw Alicia's name flashing on my phone.

Slowly, I put Sadie down on the floor and read through the texts.

Alicia: *We're in the hospital. I need you.*

Alicia: *Kaden it's crucial.*

Alicia: *Tess has been admitted.*

My pulse spiked. I slid my finger over the screen and answered.

"What's going on?"

"We're in the emergency room at St. Luke's with Tess."

"On my way," I said hanging up.

"What happened?" Sadie's eyes grew wide.

"I didn't ask," I rushed through the apartment grabbing my boots, jacket, and car keys.

Sadie watched me from the living room with her arms crossed. Alicia was a nasty bitch, and Sadie avoided her. I knew how hard it was to deal with her. Any other day I would kiss her goodbye and leave to handle the emergency. Tonight, I needed her by my side. Something happened to one of my daughters, and I needed my strength beside me to get through whatever was waiting for me.

"Come with me," I requested.

Without a word, she went back to our room for her sweatshirt and a pair of sneakers.

"I'll drive," she suggested. "You're a bit on edge. Where to?"

"St. Luke's," I responded, locking the door behind me.

"Why not Seattle Memorial?" She frowned. "St. Luke's is way too far from her house, isn't it?"

As we drove, I thought about Tess's day. I'd picked them up from her mother's house at noon and drove them to the fitting. She went with Sadie to lunch and then the spa. I dropped them back at home just a couple of hours ago. What could have happened between then and now?

"Maybe Tess went to a party," Sadie suggested.

Fuck! I slam a hand to my forehead. "Alcohol poisoning, OD ..."

"I doubt she overdosed or drank too much. You've talked to her several times about those dangers."

But it's a possibility, I thought. The drive felt eternal. Sadie remained quiet but kept squeezing my hand when she could. We left the car at valet parking and ran toward the ER.

"What the fuck is she doing here?" Alicia glared at Sadie. "This is a family matter. She's not family."

"Where's Tess?" I ignored her outburst.

"This woman killed my baby," she said with a cracked voice.

I could feel sweat drenching my skin, the throbbing of my own eyes, the ringing phone vibrating in my ears, and the thumping of my heart against my chest. My fingers were curled into a fist, nails digging into my palm. The oxygen flooded in and out of my lungs rapidly. Fear tortured my guts, churning my stomach into intense cramps, and knocking all other thoughts aside.

Alicia took a step forward and slapped Sadie. "You killed her!"

My heart dropped to the floor. "What are you talking about, Alicia?"

"Where is Tess?"

My daughter, my little girl is *dead?* I couldn't breathe. My soul left my body searching for Tess.

"I found her," Alicia sobbed, her words breaking.

I opened my eyes and watched her breaking down as she described what she witnessed. "It was dinner time. I ... we had an argument, and I told her to go to her room until she decided to do what I told her. I went upstairs to check on her, and there she was, splayed on the floor lifeless. There's a note accusing that woman."

Alicia swung her hand, and I grabbed it before she tried to hit Sadie again.

"Stop it," I ordered.

"She did this to our baby."

"Why are you here?" Alicia sneered at her. "You're not a part of us.

When will you understand that he has a family? You'll never be one of us."

"Alicia, that's enough," I demanded.

"Enough of what?" Alicia growled. "I've had enough of her. She's been destroying our family for years. Tess, my baby, suffered because of her. I should call the police and throw her in jail. She tried to murder our kid. I have evidence."

"I didn't do anything," Sadie stuttered.

"You should be in jail."

"Sade," I finally looked at her.

Her eyes were watery. She bit her lip but remained standing, quiet.

"Why don't you go home?" I handed her the valet parking ticket. "I'll come back later."

She nodded once, turned around, and left.

"Where is Tess?"

"They're pumping her stomach."

"Is she alive?"

"Yes, of course, she's alive. I found her in time."

"Why are you yelling that Sadie killed her?"

"Because she did, it said so on Tess's note. She's vicious and cruel. You always put her first, and Tess couldn't live with the emotional turmoil." Alicia covered her face and cried.

I pulled her into my arms and rubbed her back as I absorbed every word she said. The way she described her was almost exactly like the way I found Hannah, my older sister. My heart broke just thinking about the day I lost my sister. My legs just about gave up realizing that I'd almost lost my daughter too. I had no idea things between her and Sadie were that bad.

This was my fault. Just like it happened with my sister, I hadn't paid attention to the warning signs. I'd neglected my daughter, and she almost died because of it. I swore they wouldn't suffer because of me and ... fuck! I'd failed once again. My attention had been focused on Sadie who always took the blows from Tess without complaint. Several times I'd told Tess to be polite, to learn to get along with her.

Instead of listening to her, I was making her do something she hated.

"You know what you have to do, don't you?"

"I have no idea what you're talking about, Alicia."

"That woman can't be a part of your life. There's no question about what you should do. The girls come first."

"Alicia," I gasped.

"You have to end things with her, or next time, I might not find Tess in time. You can't put her life in jeopardy. Not for that bitch."

☆☆☆☆

I called Tess's doctor. She told me to send the discharge papers to her office on Monday. Unfortunately, Alicia drove Tess to a hospital where Dr. Hawkins couldn't treat her. Over the phone, she was able to give me a few suggestions, like therapy and keeping her on watch for the next few days. I didn't tell her about the note. There wasn't much to say. Alicia only told me that Tess blamed Sadie for her decision.

Once they moved her into a private room, and I saw that she was okay, I called an Uber and texted Sadie.

Kade: We need to talk.

Numbed, I pulled together the little energy I had left to end my own life. It had to be done. There was no contest. My children mattered most. Sadie knew it, she supported it, and in my heart, I knew she'd understand.

Every mile closer to my apartment became a mile farther away from our dreams. The big house with three kids and a beautiful garden burnt to the ground. Kieran, Aubrey, and our last baby would only happen in our dreams. Everything we'd planned vanished alongside my promise to her.

Once I arrived at the apartment building, I lit a cigarette, smoked it a little too fast and then smoked two more. For a few seconds, I played with the idea of escaping my reality and drinking myself into oblivion. It'd be so much easier than having to face Sadie.

How do you say goodbye to the love of your life?

You rip your heart from your chest, stomp on it, and then you face the woman you love.

"Sade," I called after shutting the door behind me.

I allowed the insensitive asshole to take over my body and perform for one night.

"In the room," she said. "How is she?"

I marched to our bedroom, remembering how only a few hours ago we'd had it all. Plans, a future, and love. I sighed, pressing my lips together and gathering enough strength to talk.

"Hey." the word barely passed my lips.

I avoided her gaze while I wracked my brain thinking of what to tell her. After several minutes of with silence, she spoke. "Is there anything I can do?"

Hold me, I wanted to say. *I can't take this, and you're the only one who can make it better.*

"Thank you for leaving before things got out of control," I offered to fill the awkward, painful moment.

I stared at the carpet and began tearing at her heart. "I care about you."

Care, fucker? Did you just tell her that you care? You fucking love her with all of your heart. Living without her is impossible. You're about to annihilate her. Where's the fucking promise that you'd never leave her?

"My children are my life. My reason to exist. Their wellbeing matters more to me than anything else in the world. The last thing I want to do is hurt you or leave you. But I don't see any other solution. I have to protect them, even if it's from you."

Suddenly, it's too much. The anger, the sorrow and my demons who are waking up, reminding me of my past. I couldn't take it. On top of that, I was hurting the best person I had met in my entire life. Without thinking I swung my fist against the wall.

She loved me. Even when I was ending things, she still loved me. I should leave her alone, disappear for the rest of the night. Lose myself with a bottle of cheap tequila. I turned around to leave the room when I saw her flying from the closet toward the bathroom. She was throwing up again. This was the third or fourth day that she's been sick. A bug we thought, but she promised to go to the doctor.

My heart felt the sadness. Everything inside her was breaking, just like me. If only I could make this less painful. We were each other's support, and we soothed each other when we hurt. Ironically, I couldn't see her anymore. How were we going to survive?

This was it. The end of a story that I swore would be happy, transcending the barriers of time. We'd be together forever. I had already printed our story in my songs and my music. I kissed her hard, taking everything she offered without apologies.

Chapter Twenty-Nine

KADE

Present

"I regret that night," I whisper, holding her hand. "Will you ever forgive me?"

"Leave!" A loud male voice orders.

I turn around to find Andrew Bell, all five feet ten inches of him marching toward me. His face is crimson, and his eyes flare with hate.

"Good evening, Andrew," I greet him.

"Leave this room, or I'll call security," he threatens me.

"Call security, I'm not going anywhere."

"You have no business in this room. You and my daughter don't have a relationship."

"We have a son together," I respond, keeping my tone down. "And I'd appreciate if you could control yourself because Kieran is sleeping."

"You're a disgusting, selfish prick," he accuses me. "My daughter is better off without you."

"Is she? Because I've been by her side since the accident happened, and this is the first time I've seen you. Where have you and Catherine been?"

"I don't give a fuck about Catherine."

Of course, he doesn't. His ex-wife could be lying on the sidewalk injured, and he'd ignore her. In fact, he might kick Catherine while she was down.

"You don't give a fuck about anyone."

"I don't need to defend myself to you. Now that I'm here, you can leave. I'll take care of my daughter."

"You want me to believe that you give a shit about your daughter?"

"I don't care what you believe. I only care about her and my grandson. Now leave, before I call security. They only allow family in this room." He pulls his ID from his pocket. "I had to show them that I am family. There's some list where I wasn't included."

"Stop threatening me, Andrew. If you'd like to call security, I won't stop you. You can try to kick me out of here, but you won't be able to do it. My son is in this room, and I have every right to be with him."

"He's not your son," he says with authority.

"You're telling me that Sadie cheated on me?"

"Well, no."

"Save your ideocracies for another day. I already got a paternity test, just in case you tried to separate me from him."

"I see." He looks at the incubator and then at Sadie. "We can ask for separate rooms."

"You'd take away his mother just to fuck with me?" I step forward and glare at him. "Stop making everything about yourself and think about your daughter for once. They need each other to heal."

"That's rich, Hades," he chuckles. "Now you're worried about the woman you abandoned, pregnant."

"Good afternoon, gentleman," Brynn enters the room and glares at Andrew. "To be in the room, you must follow protocol, sir."

"I want you to remove this man from my daughter's room," he orders.

"And you are?" She narrows her gaze.

"Andrew Bell," he roars.

"Mr. Bell?" Brynn arches an eyebrow.

"Sadie's father," I clarify.

"Where is your supervisor?" He demands.

"This is a hospital, sir. Not a boardroom. I'd appreciate it if you kept your voice down."

"I need answers," he demands. "My daughter has been here for few weeks, and no one called me. I had to find out through the internet. Those gossip sites know more than I do."

"You didn't notice she wasn't home?" I crook a brow, tilting my head.

"Our hospital must have contacted you when the patient arrived. I'm one of her doctors. You'll have to contact the administrative offices or the hospital's social worker to find out."

"Your hospital left a vague voicemail. You can't expect me to drop everything just because they need to talk to me."

"Well, there you have the answer to your question. We followed protocol, Mr. Bell, and you didn't call back or come to the hospital," Brynn responds professionally while walking toward Sadie.

"If you don't mind, I need you to put on some scrubs and wash your hands properly if you plan on staying here."

"I need you to update me on her condition. Why don't we go outside, so we can talk, Dr. Ward?"

"You can do it here," I suggest.

"This is a family matter. From now on you can't be included in any updates on her health." Andrew gives me a sharp nod and turns around.

They step out of the room and leave me with a bad taste in my mouth. This fucker is going to give me hell, but I'm ready to go to war if necessary.

"That was something," Brynn steps back in the room. "Pretentious asshole. If he thinks he's going to scare me, he has another thing coming."

"What happened?"

"He threatened to get me fired, blah, blah ..." She moves her hands like a puppet.

I laugh. "He said blah, blah?"

"No. He spewed a bunch of nonsense like every other arrogant man who thinks they're more powerful than God. My brain shuts down at the sight of them."

"Where is he?"

"He's going to find out who's in charge because I'm an incompetent woman." She rolls her eyes. "The hospital knows how to handle people like him. He's not the first idiot who thinks he owns the place."

"You contacted them?"

"The hospital did when she arrived, but that's the only call we made. Though, you knew we were going to call him soon. We need someone who can legally make decisions for her."

"You're telling me that asshole gets to decide everything."

"From this point forward, that's how it is. I'm sorry."

"Is he taking her out of this room?"

"He's going to try, but I already explained to him that this isolated area helps keep the reporters away."

"I take it the paparazzi haven't left the building."

"Yes, the story is still fresh."

"How can we stop him from moving her?"

"He won't. I explained to him that if we move Sadie, it'd be harder to keep her safe from the press."

"What else did you talk about?"

"Sadie's condition. He doesn't understand the point of using hospital resources on someone who might be brain dead."

"You're kidding?"

She shakes her head. "I'd keep your lawyer on standby."

While she takes Sadie's vitals, I pace around the room. Andrew's already giving up on his daughter. I knew it would happen, but how do I stop him? As I am about to text my lawyer, Alicia's message appears on my screen.

Alicia: I told you to stay away from her. Do you know what you're doing to Tess?

Kaden: You lied to me.

Alicia: You knocked up that woman.

Kaden: She's my fiancée.

Alicia: Tess is devastated.

Kaden: How would you know? Tess and Hannah have been living with your parents while you're in Europe.

Alicia: That's my problem.

Kaden: No, we have a legally binding agreement. I'll figure things out with my lawyer. As for my daughter, I plan on taking her back to her old therapist.

Alicia: I won't allow you to take her to a stupid shrink who has no idea what's going on with her. She already has her own therapist.

Kaden: Does she? Or am I giving away eight hundred dollars a month while you pretend to send her to a counselor?

Alicia: I'll sue for full custody if you go against my wishes.

Kaden: There's nothing you can do, Alicia. You're not even here to prevent it.

Tess and I have a long conversation ahead of us.

Chapter Thirty

KADE

Leaving Sadie's side didn't sit well, but I had to do it for the sake of my daughters and our future. The sooner I took action, the better. It's been four days since the big news that my fiancée is in the hospital broke the internet. I spoke with Alicia's parents about their current situation. They had no idea that I didn't know where my daughters were. Alicia told them they had permission from me since I was out of town.

After a long conversation with my lawyer, he suggested I file for full custody of my daughters, though I can't do much until I get a court date. However, since we have a family emergency, they will stay with their grandparents in the interim. The hearing to establish permanent custody isn't until next month. If Alicia doesn't come back by then, I'll have less trouble convincing the judge that their mother isn't fit to care for them.

"You can't make me do this," Tess insists as we drive to the therapist's office.

"This isn't torture." I hold on to the wheel, counting by twos to keep my anger down.

"I have my own therapist."

"We can go there. Give me his name."

"Mom has it."

"You don't know the name of your therapist?"

"It's Smith or something like that."

"What's the first name?" I touch the screen on the dashboard and find the phone app.

"This is stupid."

"Tess, you're lying to me—again."

"You don't know what you're talking about."

"I would if you'd tell me what's going on."

"Why would you care?"

"I care, and I need you to understand that just because I love Sadie doesn't mean I ever stopped loving you."

"You're only doing this because you're going back to her and abandoning us."

"Tess—"

"She's dead you know."

"Sadie isn't dead. She's in a coma." I gasp, coming to a complete stop at the red light.

"Potayto, potato. If you've read the news, you'd know that her brain is dead. She's never going to wake up. This is pointless."

"Where did you get that?"

"Mom told me."

"When?" I drum the wheel as I wait for the green light.

"When she called to tell me that you're going to force us to come with you to therapy, but that I should be strong. You're not convincing me to change my mind. I won't accept her. Never. Nor that kid. He's not my brother."

"He's our brother," Hannah who is in the back seat, finally speaks. "You have to stop it. I think once was enough."

"Shut up, Hannah. You have a loose mouth."

"You know that what you did was wrong. I can't keep lying to them." Hannah crosses her arms. "Sadie is in the hospital. And it might be your fault."

"You can blame me for *that*, but I forbid you to blame me for what happened to them."

I want to stop this discussion, but I have a feeling that these two will spill the lies once they begin to fight.

"Dad would've been somewhere with Sadie on their honeymoon. She would be safe." Hannah starts crying, and I'm confused as hell.

I remain silent, though. Watchful. This is like watching two trains that are about to collide, and no one can stop them, yet I can't move my gaze way. I pull the car over, parking in the first spot I find.

"Or if Dad wasn't stubborn, we all could've been in Europe, as a family. Like Mom planned. But you didn't help me convince him. That's why she left us and went on the trip by herself."

"You're not blaming me for that again," Hannah raises her voice. "She left us because she's selfish."

My poor daughter couldn't be more right.

"That's the only thing she asked from us, and you said no. They need to fall back in love like they did when they were young. High school sweethearts who danced during prom as the King and Queen."

What the hell is she talking about?

"Wait, you're still hung up on me getting back together your mother?"

"Mom says it's the only thing that's going to make her happy." Hannah exhales, dropping her head on the backrest.

"You love her," Tess insists. "Mom has told us the story. How you only had eyes for her and married her when you two were young and couldn't wait to have babies."

"That's the story she gave you?"

I close my eyes because I want to kill Alicia for putting so much nonsense into our daughter's heads.

"Look, sweetheart, I love you."

"Oh, boy. That's the beginning of *you're not going to like what I'm about to say*," Hannah sasses me.

"Hannah," I chide her, giving her a stern glare.

"Yeah, shut it."

Hannah snaps her lips.

"I adore the two of you." I inhale before breaking the crazy fairy tale. "It doesn't matter what happened with your mother. Know that I've loved you from the moment I held you in my arms."

"Oh, please. This is so dramatic," Tess grunts. "What are you going to tell us? That you barely spoke to each other in high school?"

"I met her at a concert. She was a groupie." I skip the part where she slept with some of the roadies too. "One thing led to another, and she was pregnant. As soon as I found out she was expecting you, I married her for *you*. Not for her. I need you to understand that the only reason I've been with your mother is because I adore the two of you. I respect her because she's your mother, but that's all the affection I have for her. Our marriage didn't work out because we didn't love each other. Now that I'm older, I know that I could've done the right thing for you without getting involved with her. But that's not the point."

"She says—"

I lift my hand to stop Tess.

"Believe me when I tell you that there's no lost love from her side either."

The bitch hates me.

"No matter what you try, your mother and I will never get back together."

"But that can't be true," she protests. "You composed several songs for her."

"That's also a lie."

"You're wrong."

"I'm sorry, Tess. I didn't know she raised you with the notion that we were a perfect couple with the perfect love. Actually, love isn't perfect. What makes it magical are the imperfections. Shit, if I had known ..." I trail my voice and my gaze.

"But she says you're the only one who can make her happy. That's why I did everything, so you two could finally see that you were meant for each other."

I twist my body and lean forward because her tone of voice feels like a cold bucket of water. "What did you do?"

"Nothing. Never mind." She pretends to pick at a piece of lint on her jeans and turns her gaze toward the window.

"I mind. What did you do, Tess?"

"When I found out that Sadie was pregnant, I told Mom."

"You knew about the baby?" I growl. "How?"

"Sadie was talking to the seamstress while they were adjusting the bridesmaids' dresses. She asked if they could adjust the dress in case she gained weight. The lady asked if she was pregnant, and Sadie shrugged but didn't deny it. Then she puked twice while we were at the spa, and one of the ladies gave her a tea that's great for pregnant ladies and morning sickness."

"You knew," I mumbled. "What did your mother say?"

"Mom freaked out. She told me that we had to take drastic measures, or we'd lose you. That the plan of boycotting the wedding wouldn't be enough because you always did the right thing."

"You were going to boycott the wedding?" I stare at the kid next to me, not recognizing her.

When did she become so deceitful?

"I had to help Mom. But it was too late for the wedding. We had to do something drastic. She made me take them. They were a lot, but she said the pills weren't dangerous. That we'd get to the hospital in time to have my stomach pumped. She said she'd take care of the rest. That she'd explain it to you, and you'd break up with Sadie. That after what happened to your sister there was no way you'd continue with her."

Anger boils inside my body. How dare she use my daughter like that? She could've killed her. And for *what*?

"She used Hannah," I whisper, banging my head against the wheel.

"I didn't do anything," Hannah protests.

"I meant my sister, sweetie. Do you have any idea what that did to me, Tess?" I roar, unable to control myself.

"I wanted us to be a family again."

"She set up everything to look like my sister's suicide, Tess. The fear of losing you, combined with one of the darkest days of my life prevented me from seeing what was really going on with you—and her. I let her manipulate me. She's been manipulating you, too."

"I just wanted her to be happy."

"A part of me died that day, Tess, and your mother might be happy only because she hurt me."

"You say that because of Sadie."

"No, losing you almost killed me. I've been wracking my brain, blaming myself for what I could've done to save you from that moment. I keep reaching for you, and you ignore me. Do you think it's been easy for me? I tried to talk to you about it, and you keep pushing me away."

"Because I hate that I lied." She sniffs but doesn't let a tear drop from those watery eyes. "Mom forbid me to talk about it because she knew I wouldn't be able to lie to you."

"I have to ask...if Sadie and I reconcile, are you going to do this again?"

"You're going back to her?" Tess shrieks, agitated by my question.

And I'm back to the same place where I was six months ago. Or am I? This revelation changes everything. Yet, nothing can change while Sadie remains in a coma. I run a hand through my now short hair looking outside the window. My future with Sadie doesn't depend on me at all. There's a long road ahead of us. After waking up she has to recover and then ... would she take me back after leaving her without glancing back?

"I simply don't know."

"Will you marry her because of the baby?"

"No. I'd marry her because I love her." I exhale the words, closing my eyes for one second. "But that's not what's important. We are what matters right now. You lied to me, and I can tell you're upset, but you won't tell me exactly what's on your mind. I think you need a different therapist."

"You don't understand." Tess breaks down, crying hard. "Mom won't let me, and if Sadie's back ..."

She opens the door and leaves the car but leans against it.

"What just happened?" I run a hand through my hair.

"Mom," Hannah sighs. "She's always yelling at us, telling us that we need to get you two back together, like the *Parent Trap*. She says she sacrificed everything for you and for us. That we're useless."

"She called you that?"

"Kind of, in other words."

"How long has this been going on?"

My heart stops because I never saw this coming. I thought the girls were safe with her.

"A few years, maybe more for Tess. She didn't say anything to me until I was older, but every time Sadie drove me home, Mom would be nasty with me."

"Is that why you began to change with Sadie?"

"Yeah. I tried not to love her because one time I told mom that I wished she was a lot more like Sadie." She twists her lips. "Mom...she wasn't very nice about it. Said that I had to choose between the two of you. Things got complicated."

"Is she treating you right?"

"She's Mom," she answers as if that explains it all.

"I have no idea what to do now."

"Go back to Sadie and my baby brother. You were happy when you were with her."

"For a twelve-year-old you're too opinionated, Hannah."

"I liked you more when you were with Sadie."

"Why?"

"Now you're too sad to even care if we're around you. By the way, Mom said she was going to take us away from you."

"When?"

"Two days ago, when she called us about the therapist. She told Tess to do something drastic, or she wouldn't see you again."

"What does that mean?"

Alarms begin to sound inside my head, I couldn't understand what would happen if I don't prevent Tess from ...

"Tess wouldn't do anything," she says, casually. "It scared her the first time."

"Are you safe with your grandparents?"

"They're okay."

"If I could, I'd take you home, but I can't be there."

"Honestly, Dad, we're fine." She rises from her seat and kisses my cheek. "Sorry, Dad. I didn't mean to lie to you."

"Can you promise not to lie to me again? I understand your mother forced you, but I'm here for you, to listen to you."."

"I'm sorry, Dad," Hannah apologizes.

I walk out of the car, take Tess in my arms, and let her cry for a long time. Sadie used to tell me that sometimes people need to release their sorrows before they can talk about them.

"Sorry," Tess mumbles, after a long time. "I wanted Mom to be happy."

"Tess, you need to trust me and talk to me about what's going on with you. It's hard for me to guess."

"She's going to be mad."

"You shouldn't be afraid of your mother. If anything, remember that you have me. I will make sure that she stops this nonsense. I promise."

Chapter Thirty-One

KADE

Present

After Tess promised to trust me, I took the girls to lunch and then for ice cream. It felt like the old days when they smiled freely and joked around when we were hanging out together. Then I dropped them off at their grandparents' house. I'm not sure how I'm going to work out their living arrangements, but until Alicia stops the insanity, they won't live with her.

"So much for the love you profess to have for her." Andrew leans against the wall, watching me as I enter the room.

"Pardon me?" It feels like the big break is off. I have to deal with our families, fans, reporters, and wait for Sadie. My plate is too full and my fuse too short.

"You were gone all day." He taps his watch.

"I was out for a few hours visiting my daughters," I offer a short explanation to be polite, but he doesn't deserve to know anything.

"Why don't you leave now, before things get hard with Sadie?"

"What did Brynn say about the medication?" I ignore him.

"Neither one of us will discuss her health with you." He clamps his mouth shut, crossing his arms.

"But I'll tell you that if there's no brain activity when they do the next CT scan, I'm taking her off life support."

The hair on the nape of my neck raises, my heart thunders against my chest, and my head pounds.

"You can't be serious."

"I am." He steps forward, puffing out his chest. "It's not fair to have her body hooked up to machines when her brain isn't working. My daughter isn't going to be wasting space for the next hundred years. This isn't a fairy tale where you kiss her, and she wakes up."

"It's not fair to Kieran ..." *or me.*

"I am the only person who can make decisions for her. There's nothing you can do."

"My son deserves a mother, and for that simple reason I'll make sure she has enough time to come back to us."

"Try, Hades. I'm more than ready to show you how powerful I am. If Sadie doesn't wake up in a few days, she's gone. And then, I'll fight you for custody of the baby."

"And what do you plan to do with a baby when you were incapable to care for your own daughter more than thirty years ago?"

"You have no idea what you're talking about. Sadie had a roof, food, and clothing."

"That's not enough," I argued. "She needed much more than the basics. Are you aware that Catherine severely abused and neglected Sadie?"

"You have no idea what you're talking about," he protests, raising his voice.

I take a few steps closer to him and keep my voice level. "Of course I do. We shared everything, including our worst childhood memories."

His jaw sets into a scowl. I don't stop.

"She was missing the love a father who was there on her birthday or when her mother was too drunk to remember Sadie's name."

"Catherine wasn't drunk when Sadie was young."

I growl, angry at him. "Were you always this clueless, or just don't give a fuck to realize what's happening around you?"

"You're wrong," he insists, but his attention is on Sadie.

"You never loved her unconditionally. She had to do everything the way you wanted, or you'd ignore her. And nothing has changed. You're giving her a few days to wake up, or she's dead. What kind of father are you?"

I hated leaving Sadie, but I walk out of the room.

☆ ☆ ☆ ☆

The process has been slow, but after three days, Sadie's entirely off the sedatives. Yet, she's still sleeping. There's no timeline, but they are hopeful since brain activity registered during the CT scan.

"Wake up, Hummingbird. We're waiting."

There's no answer but the machines keep beeping.

"It's time for you to come back to me. This isn't a dress rehearsal," I continue. "We're ready for you to come back. Kieran is excited to see you.

"Hey, Kade," Brynn greets me as she enters the room. "Do you ever put that baby down?"

"Occasionally." I grin at her.

"I'm sure it's great for him, but he's going to have a hard time being in his crib once he goes home."

"You sound like your nurses," I chuckle. "He'll be fine, and if I need to, I'll just carry him around until he walks. I'm sure he won't want to do anything with me after that starts."

"That's insane, Hades." She laughs. "We're taking Sadie to run a few more tests."

"What for?"

"Mr. Bell's legal team wants us to prove that Sadie isn't brain dead. The CT scan isn't enough."

"Have you heard from my lawyer?" I exhale the words harshly.

"I'm letting legal deal with all that, but know that I am rooting for you. If there's brain activity, they can't do anything." She begins to disconnect and reconnect cables as a nurse steps in with a stretcher. "Addressing the baby on the lawsuit was a great idea."

The longest hour passes, as I pace around the room with Kieran in my arms. He's awake and alert. I'm not sure how much he understands, but I'm sure he's aware that something is wrong. Once Brynn rolls the stretcher back, and the nurses put Sadie back in her bed, I breathe with relief.

"What's going on?"

"We confirmed that there's brain activity. The swelling is completely gone. They're going to have a hard time disconnecting her. I'm guessing that she might be able to breathe on her own."

"It wouldn't matter if they disconnect her then?"

"I can't guarantee that, but we might have that little ace up our sleeve."

"Thank you for updating me. I know it could get you fired."

"Only if you open your mouth," she glares at me. "I trust you not to say anything to that petulant asshole."

☆ ☆ ☆ ☆

Andrew Bell steps into the room. His hair is still wet, his dark suit perfectly ironed, and his jaw clenched.

"What do you want, Hades?"

I rise from my seat, kiss Sadie on the forehead and walk toward him to keep my voice as low as I can.

"What kind of question is that?"

"I spoke to my lawyer. He said that there's no way you can win the lawsuit, but you can make things difficult."

"I plan on giving you hell," I agree. "I won't stop fighting you until she wakes up."

"What if she doesn't wake up?" He's using a condescending voice that angers me, but I brush it away—for the sake of Sadie and Kieran.

"She will. But if she doesn't, at least I'd know that I gave her time. She does everything on her own time."

"You'll forget about her in a couple of months. She'll end up in a hospice, lifeless, waiting for someone to visit her. She'd hate that."

"If that's the case, I'll bring her home with me where I could care for her and maybe when we're both old ,we'll go away—together."

"Why would you do that?"

"Simple, because I love her. No matter how long it takes, I'm going to wait for her. You can try, but you can't just take her away from me."

"I never understood the two of you."

"There's nothing to understand about us. We just exist as one soul, one heart, and two bodies."

"You are too different."

"We complement each other," I respond, remembering how perfectly we fit together. "She challenges me, makes me better, and helps me dream. She's my light. I have no idea what I give her, but I know that I made her happy. She loves me."

"I never knew what to do with her. She's a girl. Boys are easy, but girls ... She wanted to play dolls or talk, and I didn't have the time. Even now, I can barely make time for her. I wanted her to be perfect, but she chose the wrong career and then opened a business that didn't make any sense."

"Flowers are her passion. She learned that from your mother." It's unbelievable he hasn't grasped that yet.

"Mom loved her. Out of all her grandchildren, she loved her the most."

He watches Sadie from where he stands for several minutes, his hands in his pockets.

"I love her, you know. She's my kid, and it hurts to see her laying there with little hope. I can't fix her. Nothing I do will bring her back."

"You have to be patient, wait for her to come back on her own time. To heal. Instead of watching her, you should talk to her."

"Singing to her like you do," he adds.

"Huh?" I angle my head, giving him a puzzled look.

How does he know?

"I watched you last night. I ... you told her that you've found a house that looked a lot like mine and a construction guy was ready to start her greenhouse. You talked about Kieran and how you were teaching him to say 'mama.' I didn't interrupt because the moment felt so intimate. Like talking to your partner before bedtime."

"That's what we usually did at night." I turn toward her, staring at her sleeping body.

God, she'd hate to know that she's playing Sleeping Beauty. But even if it takes a hundred years for her to wake her up, I'd wait for her.

"Don't take her away from us," I beg him. "I'll give you whatever you want."

"But what if she doesn't wake up and you find someone else?" His tone is reserved.

"There's no one else in the world like her. She owns me."

"If she doesn't make it ..." he stutters and stares at Kieran. "Would you let me see him?"

"Of course. You can visit him whenever you want. I want him to know his family. Just because I don't like you, doesn't mean I would want to put a wall between Kieran and you."

He nods a couple of times, his eyes on his daughter. Then, he walks close to me and caresses Kieran's forehead."

"I'll talk to the doctors. We'll wait."

"Thank you," I say, kissing my son's head.

We won.

Andrew stops in the middle of the doorway and turns around.

"I'll move into the pool house. Tomorrow I'll have my lawyer change the deed to Sadie's name."

I crook a brow, confused by what he just said. "What do you mean?"

"The house where I live belonged to my parents. My mother left it to me so I would give it to Sadie when she decided to marry and start a family."

"You didn't tell her?" I gape, astonished at this controlling asshole.

"I didn't think it mattered, and when you two were engaged, I ... I didn't want to give you the house."

Fucker. She was marrying a guy he hated, therefore she didn't deserve her inheritance. Though, before I say something I might regret, I remind myself that I just won the war. Sadie has time, the rest doesn't matter.

"If you want, I can buy it from you," I offer. "That house would make her happy. I can wire you the money tomorrow."

"You have no idea how much it costs."

"You have no idea what I'm worth, Andrew," I counteract. "I'm a high school dropout, but I work hard and save as much as I can. You don't have to like me or to love me, but I'd appreciate if you stopped calling me a lowlife in front of my son or Sadie."

"I can do that, but you might want to save your insults too."

"We both can be civil," I agree with him.

"I'll let you know when the house is empty so you can start moving in or redecorating it."

"Thank you," I hand him my card. "So, it's easier to get in touch with me."

☆ ☆ ☆ ☆

Days pass, and there's no news. It's been two weeks since they took her out of the induced coma, and Sadie still hasn't woken up yet. She's breathing on her own and only has the IV connected to her. I remain calm, but I wish I could speed up the process. Her condition remains the same. She's stable. But I guess she knows that now she has all the time in the world. I wish she could speed up the process because Kieran continues gaining weight and growing. Dr. Hawkins hasn't discharged him yet, but she implied today that he's ready to go home.

If only everything in my life was like him; easy, compliant, and fun. At least I can't complain with the way things with my three kids have been working out. Tess and Hannah come to visit every day. Hannah loves Kieran while Tess continues shying away from him. I don't push them. There's a lot of baggage that's waiting for us when we head out of the hospital. Alicia continues her travels through Europe. Does she even care about her children?

Though I prefer it that she's away. The girls come to the hospital freely without having to give any explanation. Andrew has visited a few times. All four times he told Sadie to wake up for him, that he loved her and missed her. I have no idea if he had ever said those words to Sadie, but I'm glad that he's changing.

True to his word, he switched the deed of the house to her name. He didn't accept any money from me. A couple of days afterwards, he moved into the pool house and helped me hire a contractor to do some modifications to the house.

"Tess and Hannah are coming in a couple of hours, Sadie," I

whisper into her ear. "Wouldn't you want to wake up to visit with them?"

Her fingers move, squeezing me lightly. My eyes stare at her, as I push the button calling the nurses. Her eyes open. She blinks a few times adjusting.

"Hey, beautiful," I whisper, caressing her cheek. "I knew you'd come back to me."

Her eyes scan the room, the machines. She frowns and then looks ahead.

Her breathing becomes erratic, she moves her hand toward her belly.

"My baby," she croaks. The machines begin to beep faster; her breathing is shallow.

"Stay with me, baby. Stay with me," I beg her.

The nurses who are stationed next door arrive with a cart. One of them signals me to go to the door.

"Sir, you have to leave," she orders.

"We're losing her!"

"No, please," I beg as they push me outside the room. "We need to stay."

"Sir, let us work."

"I love you. Fight for us. Stay with me, Hummingbird. Kieran needs you. Don't leave us."

Chapter Thirty-Two

SADIE

My heart rate slows down as I arrive at the meadow. I find grandma sitting on the bench watching the little creek and throwing crumbs to the birds.

"Why are you back?" She turns her head glaring at me. "It was time for you to go back."

"I lost him," I whisper.

"Who?"

"The baby. I lost my baby."

"I don't think you did, sweetie, or he'd be with me."

Why would he be with her? She's always so practical, finding the bright side of everything. I don't think she can understand what's happening to me. First I lost Kade. Now our baby. I can't go back to a place where I'll be reminded of both.

"You don't belong here, sweetheart."

"Where's here?"

"The middle of nowhere. You're in the valley of the lost souls."

"This is a dream, isn't it?"

"Something like that." She winks at me. "You get to continue your life. Why do you want to stay behind, in here?"

"Here? I thought you were in heaven."

"Of course, I'm in heaven. But sometimes I have to pay visits to stubborn grandchildren who decide that they don't want to face life."

"What's there to face?"

"You have a million reasons, and the most important is right there. Can you hear that?"

I close my eyes, and I hear his broken voice singing as he plays the saddest melody I've ever heard.

"Take your next breath, that second chance to make things right. You have a life and a purpose—don't waste them."

Chapter Thirty-Three

SADIE

I'm back in the same room. Hooked to machines, needles, and tubes. My eyes move to my right. Kaden's red eyes stare at me. He's barely breathing. I scan his profile. His hair is short. So short he looks different. The beard though is new. He hasn't shaven for a long time. He's dressed in a t-shirt, and in his corded, inked arms, he holds a baby.

My anxiety increases as I take in the entire picture. Where am I, and why is he holding a baby? I look at my swollen belly, but it's gone.

"Calm down. Breathe, Sadie. Everything is alright. Kieran is here." He leans closer showing me the most beautiful newborn I've ever seen in my entire life. His big blue eyes stare at me.

"Say hi to mama, Kieran,"

Kieran, I smile at the baby.

"Do you want some water or ice chips?"

I swallow, and my throat is so dry, it feels like I ate a bunch of cotton. Kaden stands up from his chair, leaves the room, and comes back with a cup.

"Here. Drink slowly and take deep breaths."

I do as he says, and after my anxiety settles, I say, "Where am I?"

My voice is raspy, and my throat feels sore.

"At the hospital," he answers, cautiously.

I drink more water giving me time to think.

"What happened?"

Kaden explains that I was in a car accident. I do remember driving the van to make the last delivery of the night when I heard a loud screech and felt something bumping me from the side. He continues telling me that a man lost control of his truck and t-boned the van. They cut me out of the car, performed an emergency C-section and patched me up. He goes on to explain about my spleen, my arm having screws, my punctured lung. By the way he describes it, I feel lucky to be alive.

Lucky or not, I remember correctly that this man and I broke up long ago and he shouldn't be here.

"They didn't have to call you." I sound ungrateful, bitter, but I'm neither one.

I'm scared.

"My girl and my baby needed me. Of course, they had to call me."

He touches some buttons, the bed elevates, and he rises from the chair one more time.

"Do you want to hold him?"

I nod, looking at my left arm which has a red welted scar. I move it a few times.

"They fixed it and came every day to do physical therapy, but you might have to continue it." He hands the baby over to me.

I stare at him confused. Is this really my baby? Something in me is rejecting the idea of this kid. But when he opens his eyes, everything in the room disappears, and it's just him. His little face glows from a light within, and his small fingers grasp mine and hold tight.

He knows!

Somehow it feels like he knows that we belong together. That I need reassurance that he's mine. He knows I need his warmth and love amid what's happening right now. I hold him tightly to my chest, promising that I'll never let him go. No matter what comes our way, I'll protect him.

"Hey, handsome," I say, holding him tight to my body.

Kieran's eyes open wider as if he recognized me.

"I told you she was coming back," Kade says. "He missed you, but I made sure he heard your voice daily."

"Thank you, I guess, for being around."

Now leave before I fall for you all over again and you break my heart.

"I'm sorry," he mumbles.

"For?" I frown confused.

I look around, check my legs, wiggle my toes and my fingers. Nothing. Am I invalid?

"Why are you saying sorry?"

"For leaving you, for not sticking around and fixing everything together as a family."

"Hey, I understand. Hopefully, everything worked out for the best."

He shoves his hand into his pocket, pulls something out. My ring.

"If you could give me another chance."

"Another chance?"

My pulse spikes, and it's not love. It's fear. The beeping sound of the machine accelerates as my heart goes into overdrive again.

"Calm down," he says with a soothing voice. "The last time you freaked out like that I thought I'd lost you forever."

"I have no idea what you're doing. We're over, Kaden. In fact, you shouldn't be here. You promised."

"What about my son?" His voice cracks, his eyes fill with pain and anguish.

"This little one is mine. He's all I have. You have your life."

He steps backward, as if I had punched him in the gut. My words were daggers puncturing his heart.

"Finally, you woke up." The doctor enters the room. "How are you feeling?"

"Sleepy, groggy, and confused."

"Confusion is typical after a trauma like the one you suffered. Let's get the first test out of the way by responding to a few questions for me."

Brynn asks my last name, date of birth, to recite the alphabet, count backwards from 100 by fives, my parents' names, the name of my flower shop, and whether I recognize the guy sitting beside me.

"Who wouldn't recognize a famous rock star?" I joke.

"And she also has a sense of humor, ladies and gentlemen," Brynn says, scribbling on her chart.

"From zero to ten, zero being nothing and ten being unbearable. How would you grade your pain?"

I study my body while figuring out if I can even feel it. My legs feel stiff, but there's no pain. The arm that's barely holding my baby hurts though. "My arm, I'd say six."

"Do you have a headache?"

"No, but my shoulders are tense."

"Kade, would you mind holding the baby?" Brynn scoops him out of my arms. "I need to check your stitches and run a couple of simple tests."

Brynn asks me to look left and right, focusing on her finger while she flashes me with her flashlight. Then she checks my reflexes, and in the meantime I observe them. Kade holds our baby close to his chest. He mumbles something into his ear while cradling him. His eyes are closed, his face etched with pain. While Kieran's head rests on his chest, relaxed, feeling protected.

I wonder what he's saying or if he's singing to him. The sight of them together is the sweetest thing. Two generations sharing a special bond. I've seen Kade with his daughters, but watching him with our baby is a different sight. The way he holds him like he's the most precious thing, the love he pours into him.

My heart clenches and twists as the memories of our story downpour like a rainstorm in the middle of a hurricane. All my dreams, hopes, and the way I pictured our future follows. This is precisely how I imagined the day our baby would be born. But our baby is a month old, and we're not together anymore. Taking a few deep breaths, I try not to cry.

"Hey, everything is alright. You're doing great, and the baby is too." Brynn glances at Kade who leaves the room. "He's been cared for and loved this whole time."

"How long has Kaden been here?"

"He arrived three, maybe four hours after you were admitted. I think you should know that he barely sleeps and only leaves when one of us is around."

I sigh, trying to figure out why he's back. Do his daughters approve?

"The first time you woke up he was crushed, thinking he lost you."

"That's a scary way to wake up," I confess feeling just as anxious and overwhelmed.

The machines were beeping, Kaden was by my side and my baby ... he wasn't with me anymore.

"You're doing well so far. I want to keep you a few more days for observation. If you have any symptoms like lightheadedness, trouble breathing, or remembering dates or names, I want you to tell us right away. You had a serious contusion to the head," she says, smiling. "If you need anything, call the nurses. We're going to make a few changes to the room, so it doesn't look like an ICU anymore."

"Thank you," I say graciously.

"Anytime." She checks her watch. "I'll be in the hospital for a few more hours. If you need me, you have the nurses page me. If not, I'll drop by before going home."

"We're done," she says as the glass doors slide open. "Kevin will be here in a couple of hours."

"I texted him," Kaden says, entering the room. "He can stay home today."

"But you haven't slept in more than twenty-four hours."

"That's okay, I'll sleep later," Kaden answers. "Right now, I couldn't even if I tried. I have to make a few calls and make sure all is in place for when we go home."

"They have to stay a few more days in the hospital. Go to sleep."

We? Home?

I'm confused. Kaden behaves like the past six months never happened. There's no home. Pathetically, I live with my father because I can't seem to find a good enough place to raise my baby. At least my Dad has a big backyard for a playset and for Kieran to run around in when he gets older.

"Now if you'll excuse me, I have to finish my rounds."

"You don't have to stay," I speak up when Brynn leaves. "We're fine. I think we can handle it from here."

"You don't get it, do you?"

I arch an eyebrow, waiting for him to explain what I don't get.

"I won't ever leave your side. Never again. I made that mistake once. I'll regret it for the rest of my life, but walking away isn't an option. Never again."

"You say that now, but I can't put myself back in that place. It was hard enough getting over you the first time. From the beginning, I knew you'd leave eventually, but I ignored my gut. This time I won't."

"No, you moved past that, and now you don't trust me."

"Either way, we're over, and you have to leave because I don't want to relive the past."

"What are you saying?" he fumes. His voice is low, controlled, and I bet it's for the sake of the baby he holds. "Are you regretting us?"

"Some nights I wish I could take everything back. My kisses, my love—all of it. But as much as I want to, I don't regret you. Because when we were together, you were exactly who I wanted to love, who I needed to love me. And because I have Kieran."

"*We* have Kieran. He's mine too."

I've seen that side of Kade, the protective father who'd fight for his daughters. But this man, he's wounded, sad, and desperate. And for the first time, I have no interest in making him feel better. Because unlike him, I know that today he wants his son, but tomorrow he'll choose his other family.

"I wouldn't take him away from you. You'll always be welcome to visit him."

"We promised to share everything when our little ones came into this world."

"That was a long time ago, when we believed that we'd spend the rest of our lives together. Now," I shrug. "I'm sure you'll change your mind when the time comes to face your daughters. Tess won't accept him and Hannah ... I'm guessing she won't either."

My lips tremble because everything I ever wanted disappeared. What's left are a bunch of memories and broken promises that hurt us both.

Everything happens too suddenly and too fast. The overwhelming sadness and melancholy hits me right in the chest. I can't take it. Not anymore. A river of tears streams down my face in full force. My chest hurts as the sadness collapses my lungs. I sob because I feel empty, drained, and lonely. I missed my baby's birth and haven't got to see him grow. Kade and I are going to have to work out a custody schedule. This isn't what I wanted for Kieran.

Kade sits right next to me. He hands me the baby and takes us both in his arms. We're inside of a bubble, just the three of us. I hate him because in his arms I feel whole and calm and protected, but I know it won't last. He kisses the top of my head and sings a tune with a bunch of nonsensical words that sounds like a lullaby. I close my eyes, and for a few minutes, I allow him to step back into my world—to be a part of me.

For one moment I delude myself into a dream where it's the three of us inside a bubble where no one can touch us. The outside world doesn't exist. Though I know Kade will leave and that I'll have to build a wall up between us to protect myself, most of all to protect my son.

Chapter Thirty-Four

SADIE

I can't remember the last time I cried myself to sleep. It's like every-thing that has happened over the past months finally hits me. Kade held me for a long time. In fact, I can barely remember when he took Kieran from my arms and set him in his crib. There's still sadness lingering inside my heart, along with despair. I'm not sure if it's a normal feeling or something that I should be concerned about.

When I wake up, instead of Kade, I find Dad sitting on the chair next to my bed. His silver hair looks slightly longer than the usual buzz cut he sports.

"Sadie," he greets me.

"Dad," I clear my throat. "You're here."

"I've been around," he says, scratching his chin with the back of his index finger. "How are you feeling?"

"Would it make sense if I answer that I can't decide yet?"

He chuckles, patting my hand. "That sounds like an answer only you'd give, sweetheart. I'm worried about you."

"You don't have to worry about me. I'll work things out," I offer, is he already considering me an inconvenience?

"Of course, I worry about you. Though I'm aware that Kaden has a plan. But if either one of you needs anything, I hope you'll let me know."

I look around the room. Kade's nowhere to be found. Nor Kieran. I open and close my eyes several times. This has to be a dream. Or I fell into an alternate universe where my father is actually a human being and not an asshole.

"Kaden has a plan?" I repeat slowly, not knowing what the heck he's talking about. "Are you feeling okay, Dad?"

"I might feel better when Kaden gets here with my coffee."

"Kade is bringing you coffee?" I can't help but laugh at the idea.

Kaden Hades wouldn't hand my father a glass of water even if he were dying. They hate each other.

"He was on his way out with Kieran when I arrived. They were going for their daily walk around the block, and he offered to bring coffee. He said that you might want some chai tea."

"Wait. Are you telling me that you and Kade exchanged words in a civil manner?" Is this the twilight zone?

The first time they met, Dad forbade me from seeing Kade. Not that he could stop me from anything, but he always tried. The second time they exchanged insults, and from that day forward I've wanted to keep them apart because they're vicious with each other.

"We came to an agreement a couple of weeks ago."

"A little too late, don't you think, Dad?"

"That depends on what we're talking about. The way I've treated him since we met, or the way I've treated you since you were little."

Dad leans forward, taking my hand. "He made me see things from a different perspective. I haven't been a great father."

Understatement of the century.

"Is this one of those, '*my daughter almost died, so you'll try to be better, but then you'll go right back to being your old self*' changes?" I gasp, regretting my harsh tone.

"I deserved that," he agrees with me. "Sadly, I can't say that it was when I learned about your condition that I changed."

Dad drops his face.

"I was upset by what had happened to you and that I couldn't fix it immediately. You were lying here unresponsive. Days passed, and you were still unresponsive. No one told me what had happened to you. I was so busy working and traveling that I never checked in on you. And you know what I thought ... it'd be easier if they just disconnect her, so I can go on with my life."

My eyes grew wide, and I can't breathe. He wanted me to die. From everything he had done, this is the worst. Forgetting my birthday, choosing to spend Christmas with his girlfriend in turn, forcing me to work with him during the summer if I wanted him to pay for my college tuition.

A tear rolls down from the corner of my eye.

"I know our relationship has always been difficult, but ..." I breathe a couple of times organizing my thoughts but coming out with just a simple question. "Why are you even here?"

"Because you're my kid, and I love you," he states, his eyes filled with regret.

"I'm sorry for the way I behaved for the past thirty years," he says, something I had hoped he'd say years ago.

Is it too late? Should I stop him and kick him out? The little girl inside me begs me to listen to him. To give him a chance.

"I never stopped to think about my feelings—or yours for that matter. All my life I just stuck to the plan. Things had to be done in a certain way. I'm inflexible. That's the way my father taught me to be. I had no patience for a child like you. You're difficult to understand, and I'll admit I never tried. It wasn't because I didn't love you, but because you showed me my flaws."

He pauses, closing his eyes and taking several deep breaths. I'm in shock and speechless. He wanted to disconnect me. That part doesn't surprise me. Andrew Bell has a schedule and rules for his life. If you interrupt any of them, he'll cut you out of it. The apology shocked me.

"What made you change your way of thinking?"

"Kaden and Kieran. Mostly Kaden," he says softly.

"I'm ashamed of my behavior," he continues. "Kaden made me realize how poorly I've been treating you since you were a kid. I have no idea how to fix all my mistakes. But I want to have a real relationship with you, to become a more active part of your life."

"This is too much for me to take."

Can I go back to sleep?

"I understand, but we can take our time. Anything you need, I want you to know that you can come to me, and I'll give it to you unconditionally."

We stare at each other for a few seconds. Feeling bold, I dare to ask him, "If I need a loan, you'll be okay just handing it to me."

"Of course. Anything you need, sweetheart. Is there something you need right now?"

"Not now, but I might need it to cover medical expenses, and I have to find a bigger place, and maybe even hire a nurse to help me."

"Isn't Kaden going to help?"

"He shouldn't. We're not together," I remind him.

"I'm assuming that he hasn't talked to you about the house."

"No, I haven't," Kade steps inside, pushing a stroller and carrying a cup-holder with three cups.

"I see."

"You don't, Andrew," Kade growls. "She just woke up, and I didn't want to overwhelm her. I was trying to avoid that face."

"What face?" I arch an eyebrow.

"Confusion, terror, and stress," Kade responds.

"Well, I'm already feeling all of those. You might as well tell me everything that's going on, please."

My mouth opens wide along with my eyes as they tell me that the house where my father has lived since Grandma died is now mine. Dad's living in the pool house. They get along because they have something in common: *me.* I am confused on how to feel about this new attitude. It took a near-death experience for him to wake-up and decide to change our relationship.

"I'll be more than happy to pay for nurses and any other medical expenses."

"I'm covering those, Andrew," Kade clears his throat.

"Dad and I can take care of this. You don't have to worry about me."

"That's for you two to discuss," Dad says, rising from his seat.

"This doesn't fix our relationship," I say carefully. "But I think it's a good start, Dad."

He smiles, bends over and kisses my forehead. "I'll take whatever you can give me."

Dad squats and talks to Kieran. I can't hear what he says to him, but my heart flutters at the moment he's having with my son. Maybe he changed, or he's working on that. It'll take me some time to acclimate to what he said and to trust him.

"Tea?" Kade walks over to hand me the cup.

"You went outside with Kieran?"

"We started this new routine a couple of days ago. He needs some fresh air."

I sigh, chewing on my lip. Kieran isn't a newborn. I missed his birth and four long weeks of his life. He's mine, I know it, but I feel like we're not as close as a mother and son should be.

"Thank you for the tea."

"Why are you upset?"

"I was out for a little more than month. But it feels like I missed an entire lifetime, and I'm lost and disoriented."

"It must be hard to play catch up, Sade. But I swear not much happened."

"You and my father are civil."

"And to think I was beginning to plan his death."

"Stop joking about it."

He smirks and takes Kieran out of the stroller. Then he's changing his diaper, dressing him in a new outfit, and pushing the nurse's button.

"You're a pro with the baby," I point out. "I thought you said you had zero experience."

"Everything I said was true. The nurses here have been helpful. They taught me how to change diapers, feed him, carry him, and we just learned how to bathe him."

One of the nurses arrives with a small bottle of formula. Kaden grabs it and walks toward me holding the baby with the other arm.

"Would you like to feed him?"

I nod, setting the cup on the nightstand next to me.

Kaden hands me the baby, the bottle, and then takes a seat right next to me. We don't say much; just watch Kieran drink his milk until he sinks into a deep sleep. The bitter words that my father said, his confusing change of attitude, along with his apology are forgotten as my heart falls a little more in love with my baby boy.

☆ ☆ ☆ ☆

Before her shift is over, Brynn stops by to check on me. It's been a long day. Every hour has lasted longer than usual. My father stopped by, then the speech therapist, and later a nurse came to draw my blood.

"Everything seems to be normal."

"Just like that, I'm doing great."

"I didn't mean to say that you're in perfect health, and you can go home. More like you're in better shape than I expected. Your memory seems to be working perfectly, and the speech evaluation came out above expectations. It's safe to say that despite the swelling, there wasn't any brain damage. We still have to keep an eye on you. The occupational and physical therapists will come by tomorrow morning to evaluate you."

"Is that necessary?"

"Your left arm needs a lot of retraining. It probably doesn't feel stiff because we had a physical therapist drop by daily to massage it. However, after being in bed for about a month, you'll need help regaining the strength in your muscles."

"Can they come to our home after she leaves the hospital?" Kaden asks.

I chew on my lip.

"Not sure if that's something my insurance covers." My coverage is crappy, to say the least.

"Whatever your insurance doesn't cover, I will, Sadie."

"You don't have to. My father might be willing to loan me some money."

"You guys can work that out later. I don't think I'll discharge you for another week. While you work your living arrangements, remember that you need 24/7 support."

"Aren't you exaggerating a little? There are plenty of single moms who fend for themselves from the first day."

"Moms who didn't just wake up from a coma and need to recover their strength," Brynn chides me. "You need someone to be with you. Think about Kieran."

"That's the plan. The house is set. We just need to add the gym."

"I am not going with you." I clench my jaw.

"If you need to reach me, just text me," Brynn smiles awkwardly.

"Love, can we talk?"

"I'm too tired to talk."

He pulls something from his pocket and marches toward me. I gasp when I see it. My engagement ring—again.

Chapter Thirty-Five

KADE

"Why do you still have it?" She looks at the ring in horror.

"It's yours, and I want you to take it back."

She laughs, but there's no humor behind it.

"Why would I take it back?"

Do you have a lifetime to listen to all the reasons?

"Simple. Because I want to do the right thing by you. Marry you."

She huffs, shaking her head. "You think that marrying me is doing the right thing?"

"We have a kid—"

"Didn't you learn the first time?" She interrupts what I hoped would be a reasonable explanation.

"First time?" I'm confused by the question and sleep deprived.

She didn't let me explain why I want to marry her, just stopped me before I could say more than four words.

"You married Alicia to do the right thing," she says bitterly. "What was it?" She taps her chin. "Six or seven years of unhappiness that pushed you to hate her."

"Don't fucking compare yourself to that bitch!"

"I'm not her, I know that. We're over, and we share a kid. But that's all we have left."

"You can't believe that. It can't be over between two people who bonded their souls and melded their hearts. We're one, Sadie."

I look down for a moment as I remind myself that she's hurt, afraid, and her father already confused the fuck out of her.

It's been a long day. A long year if I add in the fact that I left her. She almost died, and she mumbled before falling asleep earlier that she was all alone. Everything is too much for her, and I know for a fact that when she's overwhelmed she retreats into herself. But it's so hard to stay away. There's this intense need to hold her, embrace her, and never let her go.

"You got to leave the past where it belongs, move on. No matter how many times you ask, I won't marry you for the sake of Kieran."

"I have more I want to explain."

"Save your words, Hades. Nothing you say will make me change my mind."

So much for fixing this as soon as she woke up. *What were you expecting, fucker? You broke her heart and your promise.* It takes me longer than it should to realize that I'm taking the wrong approach.

"I understand that maybe I won't be able to fix what I've broken, but at least let me help you during the next few months."

"Help me, how?" She tilts her head and narrows her gaze.

"Rent me a room in your house for about a year," I propose.

"Where are you going to stay? I might have a big house, but I don't have much furniture."

"I furnished the place. We moved your things to the big house and recreated Kieran's nursery the way you wanted it. It's ready for you. If you're okay with it, I'll move into one of the empty rooms temporarily. That'll allow me to see Kieran every day. I don't want to lose him so soon."

Sadie stares at me for a long time. I hold my breath. She has my future in her hands.

"It's a big place. We won't crowd each other," she says, sucking on her lower lip. "Sharing a house sounds like a good idea for now. Kieran is used to you, and I don't want to take him away from you. But once I'm stronger, you can move back to your place."

Hummingbirds are fast and not so easy to catch. Sadie is a lot like those birds. I can't catch her, but I can set up a garden where she can stay close but still fly free. My only chance to win her back is to earn her trust.

☆ ☆ ☆ ☆

This fathering a newborn isn't as easy as I thought. I'm beyond tired. If I had time, I could've driven home to catch a few Z's. Instead, I met with Duncan and the band. The last album is doing great, and they want to expand the tour that just ended a month ago. I had to explain to them that for now, I can't leave Sadie's side, let alone the city. After that, I went to visit Tess and Hannah. They insisted on coming to the hospital, but I explained to them that for now, what Sadie needs is a lot of rest. So far, I've told everyone to wait a day or two before they start dropping by to see her.

"How are you feeling this morning?" I ask when I enter the room.

"Fine." Her somber tone matches her solemn face.

"What happened?" I lower myself on the blue plastic chair.

"Nothing. I'm fine."

"Sadie?"

"It doesn't matter. I just have to work things through." She touches her temple.

"Why don't you share? Maybe I can help?"

She huffs.

"The occupational therapist said that my fine motor skills need some work."

"She was already here?"

She nods once.

"What did she say?"

"I can't cut well with scissors or fold paper. Writing was difficult too."

"Maybe the physical therapist will be different."

"Not by much. I wave when I walk. My hip muscles are weak, all the others are atrophied, and I can't lift heavy objects. What if I can't hold Kieran for much longer?"

"What did they say?"

"It doesn't matter," she says. "It's over."

"What's over?"

"Everything. They can't guarantee that I'll be able to draw again, or cut or ... what's the point of having my flower shop? I'm going to lose it soon, and then I'll lose Kieran because you can prove that I'm an unfit parent."

"Aren't we skipping ahead? Try to take it one step at a time."

"It feels like I'm drowning, and it's almost impossible to see the bright side."

"We'll come up with a plan and follow through. You're not in this alone, even though you may think different."

"You say it like it's easy. But you have to go back to your daughters."

I sigh because there's some truth to that. We have to figure out what's going to happen with my girls. Not wanting to approach the subject yet, I make my way to the crib because Kieran is beginning to fuss.

"How are you, Little Beanie?" I greet him, lifting him out of bed.

"He's the sweetest baby," she says. "I can't wait for him to meet Sinatra."

"Sin's a good brother. He was cool with Hannah and Tess."

Sadie stiffens and since I brought them up, I might as well get it over with.

"Will it be okay if they come to visit you?"

"Me?" she touches her sternum. "They know?"

"About you and Kieran and everything. A lot has happened in the past few weeks."

She goes quiet, and I hate when Sadie is brooding or trying to push me away.

"After what Tess did in reaction to me being in your life, I can't think of how she'll handle Kieran."

"Tess didn't do anything."

"What do you mean?" Sadie touches the back of her neck, narrowing her eyes at me.

"Alicia made the whole thing up," I begin the long explanation.

While I recount the story that Hannah and Tess told me, she remains quiet but for a few exclamations of shock and anger.

"You mean to say that your ex is even crazier than we thought?" I nod in response. "She made Tess pretend that she killed herself to hurt you?"

"To break us up, so I'd get back together with her."

"That's ..." she breathes the word, slumping. "Dangerous. Do you realize what she could do to Kieran?"

"What do you mean?"

"She can order your daughters to hit him, drop him, drown him—anything." Her voice now has an urgency to it that makes me jittery too.

I don't react. I take several calming breaths instead.

"You're exaggerating," I say.

"No, I'm telling you that someone is so unstable that they'd urge their own daughter to attempt suicide needs help! And she needs to stay away from my son. That includes her minions."

"They wouldn't do anything to him."

"You trust your kids, and I respect that. I don't have to trust them. They've done nothing but hurt me while Alicia gave them orders to do so for three long years. There's no guarantee that they'll change," she says with conviction. "They aren't allowed to see Kieran—not until he can talk and defend himself from them."

"You're going overboard."

The best way to ensure their safety is by having them with me. If my girls can be close to Kieran, that means we won't be able to live together. Indirectly, Sadie is making me choose between Kieran and my daughters. Her words hit me like a ton of bricks, and my stomach feels completely empty.

"Look, I've seen it all, Kaden. Remember that I was a social worker before I opened the shop. Have I told you about the case of the little boy who died because his sister dropped him down the stairs? She did it because her stepfather suggested it. He was annoying them."

"I'm sure there's a lot more to the story that I don't care to learn, Sadie. My daughters aren't like that."

"They have a psychotic mother who manipulates them, Kade." She raises her voice and her eyes are vicious. "Think of the things they could do to a newborn and claim it was an accident. Alicia is a manipulative bitch, and she hates me. If something happens to Kieran, I won't survive."

"So what am I supposed to do with my daughters?"

"Stay with them. We'll be fine without you."

"I'm not leaving you," I say with conviction. "We have things to work out."

"*You* do. I don't have anything to do with your daughters—or you—Kaden. They're yours, remember? I'm out of the picture."

"Somehow, I feel like you're throwing what happened between us in my face."

"Not really. I'm just reminding you that you made your decision long ago."

☆ ☆ ☆ ☆

"When my kids come back from the ice cream store complaining about the flavor they chose, I remind them that it was their choice." Raven files her nails. "Nobody made them choose."

"You're comparing my relationship with ice cream, Rae?" I wring the mop and continue cleaning the flower shop.

"It's not a fancy analogy, but it's exactly what happened to you. The moment you decided to push Sadie away and deal with your family, you told her—"

"That she wasn't family."

"Exactly, and that your daughters were yours to deal with—not hers. Sadie tried her best to be a friend, a stepmother. Not once did she try to step on Alicia's toes. Yet, when it came to making decisions, you always left her out of the equation. The day you needed Sadie the most, you dismissed both her and all the years you two had been together."

She's right. I could've relied on Sadie, trusted that she could have helped me with my girls. Because we're a team.

"How do I convince her that we were better back then, when we were together?"

"You can't get back to where you were, that's not an option," Raven says watching me clean the flower shop. "Hey, don't miss that spot. Some kid came in with a root beer float and made a mess."

"I regret visiting you."

"Do you?"

"You put me to work," I complain, mopping where she told me.

"Didn't you watch *Karate Kid*?"

"What does that have to do with my problem?"

"Mr. Miyagi put Daniel to work while teaching him karate."

"You're just putting me to work."

"While I'm thinking about your psycho ex, my broken friend, and you. Not that this is a love triangle, but that Alicia is unstable. You're asking a woman who just had a little chat with the Grim Reaper herself to welcome the spawns of Satan back into her life."

"They are *my* kids too."

"Exactly, Hades. You're Satan." She laughs at her stupid joke. "Give her time."

"What do I do with my daughters?"

"Do you think they're in danger?"

"Not with their grandparents," I explain.

"Then, make sure they stay there. Talk to your lawyer and explain the situation. If things get sticky, you can bring them to me. We have space for them."

"But that's not a long-term solution."

"Patience, Hades." She rolls her eyes. "Sadie is recovering. Once she can be on her own, you can move back to your house and have full custody of your daughters."

"But I don't want to leave Sadie's side. I'm working on things between us. Which includes getting Alicia to disappear from our lives and convincing Sadie that my kids are harmless."

"There's that option too." She nods. "Which I like better, if you ask me. I say, give her time and stick to your plan. But don't offer her what you two already had. Offer her a new relationship. A mature relationship where you trust each other, and you share everything—even parenting."

It all boils down to patience.

"Are you going to visit Sadie?" I sigh, studying the floor.

"I'd love to, but Bill and the kids need me at home." She grins. "I'll call her and tell her that she can have sex in a week."

"What does that mean?" I narrow my gaze at her.

"It's a new mom thing." She winks at me. "In the meantime, you can close the shop and make sure to set the alarm before you leave. It was nice seeing you, Kaden."

Chapter Thirty-Six

KADE

Six days after Sadie woke up, we finally left the hospital. Sadie and I hadn't spoken about my daughters since she reminded me that they're my problem—not hers. I've visited my girls daily and was honest with them about Sadie. She's afraid that Alicia would ask them to hurt Kieran. They assured me that they wouldn't do anything to harm him, but as I explained to both of them, it's an issue of trust.

Alicia remains in Europe, but I have the feeling that she's coming back soon since I stopped the direct deposit to her checking account. Her parents are the ones getting the child support money since they're housing my girls.

"You did all this?" Sadie asks as we enter the house.

The room looks like it could be on the cover of an interior design magazine.

"I'm afraid to step foot into the house. It's that perfect."

"We got some of the ideas from your Pinterest. Raven and your father's interior designer helped me with the rest."

"It's gorgeous."

The couch is cream. The cushions are the same color but inlaid with delicate green silk leaves embroidered so skillfully that they looked like they could have landed there in spring. The white curtains are organza, the kind of white that's untouched by hands and devoid of dust. A cursory look to the right shows me the almost hidden cords that are used to open and close them. We added a couple of recliner chairs around the bespoke fireplace. The photographs on top of the shelves and around the walls are snapshots of family. Most of the pictures that Sadie had in our old apartment and a few new ones of Kieran. The floor is high polished wood, dark and free of either dust or clutter.

"What did Dad do with his things?"

"He donated everything and had his interior decorator furnish the pool house with brand new furniture."

"I'm not sure how I feel about living with my dad."

"You were living next door, weren't you?"

"Yeah, but it was temporary. This is permanent."

"He travels a lot," I remind her, which is what I keep telling myself every time I think about the asshole living next to me.

We're on friendly terms, but until I see that the change is permanent, I'll continue watching my back.

"What did he do with his car collection?"

"Honestly, I didn't ask, but the garage is empty. It's a big room, and I'm wondering if you'd allow me to fix the acoustics and use it as my studio."

"Don't you have a studio?"

"I lease space from the Deckers, but I have to drive to downtown. I don't want to leave you for long periods of time. Yet, I need to practice, and the garage is the best place for that. It'd save me money. Would you mind renting it to me?"

She presses her lips together and nods. "Okay, but where are we going to park the cars?"

"I'll have a contractor come over to help me set up the studio, and he can split it, so we have three or four spaces for the cars. Is that a good compromise?"

"Yeah, that sounds reasonable."

"Okay, let me get this little man to bed." I lift the baby carrier. "Then I'll help you upstairs."

Instead of taking him to the nursery, I place him in the bassinet I bought for the master bedroom. I set the baby monitor and make my way back downstairs. Sadie sits on the second step of the staircase. Her head resting on her knees.

"Hey." I sit next to her.

"How is he?"

I hand her the monitor that shows the master bedroom and Kieran.

"This isn't the nursery."

"No, it's the master bedroom. I bought a bassinet for that room and a crib for his nursery."

"You were busy." She smiles, playing with her long skirt.

"I can't take all the credit. Your dad helped me a lot."

"Thank you. You've been great. I know I sound ungrateful when I'm only taking and not doing anything to help you," she pauses, taking a deep breath. "But I do appreciate everything that you're doing for me."

"It's a lot to take in, I understand."

She stares at my arm where I have the hummingbird tattoo. "It's just ... I have to protect Kieran."

"You don't need to explain yourself. I get it."

"Your ex is scarier than we thought."

"That's something I have to figure out before she gets back."

"Just file for full custody," she suggests.

"I did. The hearing is soon. But where would they live?"

"With you, of course."

"I live here."

"You don't have to. I know they come first."

"Sade, for fuck's sake, stop that! Tess and Hannah don't come first." I shake my head.

"Kieran is as important," I say, pointing toward the stairs. I take a deep breath. "This is the last time I want to hear you pushing me away to keep him safe. My three children matter, just as much as you do. We're a blended family that has to learn how to live together. Kieran's safe with me. I won't take him away from you. There's no custody battle between the two of us. Did I fuck up a few months ago? Yes. I accept that I handled the situation poorly."

"You did what you thought was best for Tess. The way they set everything up was a replica of how your sister died."

"Alicia knew how to fuck with my head." I tap my temple.

"I wish I could help you."

Sadie sounds genuine, but I bet she doesn't have an answer right now. At least not a solution that can be used long term.

"I'll figure everything out. Don't worry."

We both stay quiet for a long time just being there with one another. I want to know what she's thinking, just like I want to tell her that I need her help.

"I still love you," I whisper with conviction.

"*Please*, Kade," she groans.

"Shut up, I got it." I salute her.

"Where's Sinatra?" She looks around.

"Still at Raven's. She's going to bring him once you're settled."

"She's amazing. I couldn't have survived the past months without her."

"Can I ask you why you didn't tell me about the pregnancy?"

"It was the surprise that I had planned for after our dinner," she says, placing her chin on top of her knees, hugging her legs. "There's a onesie somewhere with the Killing Hades logo and the sonogram. But how could I tell you when Tess couldn't even stomach me. A baby would have push her off the cliff."

"Alicia screwed with my head in the worst possible way."

"Why do you think the girls went along with it?"

"To make Alicia happy."

"I wonder how she's treating them emotionally. It must be hard for them to be held accountable for their mother's happiness. I bet nothing makes Alicia happy, but we know she enjoys seeing others suffer."

"That would be a pretty good assessment."

"She hates me."

"Because she knows that I'm in love with you. You weren't like the other women who I slept with for a night ... you made me work for it." I smile remembering the times I spent with her at the flower shop or the nights having dinner together and just playing board games.

"You enjoyed it, Mr. Hades."

"Anything that involves you is enjoyable, Miss Bell."

"I wish I could trust them—you. It's just ..." She shrugs. "Kieran is all I have."

"Hey, I get it. I'll figure it out. One way or another I'll make all this work."

She closes her eyes, and I fucking know that this is breaking her just like it's tearing me apart. Sadie's right. We can't put our baby in jeopardy, and I can't stress her either. She has so much going on that pushing my problems on her might become an issue in the long run. Without thinking, I put my arm around her and kiss her shoulder.

"For now, just focus on getting better, Hummingbird."

"Don't touch me, please. You have to keep your hands off me."

"It's hard."

"Look, I get that you worked through our breakup while I was fighting for my life, but I didn't. I'm not in a good place. I'm trying to catch up with my surroundings, my mind, and my body. I have screws in my arms, and my emotions are all over the place. I can barely walk or hold my baby."

"Hey, as long as you let me help you, I'm happy."

"I appreciate that. It'd be stupid to think that I could do everything alone when I can barely lift a cup of tea."

Chapter Thirty-Seven

SADIE

"How are you feeling today?"

Horny, mind putting on a shirt and stop holding that baby because every time I see you two together my ovaries explode. Can we have another baby?

"Sade, are you okay?"

I move my gaze away from his perfect chiseled torso and focus on the whisk and the bowl I'm holding.

"Sorry, I'm fine. How was your run?"

"It was great. This little man likes the new trail. You should come with us tonight."

Kade discovered that my father's house sits on five acres of land. He can run freely without even leaving the lot, and so he decided to create a trail. He hopes that at some point I'll be able to use it too. But I get tired too quickly. For now, I walk on the treadmill twice a day, but only for about ten minutes.

"To run?"

"Just for our nightly walk," he proposes. "It's short, and you could use a little air."

"It would be a nice change of scenery. I might join you."

"What are you cooking?"

"Nothing, I'm just whisking flour with water to loosen up my wrists."

"You can do other things to loosen them up." He waggles his eyebrows and drops that panty-melting smirk my way.

"Ah, that dirty mind, Mr. Hades. I'm not adding jerking you off as part of my daily therapy."

"I never said that, Hummingbird. You're the one with the dirty mind."

"Right, because that's not what you were thinking at all."

"A guy can always hope." He winks at me.

"For God's sake, your son is listening to this nonsense."

"There's nothing wrong with him knowing that his old man lusts after his mother."

"You're not old, and you shouldn't."

"We might not be together, but you can't stop me from loving you."

"Rules. We need rules." I close my eyes because a part of me doesn't want them at all.

If only things between us were simple. But they're too complicated to add sex into the mix right now. We have a kid who depends on us, and he has his other children too.

"Don't challenge me. You know what happens every time you do it."

"I give up!" I set the bowl in the sink. "Go take a shower, Hades."

"That's a great idea." He opens the fridge and pulls out a bottle of water. "By the way, Raven is dropping by with some flowers and Sinatra."

"Ah, the master of the house is coming home."

He smiles and takes a few gulps of water. Watching his Adam's apple move along with his naked, sweaty torso makes me shiver with desire. It's just a couple more days until I can have sex according to Raven. I had no idea there was a rule. Not that I plan on having sex anyway.

But I need to relieve the ache between my legs. The need keeps intensifying because I have this sex on a stick of a man flaunting his bare torso around the house every day.

"Do you think Sinatra will like Kieran?"

"I hope so. He liked him while I was pregnant," I say, smiling at the memories of my kitty. "Sin liked to purr and rub his head against my belly. Kieran would push against my stomach at his will. They had a good relationship."

"Good. At least I don't have to worry about it. Where do you want me to set up his things?"

"The kitchen?" I look around. "It's open and he'll enjoy the view."

Kaden's phone rings, and he rolls his eyes before answering. "What's up, Jax?"

"It's not a mansion. The gate code is in the email I sent you." He nods a couple of times, stares at the ceiling and turns red. "Are you sure?"

I walk toward him and take my sleepy baby from him.

"They found who it was? Well, I'm glad the hospital is firing her. Yeah, I'll see you soon."

"What happened?"

"There was a media incident while you were at the hospital."

That's code for someone caught me doing something I shouldn't have. Like the time a fan caught us having sex in the parking lot of a stadium in Brussels, and he posted a blurry video on YouTube. There's nothing to see, but the media made it into a big deal.

"Like they caught you having sex with some nurse while I was in the hospital?"

"Are we jealous?" He cocks his eyebrow.

"No, just guessing."

"I know your faces, love. That's your typical *who am I going to kill* face."

"You can say whatever you want, but it's not true." I'm lying because of course I'm jealous if he slept with someone while I'm still getting over him.

"What happened?" I humor him trying to satiate my curiosity.

"Someone wanted to make a little money off our tragedy and sold the press a bogus story."

"What story?"

He goes into detail about the news of him being involved in a car accident while under the influence. How supposedly I died, while our son ended up in critical condition.

"You were on tour."

"You knew where I was?" His surprised voice almost wakes up Kieran.

"It's hard not to know when it's all anyone is talking about," I say, dismissing it, while soothing my baby. "Don't you think? But back to your story."

"Do you mind walking with me upstairs? Jax will be here soon."

We follow behind to his room. He has all the furniture from our old bedroom here. Even our pictures. Nostalgia hits me right in the middle of the chest, sending the memories of our life together from the back burner to the front of my mind. I've worked hard to keep them where they belong, forgotten. It's the only way to stay emotionally away from him while he's so physically close to me.

"You're undressing," I say, sitting on the unmade bed and averting my gaze to the window.

He's going to kill me with lust.

"That's how I shower. Naked," he says with a mocking tone. "It's nothing you haven't seen before."

"Just finish the story." I wave my hand, still not looking at him.

If I do, I might jump him—right now.

"After the news broke, the press was going crazy about my alleged crime. The paparazzi set up camp outside the hospital which made it hard for me to come and go and for the guys to visit."

"I had visitors."

"Of course you did. All your friends stopped by daily, sometimes they sent me to take a nap while they were watching over you. There was a sign-in book. I can ask Jax for it."

"I wouldn't need it. I was just curious. So, who sold the story to the media?"

"One of the nurses. The bitch needed money."

"We have to discuss your vocabulary in front of Kieran," I say louder as the water is running.

A couple of minutes later the water is off, and he comes out wearing a towel around his waist. I need to ignore his muscular chest and focus on his face. He has a five o'clock shadow that I can remember created a carpet burn when he went down on me.

"And we're feeling better." He chuckles.

"What do you mean?" My cheeks heat up because he caught me lusting after him.

"You're starting to censor me—again." He puts on his jeans—no underwear.

Ugh, he's killing me.

He puts on a black t-shirt that covers his broad shoulders and lets me see every one of his chest muscles.

He kisses the top of my head.

"I'm going to be outside talking to Jax, but text if you need anything."

"Don't worry about us, we have a routine to follow. Maybe some play time if he's not too tired."

Chapter Thirty-Eight

SADIE

Kieran's a sweet baby who babbles when he wakes up. Though, we only have about a minute or two to get to him before he cries at the top of his lungs. It never fails when we take too long to retrieve him; he makes good use of his lungs. Like tonight when I didn't hear him, his shrill cries were loud enough to wake up the entire state of Washington. He's gasping for breath in-between his frantic sobs.

"Got him!" Kade announces, rushing into my room.

"I was going to get him."

"Did he babble?"

"If he did, I didn't hear him." After I put him down the last time, I crashed, blocking out everything.

"Me neither," he shows me the monitor. "I was just coming upstairs from the studio."

"So late?" I check my phone. It's two in the morning.

"The beauty of having my own studio." He picks up the baby. "We're recording a few tracks."

"New music, huh?" I chew on my lip because Kaden usually played his new stuff to me first.

Then again, I've refused to listen to him sing ever since we broke up.

"You want me to play it for you?"

"Maybe, someday." I rise from the bed and put on my robe. "When it hurts a little less."

"Can we talk about us?" Kade glances at me briefly before turning back to the changing table, giving his full attention to Kieran.

"Nope, I'm not ready for that," I answer honestly because he has too much going on in his life, and I just want simple.

"I'll get his bottle ready," I announce, leaving the room.

"You don't want to talk about it, and yet, we function like a real couple who happen to have a newborn," he says loud enough that I can hear him as I make my way down the stairs.

In a way, he's right. We are almost a couple. Except, we don't share everything, and that includes the other part of his family. He's still dealing with his daughters, and I don't ask him much about them because what's right for them could be wrong for Kieran. These moments break my heart again and again. I wish things were different between us.

Once I'm back from the kitchen, I spot Kaden sitting in the rocking chair. My heart skips a beat at the sight of him. This tug-of-war between my head and my heart is tearing me apart. I'm aware that what we share can't be replicated with another man. This love, this feeling, is just between him and me. Centuries could pass, I could travel the world looking for someone else, and I'd still have to come right back to him if I wanted true love.

Yet, I'm not strong enough to risk being broken all over again, to let myself love again.

"You should go to sleep."

He opens his eyes and smiles at me.

"Nah, this is my favorite time of night. Being with two of my favorite people."

"I wish I had breastfed him. That mother-son bonding is missing, or maybe it's not, and I'm just obsessing."

"You two are close. Kiearn is always looking for you when you're not around. But in case you miss it, you'll get another chance to do it with Aubrey and Grady."

"*We* are not having an Aubrey or a Grady."

"Is that a challenge?"

"God, you're stubborn, Hades."

"No, I'm a man of faith and who has lots of patience."

He's a man who never gives up, I know that about him. It's not just with me, but with his whole life. He's not stubborn, but perseverant. Right now, his focus is Kieran and me. Every day he's around, helping me with my exercises and caring for our baby. He takes his rehearsals and visits to his daughters right around nap-time. We spend hours talking. Even when I push him away, he keeps coming back to me.

"We have a lifetime, an eternity. It'll happen sooner or later. Your heart can only be far away from mine for so long."

"Why would you say that?" I close my eyes, paying attention to his voice.

"Because mine is withering without yours, and our hearts are a lot alike."

"Lines, stay behind them."

"Walls, Sadie. You built walls of steel that I'm not interested in breaking because you feel safe behind them. For now, that's what you need."

"Do you know what I need?"

"To sleep and stop this nonsense."

He begins to sing, a lullaby I don't think I've ever heard. Once he's done feeding Kieran, he walks around the room with him, patting his back. After the baby burps, he sets him in the bassinet that's next to my bed.

"You're still awake." He walks toward me.

"Sometimes I have trouble falling asleep after he wakes up."

"How are you feeling?"

"Sleepy?" I shrug. "I don't know. This is the time of night I like to focus on tomorrow's schedule."

"May I?" He asks, sitting on the bed.

"I should say no."

"Promise not to do anything other than hold you until you fall asleep."

"Kade," I sigh.

It's impossible to stay away when he knows exactly what I need—

him. His arms, and that safe bubble he builds around us at night that no one else can penetrate. It's just the two of us.

"Yes, Hummingbird?"

"I wish I weren't afraid."

"Me too, love. Me too."

"Are you afraid of anything?"

"Too many things to count, but a wise woman once taught me to lead with my dreams and not with my fears. Focus on building my future, not what destroyed my past."

"What's your focus?"

"Co-parenting, helping you recover your health and in doing so, recuperate my friend."

"You want to be my friend."

"I enjoy your company, Miss Bell. If you allow it, we can be friends."

"I thought we were friends."

"Friends don't have barriers the size of the Great Wall of China."

"One day I might let you back in, Hades."

"I hope so, love," he whispers as I'm falling asleep.

☆ ☆ ☆ ☆

Battling my sore, unsteady legs, I am finally going faster on the treadmill. Despite my heart pounding, throat rasping, leaden feet, and wheezing as my burning lungs gasp for air, I did it.

"Look at you, running."

I move my gaze from the dashboard toward Kaden who leans against the doorframe and holds our little boy.

"It's more like fast jogging," I correct him, smiling at the sight of my guys.

"How was your run?"

"We broke our record." He grins, lifting our son's arm as a sign of triumph.

"Little Kay and I just decided that you have to come with us tomorrow."

"No, no, and no. Little Kay sounds like a cereal. Stop that nonsense."

Jax made up that stupid nickname, and they're trying to make it stick, but I'm not allowing it.

"Kieran isn't going to have the name of a rapper from Sesame Street. Today's song is brought to you by Little Kay and the number three."

"You can be funny, Hummingbird," he laughs.

"And mean, so stop calling him that or else."

"Are you going to punish me?" he throws his sexy smirk my way.

My legs wobble, and it's not because of the treadmill, but because of the lust that I'm carrying.

"Ugh, you're impossible, Hades," I feign annoyance and slow down my pace.

"The flowers arrived." He changes the subject.

We're making a few changes to the landscape. I'm adding iris, lavender, and sweet pea to give my backyard a purple tone that matches perfectly with the already white and blue ambiance I have.

"Are you helping me?"

"Yes. I got a baby swing for the task, so Kieran can watch us."

"When do you want to start?"

"In a couple of hours. I have to check on the girls if you don't mind."

"How are they doing?" I dare to ask.

"They're fine. Their grandparents are driving me crazy. You know they like to say that I'm a worthless piece of shit in front of my kids."

"Sorry about that."

You're sorry, but you don't plan on doing anything to help, do you?

"It is what it is. Don't worry about it." He walks toward the door. "I'm going to take a shower."

I stop the treadmill. I have to take a bath before he leaves the house, but as I'm heading toward the stairs, I hear someone knocking on the door.

I open the door, and Tess stands there stoically.

Chapter Thirty-Nine

SADIE

"Hi," Tess waves from the other side of the door.

She stands right in front of me, and she's now a couple of inches taller than me. Her red, straight hair is pulled into a ponytail. Her brown eyes find mine, holding my gaze for a long time. The silence is deafening. I'm not sure what to say, but I'm not afraid of her. A part of me still wants to hug her, but I'm not sure how to behave around her.

"Do you want to talk to your dad?"

"No, I'm here to see you." She looks around, hugging herself.

"I don't want to sound harsh, but you can't be here."

"Dad told me." She lifts a shoulder and drops it slightly.

"He did?" I arch an eyebrow.

"Yes, we try not to keep secrets between us," Tess says, looking around. "Is there someplace we can talk without him?"

I can't help but release a laugh. "So much for not keeping secrets."

"Later I'll tell him about it, but I don't want him here now."

"Follow me," I say, closing the door behind me.

We walk toward the pool house, while I text Kaden to let him know that I have to check on something at my father's home. Dad's out of town which means we have the place to ourselves.

"He might come to look for me soon," I warn her.

"Did Dad tell you what happened?"

"Yes, everything. How do you feel about it?" I punch the code on the electronic lock.

"You sound like my therapist." She rolls her eyes.

"I'm here for another reason, but Dad and I have been talking, you know. I'm trying to change because he said that I should stop trying to please Mom. That what I did hurt him. Not only because of you, but because it reminded him of his sister."

Tess looks around my father's house when I swing the door open. She doesn't say anything more until I close the door behind us.

"He said that either I mature and become my own person, or I'd lose him."

"A little harsh. He knows better than to threaten you like that."

"Well those weren't his exact words," she clarifies. "He said it fancier. The point is that he was hurt by what I did and there are consequences. He doesn't blame me, but I know that it's my fault that you two aren't together. That he lost everything because of what we did."

Tess walks around the living room stopping in front of me after several passes.

"He said he was done with my behavior. That he loves me, but he doesn't like me when I'm behaving like my mother."

"He's right in a way. At some point, you have to become your own person."

"Well, yeah I'm working on that. Dad and Hannah also made me think about what's happened since you came into our lives. He's different with us. He listens to us more and you ..." she shrugs. "You cared for us. And when we were sick, you never sent us somewhere else, like Mom usually does."

"I was happy to take care of you guys."

"Yeah, but I didn't see that because my mother tortured me every time I came back from Dad's."

"Everything is so clear," I say, shocked by my stupidity. Why didn't I see this when it began? "You hate me not because of me, but because of the emotional torture you had to endure."

"Something like that." She presses her lips together.

"I don't hate you though, more like I was working hard at trying to, but it's kind of hard. You're too nice."

My heart feels sad for her. I can't imagine what she's been going through. She's a victim of her mother's insanity.

"But I want you to know that no matter what, I would never hurt my brother."

I remain still, silent, observing her and waiting for more.

"Mom called earlier today, and it was kind of disturbing you know. She insisted that the baby is taking Dad away from us and that we have to do something. That scared me and also made me realize that the only person who keeps me away from Dad is Mom."

"No matter what, your dad will always put his children first. He's an amazing father and what your mother did to him is unforgivable," I reassure her. "Not because it broke us apart, but because of how she exploited your father's trauma. It hurt to know that you hurt yourself. I care about you."

"I just wanted Mom to be happy," she says without acknowledging that I care for her.

"It's hard to please your parents. I tried with mine for a long time. It took me awhile to understand that I'm only responsible for my own happiness. I hope that one day you can see that too."

"I just wanted to say that I'm sorry, though." She shuts her mouth closed.

"Okay."

"And I wanted to ask you for a favor."

"What is it?"

Leave my dad alone!

"I'll be going to college next year, and I'm hoping that soon you and Dad can work things out. He loves you, like a lot. He says that one day I'll understand what it means to have a soulmate."

"That man is a hopeless romantic."

"You make him happy. And I want him to be happy."

"Things are complicated between us."

"I know, but when two people love each other so much, they have to find some way back to each other," she pauses for a second, swallowing hard.

"But I'm not here to fix things for him. I'm here because I know you two will work things out. And when you do, I'm begging you to let Hannah stay with you. I don't want to leave her with Mom when I can't be there to protect her. She loves you, and she's always saying that she wishes Mom were more like you or that you were her mom."

She flinches. "Mom knows that, and she's been making her life difficult. Mom treats her worse than trash. I don't know what to do."

My chest burns, and I'm about to go and drag Alicia all the way back from Europe by her hair. How dare she treat my Hannah like that. But I remember that this isn't my family to meddle into and that I can only give a little advice.

"You tell your father, so he can take care of it. I thought you were practicing honesty with him."

"Yes, but we're not allowed around the baby."

The guilt hits me right in the gut. They feel unsafe because of me.

"Again, not something you two should be worrying about. We, as adults, have to look after you two."

"You make it sound easy."

"Honestly, Tess, it has to be easy for you and Hannah. You're not responsible for your sister's safety. You should feel and be safe."

"We are," she insists but her voice wavers.

"Not emotionally. The things your mother has done have scarred you, psychologically. I know for a fact that your dad will do everything in his power to make sure you two don't have to deal with it."

Because one way or another, I'll help him. I'm strong enough to be in this house by myself. They need him.

Her phone rings, she pulls it out, and sighs.

"It's time for me to go."

"You want to come back with Hannah and have dinner with us?"

"Thanks, but Mom arrives soon from her vacation. Maybe another day."

☆ ☆ ☆ ☆

I don't enter the main house until I watch Tess's car drive away. My breath caught up several times as I listened to her worried voice. Her stories remind me of my own mother and my own little hell.

We have to do something, yet I feel as if my brain is firing a million thoughts at once, and I can't understand any of them. What do we do to keep everyone safe?

"Where are you?" Kaden's voice drags me back to reality.

"What?"

I stare at the hot, sexy, freshly bathed Kaden who is right beside me.

"You were lost inside your head," he explains, his hungry eyes holding me prisoner. "Are you thinking what I'm thinking?"

"Probably not, Hades. Most of the time you only think about sex."

"At least you know what I'm thinking about. In exchange, you should tell me what's going on in there." He touches my head briefly.

"Alicia arrives tonight."

"I got her message. She's pissed. I'm on my way to pick up the girls. Raven said that she can keep them with her while I figure something out."

"Why there?"

"Because that's my only option," he responds. Though guarded, there's no resentment or anger in his voice. "You don't want them close to Kieran."

"You need to understand that I was scared, hormonal, and I hadn't yet talked to the girls when I said that. However, I need to know your plan, too."

He narrows his gaze and exhales harshly.

"I plan to keep them away from Alicia. As you know, I already filed for full custody. The hearing is set for next week. The judge already granted me temporary custody since Alicia went out of town and left the girls with her parents—without my knowledge. Also, we have the other infractions like the fact that she's neglected them and abandoned them alone for weekends when I'm not in town."

"She did?" I tremble with anger.

"Tess and Hannah have plenty of stories that they're willing to share with the judge."

"Hmm." I chew my lip thinking about what he's done so far.

He can place them with Raven, have as many documents as he wants, but that doesn't keep Alicia away from them.

"Is there a way you can get a restraining order?"

"On what grounds?" He narrows his gaze.

"Emotional abuse," I explain. "You don't need proof for that, only your word against Alicia's since they are minors."

I walk toward the home library where we keep the computer on all day long.

"We need it by tonight."

"It shouldn't be hard. You have people for everything," I remind him. "Get a therapist to testify that the girls are in fact being emotionally abused for the custody case. Any judge would sign that, but I know one who might help us expedite this."

"In the meantime, they can come here. You can take them to Raven's afterwards."

I fire off an email to Judge Summers. She always expedited my cases if I explained everything clearly and felt like the children were in danger. I do exactly that in my email, describing everything from the 'suicide' to what's been happening over the past three years as described by Kaden and Tess. I read it out loud to Kaden who adds the accounts of when the girls were sick and when she dropped them at her parents without Kade's consent.

"What's your lawyer's email address?" I ask, copying Kaden on the email.

As soon as he gives it to me, I copy him and send the email. I place a call to her secretary too, leaving a brief message that I sent an email, and it's urgent. She knows that when I do that, I'm not joking.

"Just in case, I recommend that you hire security. A bodyguard or two to be close to them around the clock."

He stops in the middle of the library watching me.

"That's a good idea," he says before leaving the house.

For a few minutes, I remain in my seat, thinking about Tess and Hannah. Raven is a wonderful mother, but those girls belong with their dad. They have been through a lot and jumping through houses isn't the best for them.

I dig into my feelings, and for the first time, I recognize that it isn't only Kaden that I'm afraid of, but them—his daughters. Loving them unconditionally just brought me pain. I was cut out of a family that I believed was mine, and the mere thought of going through that again makes my pulse accelerate with anxiety.

But someone must think about those girls, and maybe this time around things will be different.

Chapter Forty

KADE

We had a long day. My therapist agreed to interview my daughters, and he wrote a letter where it states that they've been neglected and abused by their mother. Judge Summers granted me full custody of the girls once Tess and Hannah relived the suicide attempt and told her about their mother's outburst.

Once I helped them pack their things at their grandparents, we drove to Sadie's, who said she expected us for dinner. I have no idea what to expect from her or this impromptu family reunion, but I am hopeful about it.

"Are you sure this is okay, Dad?" Tess stares at the house.

"He said it was, and I saw the text," Hannah says, excitedly.

"What if she changed her mind?" Tess fidgets with her bracelet and looks at me.

"She won't," I assure her. "It's just dinner."

"Come on, Tess. You said she was cool today," Hannah pats Tess's hand lightly.

"Well yeah, but that doesn't mean that she's fine with me in the house."

"It's a step, Tess," I encourage her. "She's not mad at you, if that's what you're thinking. Sadie cares about you two."

"She said that earlier, but after everything I did ... Mom would be livid and cruel."

My poor daughter is finally opening up about her life with Alicia, and I feel like the worst fucking father ever. What do I do to make it better? There's nothing I can say that will erase what she's been going through. I scratch my forehead and take a deep breath.

"Sadie isn't like your mother." That's the best I can come up with, without trashing Alicia.

"Mom's a bitch," Hannah concludes. "If I had to choose between the two ..."

She drops her head. "Not that Sadie would want me anyway."

"Stop this nonsense and let's go down," I suggest before they end up crying.

As we step inside the house, the place feels more like home. It smells like chicken soup and grilled cheese.

"Cookies!" Hannah flies toward the kitchen.

"You know the rules," Sadie calls her out from upstairs. "Dinner first, then you can have as many as you want."

"She still has rules," Hannah whispers, grinning at me.

We both broke a few from time to time. It was fun to have an accomplice when I stole sweets from the kitchen.

"And cookies." Sadie walks into the kitchen. "Hannah, the plates are in that cupboard, the utensils in the drawer next to the stove."

Hannah doesn't say anything, but she gets to work.

"Kade, can you help her with the cups and placemats, please?"

"What can I do?" Tess swings her body back and forth watching us do our usual chores.

Sadie turns her attention to her and twists her mouth, then looks at me. I shrug because I'm at a loss. Tess has never offered to help. When I assingned her chores, she refused to do them.

"Why don't you come over and help me?"

In no time, we have the food on the table, the places are set, and we all sit down. We have comfort food. The girl's favorite. Chicken noodle soup and grilled cheese sandwiches—oven made.

"Where is Kieran?" Hannah looks around the table as she eats.

"In bed, he should be waking up in an hour or two," Sadie answers with a guarded voice.

"Do you think we can see him before we leave?" She smiles at Sadie. "Just from afar, I promise not to touch him."

Sadie looks at me, then at the girls, and sighs.

"They should stay with us," she proposes.

"What?" I perk up, but hold my breath.

I study her because the offer is huge. What would make her change her mind?

"Only if you two want to," she continues, looking at my daughters. That's when I see it, the fear. What is she afraid of?

"I mean, I'm sure you don't want to stay here, but it would be temporary." Her voice is low, and she sounds rejected. "At least until your dad leaves. Soon, I'll be well enough."

"Leaving you isn't an option," I warn her, studying her closely. "You promised to give me time with Kieran." *...and you.*

"It's just a suggestion, but maybe they don't want to stay here."

"I want to stay here forever with you and Dad." Hannah stands up and hugs Sadie around the neck. "Unless you don't love me anymore."

It hits me right in the chest. Sadie's afraid of their rejection. They did it too many times for her not to feel the way she does. And one fine day I snatched everything that I had given her without looking back.

"Love doesn't stop on command, Hannah," Sadie sobs, hugging her back. "Of course, I love you. Everything just got so complicated and ..."

"I love you too, Sadie," Hannah is crying too.

Tess just watches them, tears streaming down her cheeks. I reach for her hand and squeeze it lightly.

"Can we stay here?" Tess asks timidly.

"You heard the lady, as long as you want to be here, she'll be happy to have you." I lean forward and whisper, "She's nice, and I'm sure you two can become real friends."

She nods a couple of times and wipes away her tears with her sleeves.

"I'm going to move the security from Raven's house to here," I alert them, rising from my seat. "Also, I need to update the address change with my lawyer—legalities are a pain in the ass, but I'd rather cover mine."

"Don't worry about us," Sadie smiles at me. "We can start cleaning up the table while eating some cookies."

☆ ☆ ☆ ☆

"Are you sure you'll be fine staying on the couch?"

"Unless you let me stay with you," I say suggestively.

Since we don't have enough beds, Tess and Hannah are staying in my bed while I take the couch.

"In your dreams, Hades." She chuckles, turning off the kitchen light and heading up the stairs.

"Thank you for accepting them." I walk right behind her. "And sorry."

She stops, looking over her shoulder. "What are you sorry for?"

"When we broke up, I didn't think about your relationship with the girls."

"It was too rocky," she says quietly as she enters her room.

"Yes, but you cared about them. You were like a mother to them."

"But I wasn't. I'm not." She sighs, the sadness lingering between us. "There's no point to this discussion, is there?"

"The point is that I'm sorry for how I reacted," I begin my apology.

She lifts her hand, nodding her head. "And I'm going to stop you right there. Tess and Hannah are safe and happy. That's all that matters."

"How about us?"

She rolls her eyes. "For now, we are two adults who happen to live under the same roof and share a baby."

"I get it. You're not at a place where we can discuss our relationship. But since you're not closed to the possibility, I'd like to argue that this time we're all in."

"We?" Her brows furrow.

"Hannah, Tess and I want to be a part of you. We want to become a real family. We are sorry for the way we handled things in the past.

This time we promise not to push you aside. We are so sorry for not knowing how to handle it before."

"That's a lot to absorb for one day," she murmurs, checking on Kieran.

My phone buzzes at that moment, when I pull it, I read a text from my lawyer.

"Who is it?" she whispers, walking silently toward the door.

"They've served Alicia with the restraining order and the custody agreement," I announce, closing the door behind us.

"What do you think she'll do?" She closes her eyes, hugging herself. "I just don't want her close to our girls."

"She won't get close, I promise." I wrap her inside my arms. "We'll be fine."

"I trust you," she whispers, leaning her head on my chest.

Progress, I think as I assimilate her words and breathe her scent.

☆ ☆ ☆ ☆

It's been a day and two nights since my daughters moved in with us. The first night they stayed in my bedroom. This morning, we bought them furniture and paid extra to have it delivered the same day. Both are happy, and Tess is starting to be more open with Sadie. *Baby steps,* Sadie told me when I asked Tess to empty the dishwasher and she made a little drama.

We have to be patient, but as long as we work with them—as a family—she should change little by little. I tried not to change Sadie's or Kieran's schedule. Tess helped me driving Hannah to her ballet classes since I no longer go to the studio across the street anymore. Tonight, I decided to cut practice early and send the guys home with the promise that they can stay here on Sunday for dinner after practice.

As I walk toward the mainhouse, I see one of the security guys running toward me.

"What's going on?"

"Someone is breaking into the pool house." He continues his way, and I follow him.

As we get closer, I spot the other security guard tackling someone to the floor. When I reach Andrew's home, I recognize her. Alicia.

I fire up a text to Sadie.

Kade: Alicia's here. Make sure you lock the door.

Sadie: I will. Be safe.

"What the fuck are you doing in Sadie's house?"

"My daughters are here, I want you to hand them back to me, fucker," she growls. "You owe me a month of child support too."

"Tess and Hannah won't be going with you." I use a stern voice with her. I have to be careful before she makes up shit to say to her lawyer. "After hearing their case, the judge granted me permanent custody."

"I won't allow it, you fucking drunk. You and that fucking bitch are going to pay for this. I'm going to kill that bitch."

"Alicia, give it up," I suggest. "They already told us what you did to them. I will never let you near them again."

The guard helps her stand up, and she jumps on top of me, choking me. I push her away, dropping her to the floor.

"Sorry," the guy apologizes, pushing her to the floor and putting the handcuffs on her.

"Tell them to release me, fucker!" Alicia, who is in no position to make demands, orders.

Alicia's eyes flare. I knew she arrived last night, but I had no idea she would look for them right away, or that she'd violate the restraining order. My lawyer made sure to hand it over to her the moment she walked through the gate.

"You were served with a restraining order. The paper explains that you're not to even contact our daughters—you texted them." Though I had Duncan cancel their numbers and get them new ones right away. A police officer was even sent to her house to warn her about what could happen if she tried to violate the order again.

"You can't go anywhere near them either. And yet, here you are breaking and entering, threatening us, and trying to attack me."

"That's a lie. I never touched you or threatened you."

"'I'll kill that bitch,' sounded like a threat to Sadie." I cross my arms, staring at her in pity. "Things shouldn't be this hard, Alicia."

"This is supposed to be the kind of house you bought me, not that hut I live in. I was supposed to give you a boy—not her. Everything I did meant nothing to you. Now you're taking my kids away from me."

"I'm keeping them safe from you. They need a safe home, and love. If you want a relationship with them, I suggest you work on yourself first."

"The cops are almost here, sir," the private security agent says before picking Alicia up from the floor.

I text Sadie about the incident and to check on the girls while we wait for the cops. It doesn't take long for them to arrive and to haul her into their car. I watch the red light of the police car disappear as they drive away. This wasn't how I wanted to confront her.

"I'm fucking exhausted!"

"It's been a long couple of days, Mr. Hades," Sadie comes out of the kitchen holding a mug. "Here. Drink some tea."

"Did they wake up?"

I grab the cup and drink from it. It's slightly bitter. I'm sure she forgot that, unlike her, I like sugary drinks.

"No. I'm glad they caught her outside. Tess and Hannah are still asleep."

It's a blessing that the girls didn't witness their mother's show.

"How are you feeling?" Sadie goes to the staircase and sits on the second step and looks at me.

"I'm still upset at myself for letting things go too far," I say, pinching the bridge of my nose.

"You shouldn't blame yourself for what happened. They hid it well, plus neither one of them was sure if talking would help them at all. One of the adults they trusted the most was hurting them. What if you turned out to be the same? Not that you would, but that's how it can be interpreted from their point of view."

"You're back," I say taking a seat next to her.

"Back?" she rests her crossed arms on top of her knees and yawns.

"The happy, take action, kick ass woman that I love."

"It's a slow process," she sighs. "I wasn't myself for several reasons."

"Care to share?"

"There's this part where I lost my family. One day I was pushed away and not only lost you, but the girls too."

"I'm sorry, I didn't think about it until it was already too late."

"Then, there's the accident. When I woke up I was afraid of everything. I couldn't see the bright side and didn't believe that I could get back to myself. There's so much I should be thankful for. I'm alive. My father is changing. We have an amazing son. I forgot that life is a sequence of beads of many sizes, colors, and textures. Just because I encounter a few ugly ones, doesn't mean that it's over."

"You can't predict what happens next." I caress her jaw, brushing a strand of hair behind her ear. "But you can always make the best of every situation."

"We should never lose hope, and we should never live in fear."

"She still remembers her vows," I mumble resting my chin on top of her back.

"I can't remember why we wrote them together."

"You said I was great at writing love lines, and I told you that you knew a lot more about life. Mixing them and saying them together seemed like an original way to promise each other that no matter what, we would always be together."

"Even after 'death do us part.'" The words are muffled since her mouth is resting on her arm.

"I was too afraid of life. Of you," she confesses.

"After what happened between us, even without the accident, it's logical to feel the way you did. That's why I didn't fight you. I know that you don't leave family behind, and for that I'll always be sorry. That day in the hospital I should've demanded more answers, I should've let you take the lead because I was crumbling."

"It was scary to think we could have lost her."

"She's here, and Hannah too," I breathe the words and finally relax. "I'm sorry for the pain I created. You didn't deserve that."

"Are you happy?" She brushes away my words.

"Almost, Hummingbird. Do you forgive me?"

"Of course, I forgive you. Because I love you."

Her words, coupled with everything that's happened today and in the past weeks we've spent together heal something inside me. It's like my entire existence was dormant and suddenly something is blooming. Spring is finally here, and a long summer is ahead of us.

"I love you too, with all my heart and all of my being."

I lean in a little closer, our foreheads touching, our lips brushing. I take her mouth, kissing her for the first time in months, and the world falls away. The kiss is slow and soft, comforting and healing in ways that words could never be. I slide her body on top of my lap, hugging her close to me. She wraps her arms around my shoulders. She runs her hands down my spine, pulling me closer until there's no space left between us. I feel the beating of her heart synchronized with mine.

Carefully, I pull her ring from my pocket and break the kiss.

Sadie gasps, her eyes open wide.

"Do you always carry that with you?"

"All the time. That's the only way I feel you close when you're not around."

I set her aside, rising from the sitting position and then drop down to one knee in front of her.

"The first time I saw you, something inside me knew that we were meant to be together. Every time we are together, the world stops, leaving just the two of us to wander—as one. Being with you can't be described, only felt. We have a story that I never want to end. It was hard to survive without you, and I can't bare losing you again because only you make me feel complete."

Tears stream down her cheeks, just like the first time I proposed. Her eyes are filled with love and whatever I broke inside her has been repaired. What we have now is different, mature, and so much more.

"Sadie Bell, would you be my wife, my lover, my eternal companion, and the mother of my children?"

"I would," she sobs, as I slip on the ring that shouldn't have come off and that should stay with her forever.

My hands drift to her hips, I pull her toward me, and slam my lips to hers. She inhales sharply as I thrust my tongue inside her mouth. Sadie splays her hands against my chest, running them up and wrapping them around the back of my neck. The entire world disappears as I lose myself into the sweetness of her taste. Her hands roam over my body, while mine can't stop touching every inch of hers.

Our flame ignites, running like wildfire and burning us from the inside. My heart restarts, and I see her light.

I'm back into her world.

I'm alive.

In this moment, I want to give her everything, take everything.

Fuse our bodies and become one.

I kiss her deeper absorbing all the pain I inflicted on her and replacing it with love.

"Love, I need you," I gasp.

"Take me upstairs," she says with longing and need.

I lift her and automatically she wraps her legs around me.

"You know I can walk," Sadie protests as I carry her toward my bedroom.

"Be quiet, Little Minx, or you'll wake up the troops," I squeeze her butt cheek.

"Stop manhandling me." She wiggles her ass.

"That's why I carry you, so I can play with your perfect butt." I close the door of my room behind us, pushing her against it. "I believe you owe me a good fuck."

"The dirty talk is about to start."

She unwraps her legs from my waist, setting her feet on the floor. She stares at me, her chocolate eyes melting with lust. Slowly, she unties her robe and lets the silk fabric slide over her shoulders. A smile is painted across her face while she pulls down her tank top and the shorts she's wearing.

No underwear.

"I fucking died and went to heaven," I mutter staring at her.

She's always been so fucking hot, but now she's fuller, curvier.

"You're wearing too many clothes, Mr. Hades," she says with a sultry voice.

My dick hardens with her tone and those sexy eyes she's giving me. I want her. Not only her body, but her heart and soul. I need to lose myself inside her before I take my next breath. I pull off my shirt, push down my pants, and lick my lips.

"I can see what you're planning, but I can't wait that long.

Tomorrow or after the next feeding you can taste me. Right now, I need you," she begs.

"Sorry, can't accommodate you," I push her lightly toward the bed and kneel right in front of her. "You know the rules."

"We have rules again?" She gasps when I trace a line with my tongue parting her labia.

"Of course: I please, you enjoy. That's our only rule, Hummingbird."

I push her knees lightly, parting her thighs. I inhale the musky scent of her arousal that drives me to the edge. For a second, I toy with the idea of thrusting myself inside her and fucking her until she can't walk. She was wet, ready, and waiting for me. But I refuse to give in to the urge. We both needed to savor each other, make it count as a first, even when we've made love a hundred times.

Taking my time, I trail my fingers up her soft thighs until I find her clit. I tease it a couple of times making her jerk with a loud moan. Fuck, she's so ready. I press my tongue flat on her bud, dipping two fingers into her channel.

"Yes, like that," she orders, pushing her hips toward me, moving them to the same rhythm as my head.

Sadie tries to thread her fingers through my hair, but she's having a hard time.

"Focus on the feeling, forget about my fucking head, Sadie, or I'll tie you up."

"I like you bossy, but I'm not in the mood for bondage. Just give me more fingers. Your big cock. I need you."

She moans when I thrust my thumb into her back entrance.

"Stop, or I'll gag you," I order and return to her pussy swiping my tongue along her slit.

God, I missed her taste, her scent. This fucking body. Nothing has ever tasted like her. She was made for me. My tongue swirls around her labia while I continue fucking her with my fingers. Her whimpers work me up, and I keep flicking, nipping, and licking until she clenches around my fingers and her body trembles.

Sadie's moans are a melody I've never been able to replicate with an instrument. Her spasms and the chant coming from her beautiful mouth fuel me with desire.

"You're so beautiful, love," I say holding the base of my dick. "Are you sure you want this?"

"More than anything, Hades."

I lean down and start sliding through her soft wetness.

"Fuck," I groan as her pussy suctions me slowly inside her.

It's all perfect once again. The world makes sense as I push myself in and out of her entrance. We remain still for a few seconds, staring into each other's eyes. And I see it—what she's been hiding from me since she woke up from the coma—her love for me and our deep connection. We fuse as I continue making love to my other half. My heart. Thoughts of her and our future together swirl around my mind. Lowering myself closer, I take her lips, kissing her delicious mouth.

The tenderness of the moment never leaves. However, her hips begin to move faster demanding more from me. She wants to come, she needs to come. I match her pace. Our breathing becomes shallow. The pace, the moans, and the slap of our sweaty bodies become all that there is. I can hardly breathe, but I don't stop. Instead, I push harder and deeper when her fingers dig into my back and her pussy convulses around my dick.

Every muscle in my body tightens as I reach the peak...I spiral out of control as my cum spills inside of Sadie. My heart beats at a fast tempo, thundering inside my ribcage, and it's all for her. It's because of her.

"I love you, Kaden Hades," she whispers, a tear falling down from the corner of her eye.

"I love you, future Mrs. Hades." I kiss the wetness on her face away.

"Are you happy, Hummingbird?"

"Your love makes me the happiest woman on earth, Nightingale."

EPILOGUE

Kade

Three Years Later

Sundays are the best days at the Hades household. We wake up early, go out for a run, and come back to prepare waffles with chocolate chips for the kids. We also spend time working on the garden. Andrew Bell visits his grandchildren, and Tess Facetimes instead of just sending a few texts to let us know that she's okay.

"Hey, Dad," she grins, her auburn hair pulled back into her usual ponytail.

"How's my little girl?" I smile back at her.

"Dad," she protests. "I'm not little anymore."

"Don't challenge him," Sadie cries from the kitchen, holding our six-week-old baby, Aubrey. "How was last night, sweetheart?"

"What happened yesterday?" I glare at Tess.

"She had a party." Sadie makes her way to the living room.

She kisses my cheek and takes my tablet away. I lean and grab my sweet Aubrey, snuggling her against my chest.

"Did the costume fit?" Sadie asks Tess.

"It did and looked cool. Thank you so much for sending it. I love you." Tess blows a kiss her way.

"What party?" I growl.

"Just a typical college party, Hades. She's there to learn, but also to enjoy herself." Sadie gives me a warning glare.

I clamp my lips together and take a deep breath. Leave it to Sadie to be the ambassador of all things fun when it comes to our children. Just the other day, I heard Hannah and her discussing a boy from her drawing class. If I don't watch those three, Tess is going to drag some stupid boy during Thanksgiving into the house and introduce him as her boyfriend. Hannah won't be far behind. I'll be damned if I allow that to happen.

"Is Aubrey awake?" Tess asks excitedly.

"She's sleeping as usual. You should come home next weekend."

"I can't be flying every weekend, Dad," Tess pouts. "Thanksgiving is close, though. Just keep sending me pictures of her."

"Please don't get them started," Hannah waltzes into the room with Kieran right behind her. "Dad's always filming her or taking pics. You'd think he's never seen a baby in his entire life—he has four children."

"Stop complaining, Hannah," I say, taking a picture of her.

"Mama!" Kieran runs to Sadie to hug her.

"Baby!" She hands me back my iPad and bends down to hug him back. He gives her a sloppy kiss—her favorite kind.

"Can I cawy Auby, Dad?"

"After you wash your hands, bud."

"Awe, take a picture of that and send it over. They look so cute together," Tess points out the obvious.

"Hi, Tessy!" Kieran waves at his big sister.

"Hey, handsome. How are you?"

"Okay," he smiles. "Can I have the phone, pwease, Daddy?"

"You may, but don't keep her long, okay?"

"We lost her," Sadie declares. "I'll call her tonight to get more details about the party."

"She met a guy," Hannah giggles. "He's cute and majoring in marine biology, like Tess."

"Where is he from and why haven't you told me any of this before?" Sadie sits right next to Hannah.

"He's a local—from San Diego," Hannah says, pulling her phone. "He's a *senior* according to her last text."

"Too old for her."

"Oh shush, Hades." Sadie rolls her eyes. "Let Hannah speak, or I won't find out what's going on with Tess until next week. Kieran took her away from me. You know she's going to spend the next two hours on the phone with him."

Kieran is Hannah and Tess's favorite person. They do everything and anything for him. He adores them back. When the girls moved in with us, I was skeptical at first about our family dynamic. Two grown teenagers and a newborn didn't seem to work well. They surprised us. Or maybe Sadie is right, and we taught them how to love each other and be there for one another.

"Are you ready to go to the greenhouse?" Sadie looks over at Hannah.

"Always. I want to check on the orchids you brought last Wednesday." Hannah joins Sadie, and they walk toward the backyard.

Sadie glances at me. "Will you be okay if I leave you with the little ones?"

"You forget that I'm a pro." I kiss Aubrey's forehead. "She just fell asleep. I have a couple of hours."

Slowly, I make my way toward Kieran's room, where he's telling Tess about his new drawings, Aubrey, and the baby brother he wants us to have. He wants us to bring him a boy so he can play with him. He already has a lot of sisters. There's a plan to have one last baby in a couple of years. If it's a boy or a girl, we'll love him no matter what.

"Hey," Sadie approaches and slides her arms around my waist resting her head on my arm and looking at our little baby. "You have that happy face that I adore."

"Tess is okay," I sigh wrapping her up in my arms along with Aubrey.

"They're doing fine. You still worry about her, don't you?"

Tess endured a lot of abuse from her mother. There are certain things that she never mentioned until she felt safe and loved. Instead of going to college after graduating from high school, she took a year off to heal. She went to therapy, support groups, and worked for Sadie full time. They finally bonded and became close friends. I dare to say that all three of my girls are best friends.

Alicia was in jail for a few days. She gave up filing for custody when she found out that I wouldn't pay for her lawyer and she wouldn't get any more money from me. It's sad that once she realized that our daughters weren't going to benefit her, she never tried to reach out to them either through my lawyer or myself. Of my two daughters, Tess is the one who never wants to see her mother again. Hannah says that maybe one day she'll reach out to her.

"No matter how old she is, she's my baby. I will always worry about her."

"They are lucky to have you as a dad." Sadie grabs Aubrey's hand.

"I wish Tess had chosen to stay in town. San Diego is too far."

"She's doing great, just like Hannah. Their mother didn't do any permanent damage."

"You identify a lot with them, don't you?"

"Let's not talk about Catherine." She sighs. "Not today."

Her father's change was slow, but permanent. The asshole side of him still might exist outside the family, but with us, he's different. He even treats my daughters as his grandchildren. Sadie loves seeing him every Sunday evening, and he calls her often just to check in. Catherine though, she has a routine that I doubt she'll ever break. Rehab, a few months of sobriety, and then another trip back again once she falls off the wagon.

"We have to take this little one to her bassinet, Mr. Hades." Sadie tries to take Aubrey away from me. "She's going to have a hard time once you start rehearsals again."

"The band is on hiatus," I remind her, not letting Aubrey go.

Killing Hades matters to me, but not as much as my family. I'd rather spend my days at home or at the flower shop with my wife. Instead of opening three different shops, we expanded it and hired more employees who help Rae, the flower shop manager, run the place.

"Don't you miss it?"

"I'd miss you and our children more. This little one needs the same amount of arm time as Kieran."

"Until one day she'll start crawling around the house." Sadie laughs. "It's going to be fun watching you chase after her."

"I love you," I find her gaze, Lifting her chin, I brush her lips with mine.

"After all these years, Hades?"

"Evermore I will love you, Hummingbird. I will love you until the end of time. As long as the stars shine their bright light into the dark night."

Dear Reader,

Thank you so much for reading My One Regret: A story near and dear to my heart. Well, all of them are, aren't they? There's always a relatable piece of the story. Sadie's story came to me back in November 2016. It was an idea that I set aside while I worked on Until I Fall.

Not sure if it was the mood, or my personal health that pushed me to dust this plot and work on it. Either one, I began to work through it slowly as a side project. Then, the news that a dear friend from high school was in a coma appeared on Facebook. The last time I talked to her was back in November when I congratulate her. She was pregnant.

Nirza was one of the first friends I made in freshman year. She always had a smile for everyone. She was a fighter, and I know that for two long months she fought for her life. Heaven has gained two angels, Nirza and her baby daughter.

For a second, I almost stopped writing this book. It became too real, too close. My own physical and mental health are unbalanced. But I decided to finish it. Create an alternate happily ever after for her and her family.

Thank you for reading this. For accepting a little piece of my heart.

After you finish the book, and if you enjoyed it. Please, do me a big favor and leave a review. Let other readers know about it and spread the word. I love to hear from readers, so please don't hesitate to email me

Thank you much. Love you all,

Claudia ♥

ACKNOWLEDGMENTS

Acknowledgements

This is one of the most difficult parts to write for me. I have a terrible memory, and I am afraid to forget anyone. Please forgive me if I do. Before I continue, let me tell you that I'm grateful for all of you and for being part of the world that I've created.

So where do I start?

First and foremost, I'd like to thank God for all the blessing in my life.

To my family, thanks you for all your support—even when some of you haven't read the stories. My husband who is my inspiration, my partner and my everything. We always keep going, no matter what kind of beads we find along the journey. To my amazing kids, you're the engine that keeps me going. Paulina, you're a light, keep shining. I'm so grateful for your help and for choosing me as your mom.

Thank you to Letha, my NanoWriMo partner on 2016. She was the first one to learn about Sadie's story and though we both realized it wasn't strong, she encouraged me to set it in the back burner and bring it to life when I was ready. Thank you for your friendship.

My alpha readers, Michelle, Patricia and Yolanda. Thank you isn't enough, but I am grateful ladies.

Michelle, you're a blessing. Your patience, your support, your friendship mean so much to me. Thank you so much for reading the story and for all your feedback. Love you.

Patricia, I value your friendship, your support and your time helping me with this story.

Yolanda, girl, words can't cover how thankful I am for your friendship and support.

Christine, it's only been a couple of years, but I feel like we've been best friends since forever. Thank you for your patience, for listening to my crazy plots and for everything. You might be in Canada but somedays it feels like you're right next to me. Thank you.

To Colleen, Kerry, and Melissa, this book worked a little different due to health issues, I'm so thankful for your support and your love.

To Hang Le—you complete my books, always. I can't thank you enough for everything you do and I love the time we spend making decisions on the covers. Love you my friend.

Mara White, for taking a chance with this book and enriching it. Thank you for your patience.

Kristi, where do I start? Love you from here to the moon and back. Thank you so much for your friendship, for listening to me and holding my hand when things are just a little too much. For always being there no matter what. This business is a lonely one, and yet I always have you. Most of all, thank you for taking a leap and proofing this baby.

Jess Estep, thank you so much for the long calls, the support that you give me and everything that you do to spread the word about my book.

Kaitie, thank you for cheering me up, your pms are everything some days. Never apologize for being you. In fact, the world needs more people like you.

Melissa, not sure if thank you is enough, but again, thank you for being part of this team.

To Becca, my sweet friend who taught me to make her feel and for cheering me up when I'm down.

Lara, my favorite hooker. The past months you've been that little voice that keeps me going. I can't thank you enough for being such a blessing.

Lesa, thank you for helping me change my life one breathe at a time.

To the Book Lovin' Chicas group, thank you so much for your continuous support. For your daily cheers, and the words of encouragement. I'm grateful for you.

Thank you to all the bloggers who help spread the word about my books. I guess thank you doesn't cut it, your energy and support is what makes every release a success.

To my readers, I am grateful to you. Thank you for reading my words, and for supporting my books. Thank you so much for those emails and notes, they mean so much to me.

All my love,

Claudia

ALSO BY CLAUDIA BURGOA

ABOUT THE AUTHOR

Claudia is an award winning, international bestselling author. She lives in Colorado, working for a small IT. She has three children and manages a chaotic household of three confused dogs, and a wonderful husband who shares her love of all things geek. To survive she works continually to find purpose for the voices flitting through her head, plus she consumes high quantities of chocolate to keep the last threads of sanity intact.

Sign up for her newsletter to receive updates about upcoming books and exclusive excerpts:

https://app.mailerlite.com/webforms/landing/m6l6v4

To find more about Claudia:

http://www.claudiayburgoa.com/

Or stalk her:

Reader group:
https://www.facebook.com/groups/ClaudiasBookaliciousBabes/

https://www.goodreads.com/group/show/176276-claudia-burgoa-reader-group

https://twitter.com/yuribeans

https://www.facebook.com/ClaudiaYBurgoa

http://www.pinterest.com/yuribeans

http://www.amazon.com/Claudia-Burgoa/e/B00EADAOLI

http://instagram.com/claudia_b30/

https://www.bookbub.com/authors/claudia-burgoa

Made in the USA
San Bernardino, CA
07 April 2018